DARING
THE
Hockey
Player

WILLOW FOX

ONE
AMBER

I'M NOT USUALLY the girl who asks a guy out, but here I am. The butterflies in my stomach make me nervous, and I shift awkwardly on the bar stool, wondering if he's going to stand me up.

I have a date tonight with Tripp. I don't know his last name. It's probably for the best. Not that I'm looking for a hookup because I've never done that. I'm the queen of taking things slow, although that doesn't mean that I don't crush hard and fast.

I've been scouring the dating sites, but I haven't talked with anyone online. But a few weeks ago, when I swung by Steele Concierge Medical to pick up my friend Charlotte, who had slipped and twisted her ankle while ice skating, I literally walked right into Mr. Handsome—AKA Tripp.

She did the tripping, and I did the walking smack into his chest. And I imagine it was a gorgeous chest. He certainly was rocking a six-pack, and those dark-rimmed glasses made him look a hundred times sexier.

When did I get so fucking horny that I started asking guys out? Not that there's anything wrong with a woman making the first move. It's just not what I do, and I'm uncomfortable waiting at the bar alone for him.

I grab my phone from my purse and text Charlotte.

Hot date tonight with Tripp, the nurse from the hospital.

Charlotte and I met last summer at a frat party at NYU. We have an agreement that if we ever go out with a stranger, we meet him in a public place but also let each other know the details, just in case they turn out to be a kidnapper and toss one of us in the back of their trunk.

Charlotte watches a little too much true crime, and I think she's starting to rub off on me.

Details, and text me when you get home.

I bite down on my tongue, tempted to answer her with a "Yes, Mom," but I think better of it.

Of course, I text and shove my phone into my

purse. I don't want to be that girl on our date—the one who's staring at her phone and more interested in her text messages than the man she's conversing with.

I order a Long Island iced tea, and the bartender asks to see my identification. I grab my fake ID from my wallet and slide it across the bar to him.

He scrutinizes it for a minute before handing it back.

I'll be twenty-one in a few months, but I've been pulling off the fake ID for well over a year. The bar is loud already, and then the front door swings open, giving way to a group of guys barreling in together, happy and full of spunk.

One of them leans across the bar and asks the bartender to change the channel on the television, and a sports recap is playing on the screen. I glance from the screen to the guys, and I swear, the one with dark hair and the cutest smile is the same guy on the screen.

The screen displays an interview following the hockey game. The name at the bottom of the screen reads *Jasper Greyson*.

It's definitely him, unless he has a twin brother or a body double.

I can't help but stare, and when he notices, he

offers me a friendly smile. He stands at the counter, ordering drinks for the table, and then he saunters off without so much as a hello.

At least I got a smile.

Not that I should care.

I'm waiting for Tripp to show up, and I try not to glance at my watch, but he's definitely a few minutes late.

He didn't mention having to work today, but it's possible he could have gotten stuck at the hospital. He's an ER nurse, and it wouldn't be unusual for him to have to work a double shift or something. At least, that's what I'm telling myself in light of him showing up late.

I sip my drink and glance at the door.

Tripp comes walking in, looking sexy as hell. I exhale a tiny breath, my hands trembling from nerves.

I'm a virgin. Never been kissed. Completely inexperienced with guys. But that doesn't mean I haven't been out on dates. I just like to take my time. I don't want to jump into something that I'm not ready for, and quite frankly, all the guys in high school and at college are super immature.

I take another swig of the Long Island iced tea,

doing my best to settle the butterflies that are making me nauseous.

I'm not sure why this guy, Tripp, makes me nervous. Maybe it's because he's a few years older than I am. He's also hot. Like, just staring at him for a few minutes will give me fantasies to live off of for the next couple of months.

"Hi, Amber," he says and gives me a friendly hug.

He's tall and smells good. I try not to embrace him for too long. I don't want to seem clingy or weird. "Hi," I say and force a smile. My stomach is tumbling, and I gesture to the seat beside me at the bar.

Tripp grabs the stool and waves the bartender over, ordering a vodka.

I can't imagine drinking vodka straight, but I'm trying not to judge him.

"Did you have work today?" I ask. What I really want to know is, did he have a bad day? Is that why he's going straight for the hard stuff?

Tripp shakes his head. "Day off for the week. I'm on for the next two weeks starting tomorrow."

"Oh, wow." I'm surprised by his schedule. "The hospital has you work fourteen days in a row?"

"I like the overtime. It keeps me busy, and the pay is great, too," he says.

I take another swig from my drink. Handsome. Check. Workaholic. Red flag. But he's an adult, and I'm still in college. Maybe that's what it's like when you get out of school? You work yourself to death. It doesn't sound fun.

At least this is a red flag, I can see. And the vodka might be one too. I'm not sure. It's still too early to tell.

"What about you? You're still in school?" Tripp asks.

I blush and nod. "Yes, I'm studying microbiology. I have another year until I graduate."

"What do you plan on doing with that?" he asks.

"I'm hoping to get a job at a hospital or university laboratory," I say.

"Let me know when you graduate. Maybe I can help you out." Tripp downs the shot of vodka and orders another.

"Thanks. How do you like working for Steele Concierge?" I ask. It's a privately owned and funded medical center in the heart of downtown New York City. Charlotte comes from money, so when she injured her ankle, she had the cab driver take her where there wouldn't be a long wait in the ER.

"The sixteen-hour days are a bit brutal. The

nurses, you wouldn't believe what some of them are up to."

"What do you mean?" I ask.

"The charge nurse was caught in the stairwell with a bag of fentanyl, passed out. We thought for a minute that she ODed."

"Oh my gosh. Did they fire her?" I can't imagine anyone being allowed to keep their job after that type of ordeal.

"They forced her into thirty-day rehab. She's back on the floor again, was clean for about a year..."

"How did she not lose her license?" Shock floods through me.

Tripp shrugs. "The board doesn't really do much since the hospital is the equivalent of a drug dealer. Making her give patients drugs, it's like it's there and tempting her."

I'm utterly speechless, and I stare at him like the world suddenly makes absolutely zero sense.

"But she stole fentanyl from the hospital."

"She wasn't the only one using fentanyl. Three, no, four other nurses were taking part. They'd all steal something and share it amongst one another. Super easy, post-Covid, when the inhalers for an asthma attack are in the same cabinet as the narcotics. A nurse unlocks the cabinet, rushes to get what they need, and doesn't bother locking it."

"That's insane." I can't wrap my head around how any of this is acceptable or how it could be true. But he doesn't seem like he's lying. He looks stressed, with dark circles under his eyes and his fingers drumming against the bar counter.

Tripp shrugs like it's not that surprising anymore. He's grown cold to it, like it's just another day at the hospital. He finishes his second shot of vodka and orders a third.

Maybe he's just making himself numb.

"I mean, I get it. I work sixteen-hour days. I've had to ask the doctors for methamphetamines."

I stare at him, shocked by where this is going. Because, already, my mind is telling me it can't be good.

"You do know what methamphetamines are?"

I wasn't born yesterday, but my drug knowledge is limited. I've never done more than a few edibles of the marijuana variety. I just stare at him, too shocked to answer, and he continues speaking.

"Meth salts? Yeah, I'd have the doctor give me that when I'd have to work a sixteen-hour shift or drive home after."

I think my mouth just hit the floor. I tip my drink

back, finishing the Long Island iced tea. I gesture the bartender over for a second because this conversation took a turn that I was not expecting.

And any warm, tingly feelings that I had toward Tripp have grown ice cold.

Crush obliterated.

I should high-tail my ass out of the bar and leave while I'm sober enough to drive myself home. Not that I'm technically sober enough to drive legally, given I'm twenty, but whatever.

Laughter and high-fives pull my attention briefly away from Tripp.

Another glance at the rowdy group in the back, and I'd bet it's the Ice Dragons having drinks after a win. They're one of New York's NHL teams. I don't know a ton about the team, but from the short segment on the news, I recognize a few faces.

The man who had asked the bartender to change channels and bought a round for his buddies, Jasper Greyson, makes eye contact with me.

At least, I think he does. He could be glancing past me at the television screen, but I'd like to think I caught his attention. I wish there were a secret signal that I could give him to come and rescue me.

A girl can dream, right?

Tripp is talking, and I'm grateful when my

second Long Island iced tea arrives because it helps dull my senses and the fact that my interest in him is waning. Okay, it's technically gone, but I'm not sure of a nice way to excuse myself and run.

I'm too nice.

Too friendly.

He seems to think I'm interested because he puts his hand on my thigh.

My eyes widen, and I remove his hand, putting it back on his leg. Tripp keeps on talking, and I'm not sure that he's even noticed my disinterest. He's now rambling about how he vandalized the local skate park, how he brought out his tools at night and tore down the metal fencing because he didn't believe it should be shut down.

"Kids should have a place to skate," Tripp says.

I stare at him with a smirk. "My best friend, Charlotte, she works for the park district," I say.

His eyes widen. "You have to promise not to tell her."

I make no such promise. I just stare at him like he's the biggest dumb fuck in the world right now, confessing his sins to me. Although, he doesn't have any remorse for what he's done.

I don't ask him if he was on meth when he

decided to tear down the metal fencing around the skate park. I honestly don't care.

"I think I should go," I say, finally gathering the courage to get my ass out of the bar before he starts thinking that he's going to get lucky because this guy clearly can't read the signs.

Tripp puts his hand on my arm, pulling me back onto the stool. "It's only been an hour. The night is still young," he says.

He shifts and stands, blocking me from getting up. There's the bar behind me and a small group standing on the opposite side, blocking me from exiting easily through their crowd.

"We're just getting to know one another," Tripp says.

"Yeah, Tripp, this isn't going to work out." I'm trying to be direct and as nice as I can be. His eyes are dilated, and I can't tell if it's because he's on meth right now or if the lighting in the bar is to blame.

"There's chemistry between us. It doesn't have to be anything serious. Have you ever had a fling before?" Tripp asks.

"Hold that thought. I need to use the ladies' room," I say, taking my purse with me. He lets me pass as I head toward the back of the bar.

There has to be an exit out of here.

I hurry down the hallway past the bathroom for the back exit. The sign on the door reads *emergency exit only*. Yeah, it's an emergency, but if it's armed and has an alarm, I'm not sure that's quite what they mean. I've never been much of a rebel.

My hands tremble, and I remain in the hallway near the bathroom, trying to figure out another way out of the bar without being seen. In order to leave, I'll have to waltz right past Tripp.

Jasper Greyson heads toward the men's room.

"I need—" I whisper, my voice trembling as I speak, trying to corner him.

"You want an autograph?" he asks with a warm smile and tilts his head at me. His brow furrows the longer he stares. "Are you okay?" he asks, taking a soft, tentative step forward, a hand reaching out for my arm.

My breath catches in my throat, his concern overwhelming. "I need help."

He slowly nods and glances past me. "Bad date?" he asks.

He has no idea the definition of a *bad date* right now. "The guy I'm with, apparently, he's done meth, and I don't know. He might be hopped up on something right now. I'm trying to get out of here, but my credit card is with the bartender, and the back exit is an emergency door. I'm kind of freaking out here," I say.

"I can grab your credit card from Pamela at the bar. Do you need me to walk you to your car?"

I hesitate.

"I promise I'll keep my distance and my hands to myself. I just want to make sure that he doesn't follow you to your car."

"Thanks, that would be great," I say.

"Just hang here for a second," Jasper says. He hurries to the bar, standing a few feet away from Tripp. He leans forward, talking with the bartender. It looks intimate; anyone else might think he was flirting, but she glances past him at me and gives a nod.

A minute later, Jasper is hurrying toward the hallway, handing me my credit card. "Truthfully, the meth head should have paid for your drinks."

I shove the card back into my purse and grab my keys. "Thank you," I say, my voice gathering a tiny bit more confidence.

"Come on, I'll walk you out to your car." He stays on my right side, walking close but not touching me as he protects me from Tripp.

The minute that I exit the hallway and am back

in the bar, Tripp's eyes are on me. He stands and approaches Jasper and me.

"What are you doing?" Tripp asks, staring at Jasper. Not once does he meet my gaze.

"Back off," Jasper says. "She isn't interested in you."

Tripp huffs under his breath. "And you think she wants you? Come on, baby doll, I'll take you home if that's where you want to go." Tripp reaches for my arm, and Jasper stops him before he can even lay a hand on me, yanking the man's arm behind his back.

"Keep your hands off her and stay the hell away," Jasper growls and shoves him into the bar, forcing Tripp to stumble a few feet.

Tripp huffs and shoves his ass back down on the stool. "You jocks are all the same."

Jasper ignores him. His attention is entirely on me. The level of devotion makes my stomach flop. "Where's your car?" he asks.

"I parked around the side," I say and gesture to the right. I could probably walk myself to my vehicle at this point, but there are a few people outside, and it's dark. The parking lot isn't very well-lit.

"Come on," he says and walks me outside,

opening the bar door for me as I step out into darkness.

Jasper walks me to my beat-up, two-door car. "I know it doesn't look like much, but it's dependable," I say.

He doesn't say a word, and if he's judging my ride, he's silent about it. "Does that meth head know where you live?" he asks.

I shake my head. "No." I hit the unlock button on the car and reach for the door handle, yanking it open. "Thank you."

"I never got your name," Jasper says.

"That's because I never gave it," I say.

He watches me climb into the car and shut the door. I lock it before starting the vehicle, and he takes a step back, watching to make sure that I'm safe. I'm backing out of the parking space when he starts heading back toward the bar.

I hope that Tripp doesn't give him any more trouble.

But I can't worry about Jasper Greyson, and I'm pretty sure he can take care of himself, being a hockey player and all that.

Heading out of the parking lot, I dial Charlotte, having to unload all of my drama on her.

TWO
JASPER

"Not that I want to talk you out of it, but are you sure you're ready for that level of commitment?" I ask my older brother. He's only older by three years, but I swear, it's like there are decades between us at times.

He's got his shit together. Not that he had much of a choice, with a six-year-old daughter and an NHL career on the line. He's done well for himself, investing his half of our parents' life insurance policy when they passed away.

Kyler has always looked out for me. I'm not jealous of him, just what he has with his new girlfriend, which is more complicated than a daytime soap opera.

I'm happy for them, most of the time.

I do miss hanging out with Kyler, and I almost never see him after a game when we have drinks and hang out. He's always spending it with his daughter and fiancée. Although, the fiancée thing was part of his fake girlfriend act.

Complicated.

I'm still trying to unwrap that whole thing in my head.

"I'm in love with Em," my brother says.

I'm happy for him. It's obvious that he's had feelings for her for months, but I just haven't been able to tell if they're real or if it's more out of lust. It's been a while since he's gotten laid. I mean, he's got a kid. Kyler can't just bring home random women and fuck them when he wants, not without Bristol asking a thousand questions. And that girl can talk.

"Yeah, but is that enough? I mean, she's cute and, from what I can tell, great with your kid, but do you guys connect?" I ask, gesturing with my hands to his dick in her vagina.

He smacks me upside the head.

"I'm not telling you about our sex life," Kyler says.

I throw my hands up into the air. "Fine. Your funeral when you marry her and realize she's as vanilla as a soft serve cone."

"Trust me, she's not vanilla," Kyler quips. "Hell, you saw her giving me a BJ when I had the guys over."

I laugh. That had been nearly a year ago. "Yeah, I guess I did," I say. "Never thought I'd walk in on that going on in your house. Noah, yes, he's always banging the next chick he can get his hands on, but you've been cautious since having a kid. Worried that you might create another spawn?" I joke.

He smacks the back of my head again. "Watch your tone. We're meeting Em's sister at the jeweler."

"She has a sister?" I'd asked her once if she had any siblings. She'd mentioned her sister liking pussy, but I'm not sure she wasn't trying just to tell me to go fuck myself. That would be a very Emerson thing to do.

"Yeah, Amber Ryan. She's meeting us at Tiffany's."

"Of course she is," I say. Why would I think that he'd shop anywhere else for an engagement ring? "You do know that Em doesn't care where you get the ring, right? She's not marrying you for your money."

I may not know Emerson well, but I've never gotten the gold digger vibes from her. And I'm usually a pretty good judge of character.

"I know, but I want to surprise her, and with the

fake proposal at the hockey arena, I owe her a real proposal."

I pat Kyler on the back. "Well, hopefully, she'll say yes."

Kyler's jaw tightens. "Do you think that she won't?"

I've never seen my older brother actually look worried. He's usually got his shit together, and when he doesn't, he hides it pretty well from the rest of the world.

We walk up to the front of the building, and there's a cute brunette with red highlights in her hair. I try not to stare, but I recognize her. She was completely brunette the last time that I saw her, and her cheeks had been bright red.

She's the girl from the bar—the cute, young brunette who asked me to save her. Actually, more specifically, she had asked for my help.

I doubt that she remembers me.

The brunette gives a quick wave and a smile. She pulls her jacket closer and tighter. The air this morning is chilly. "Hi, I'm Amber," she says.

"Thanks for meeting with us, Amber. I'm Kyler, and this is my brother, Jasper."

Does she recognize me?

"It's nice to meet you," Amber says, and I'm

guessing she doesn't remember me. I guess I didn't make a lasting impression.

"Likewise," I say and hold out my hand to introduce myself. She takes my hand and shakes it, and I hold on to her hand a moment longer than necessary, trying to see if there's any recollection on her face.

She smiles and lets go of my hand, grabbing the door handle. "Should we go in?" she asks.

Amber steps inside first, and I'm one hundred percent confident that this is the same girl I rescued months ago during her date from hell. I'm curious what she's been up to, if that meth head has bothered her since, and a number of other fleeting questions.

"Jasper, are you listening to a word I'm saying?" Kyler asks.

"Clearly not," Amber says with a grin.

I clear my throat. "Sorry, you both have my undivided attention," I say.

Kyler is looking at rings and is interested in Amber's opinion on what she thinks her sister would like, mostly the style and cut. He has Amber help with the sizing, and other than knowing her fingers are slender, he's not really confident in her ring size. Apparently, she doesn't have any cheap rings at home that he could borrow to determine her size.

I glance around the shop, but the fanciest rings are brought out for Kyler to admire and choose from without being locked behind the glass.

The price tag nearly knocks me on my ass when I hear the jeweler tell Kyler the value of the ring.

"My sister has never been one for anything flashy," Amber says, "but I think she'll like it."

"You think?" Kyler repeats, and sweat glistens from his head. He grabs a handkerchief from his pocket and dabs his forehead. "Bro, I need your opinion."

I stalk across the floor and glance at the ring Kyler has picked out for Emerson. It's a huge rock and clearly costs a boatload, but money hasn't been an issue for my older brother. He's a billionaire and in the NHL.

Flashy is expected when you're an NHL wife.

"I think it's great," I say and add, "for the two of you." I really don't have much of an opinion on engagement rings. I'm sure that's why he brought Amber. I'm just around for moral support.

Kyler chuckles under his breath. "You wouldn't be caught dead buying one, am I right?"

I smirk. "Yeah, you know me too well."

"While I finish up here, do you want to grab us three coffees from the place down the street?" Kyler asks.

Amber stands. "My work here is done. I'll join you," she says.

I quirk a grin. "That'd be nice." We leave Kyler to finish with the jeweler and pay for the ring. I open the door, heading into the brisk autumn air with Amber at my side.

"So, you and your brother, you both play for the Ice Dragons?" Amber asks.

"We do," I say. "I'm guessing Emerson told you."

There's a smile adorning her face. It's cute. Her cheeks redden, but the air outside could be to blame. "She does mention ice hockey a lot. We never watched it as kids growing up, but I've got into the sport lately."

"Do you play?" I ask. We stand at the crosswalk, waiting for the light to change.

She's bouncing from one foot to the other in an attempt to keep warm. She's got a black wool coat that's buttoned and reaches halfway across her thighs. She shoves her hands into her pockets and retrieves a pair of bright purple gloves, slipping them on as we wait to cross the street.

I don't have to ask if she's cold. We can see our

breath, and she's shivering beside me. I grab my winter hat from my pocket and secure it on her head.

"What are you doing?"

"Helping you get warm," I say. Emerson will kill me if her little sister catches a cold, especially before the wedding. Not that I know when Em and Kyler will be getting married. He hasn't officially proposed yet.

I mean, officially, he did on the ice during a game, but it wasn't real. They've been pretending to be in love, and somewhere between pretending and spending time together, they fell in love.

"Thanks," Amber says, and this time, I'm sure she's blushing. "The light," she gestures, and we stroll alongside one another as we cross the street and walk another block down to the coffee shop.

I open the door for her, letting her inside where it's toasty, and I follow behind. We order three hot coffees, and once our order is up, she grabs her drink and a cup of water and heads for the door.

"Where are you going?" I ask, slowing her down. I'm carrying my coffee and my brother's.

She points with her gloved hand at the door. "Back to the shop."

"Kyler will find us. And I don't think they'd appreciate open beverages in their store."

Amber presses her lips together. "You're right." She relents and follows me to an open table in the corner. Before she sits, she places her coffee on the table and then slides off her gloves and the winter hat, handing the black beanie back to me.

"Thanks."

She runs a hand through her messy hair. Amber looks absolutely adorable, like she's got messy bedhead after a wild night, but I keep that thought to myself.

I have half a mind to tell her to keep it, except it's cold, and after we part ways this morning, I may want it back. I was planning on doing a little practice on the ice rink and prefer to be nice and warm.

"So, your brother and my sister," Amber says, sipping her coffee. She's wearing a light blue scarf that matches her eyes and a cream-colored wool sweater that hugs her down to her knees.

"Is this your first-time meeting Kyler?" I ask.

"It is," she says with a laugh. "Honestly, I thought my sister would introduce me to him before he called me up to ask me to go ring shopping with him."

I smirk. My brother never does things by the book. "That was bold. And you said yes."

"I wanted to meet him before the wedding."

I can't help but laugh. "There are other ways to do that, like have dinner together."

Amber shrugs. "This is more fun than some lame-ass dinner where everyone is on their best behavior. This way, I get to meet him and his brother." She clasps her hands together on the table, staring at me. "So, spill the dirt. You're his brother. What's wrong with him?"

She's grinning, and I sit back and laugh, glancing up at the ceiling. That could be a very long list. "Aside from him being stubborn and a pain in my ass?" I ask.

"Aren't all siblings? What else? I want the juicy details."

"Honestly, he's a pretty great guy, and from what I've seen, the two of them make each other happy."

She dips her fingers into her water cup and flicks it at my face.

"What was that for?" I laugh, wiping away the wet drops from my cheeks.

THREE
AMBER

I FLICKED water at him like a child because I suck really hard at flirting. He grabs a couple of napkins from the table and wipes the remnants of water away, scowling at me, but there's a hint of a smile on his face.

"Just be glad your brother isn't marrying me. Then we'd be family."

"We kind of are family," Jasper quips.

The smile falls from my face. "Right." I sip my hot coffee, grimacing when it burns the roof of my mouth.

"Did you ever hear from that bad date again? What was his name?" Jasper asks.

He does remember me. "Tripp, and no, I made sure to block his phone number."

"Good choice," he says.

"Yes, although I won't ever date a nurse again. But at least I don't have a private membership to the Concierge Medical Center, where he works."

Jasper grins. "Might have to move if that were the case, can't have an ambulance take you to his hospital."

I wince. He makes a valid point. "Maybe I'll date outside of my zip code."

Jasper nods. "Not a bad idea. Then you won't run into them at the grocery store. That can be hella awkward, especially when they're married or have kids."

He's piqued my interest. "Are you speaking from experience?" He has to be, because that just sounds way too specific to be anything else.

Jasper takes a sip of his coffee, ignoring my question. "This stuff is good. Do you come here often?"

"You mean to the coffee shop?" I glance at him with a laugh. "You hang around the guys too much if you're asking girls that as your pickup line."

He chuckles, and Kyler heads into the café. Noticing us, he gives us a nod as he approaches.

"It wasn't a line. I was genuinely curious," Jasper says.

Kyler grabs the empty chair next to us and pulls it back to sit.

"No ring?" I ask, not seeing a bag in his hand. When we left, he was just about to hand over his black Amex card to purchase it.

"It's being sized. They'll have it later today."

I glance at my watch. My morning has been fun, but I have classes this afternoon that I can't miss. "I should go," I say, standing.

"Hand me your phone. If you're ever in a bind and need me to help you on another bad date, just text me."

"That isn't necessary," I say, fiddling with my phone in my hand.

Jasper holds his palm out, and I hand him my phone.

Kyler watches the exchange between us but doesn't say anything. I'm sure that the moment I leave, he'll probably grill his brother about it. Hopefully, it doesn't get back to Emerson because she doesn't know that I have a fake ID, and if she finds out I was in a bar and met a bad date and Jasper helped me out, I'm so screwed.

"I texted myself," Jasper says. "Save me as a contact."

I glance at my phone and add Jasper as a contact. "I really have to go. It was nice meeting you, Kyler, and it was good catching up, Jasper." I grab my coffee and hurry out into the cold, taking my warm drink with me.

———

"You saw Jasper Greyson?" Charlotte's mouth practically hits the floor. "Like, in person?"

I show her the text on my phone. "He gave me his number."

She kicks her legs and squeals while lying on the bed in my studio apartment. "Oh my gosh! You have to call him."

"I can't do that." I quickly lock my phone screen so that Charlotte can't embarrass me. We're best friends, but the girl has more guts than I ever will.

"We should go to one of his hockey games."

"What?" My eyes widen, and I inhale sharply. "My sister will be there."

"She's like the fiancée of one of the players, right?" Charlotte asks. She pushes the red locks out of her eyes and puts her hair up into a bun without even needing a mirror.

It isn't that I couldn't do that, but it's impressive how she makes messy look sexy and can rock it out. The girl is a ten. Gorgeous. Fit. Funny. I don't know how she doesn't have a boyfriend, although she doesn't want to lock one down while going to school and working full-time. I don't know how she does both. I struggle with part-time work and going to school.

"Yes, she's dating Kyler Greyson," I say.

"I saw that on the news. It was super romantic, proposing to her on the ice. I hope I find myself a man who's half as sweet."

"You and me both," I say with a laugh. I can't tell her that it was all fake. My sister would kill me, and while I don't see Emerson very often, I still have a lot of respect for her. I'm sure that she knows what she's doing.

I mean, Kyler is proposing, just not in the spotlight.

"Well, are you going to text Jasper?" Charlotte asks.

"Absolutely not!" The thought makes my stomach curdle like spoiled milk. He's sweet, but I'm not good with dating and guys. I get way too anxious, and after the last date with Tripp, I'm so over men.

"Then it's settled. We have to go to one of the Ice Dragons' home games."

I whine under my breath. "And what if I run into my sister?"

"You won't, and so what if you do?" Charlotte asks with a shrug. "You're not allowed to go to a hockey game because, what, she owns the arena?"

"No, of course, that's not it."

Charlotte is waiting for me to elaborate.

"She can't know about Jasper!" I flop back onto the bed beside Charlotte. "She'd freak out if she knew about Tripp, the drugs, the fact that I went to a bar, the fake ID, the list goes on," I say.

"Whatever, live a little." Charlotte sits up and grabs my arms, pulling me off the bed with her. She grabs her phone and looks up the date for the next home again. "Two tickets for Friday night. No excuses." She glares at me.

"Fine, just get the nosebleed section," I say.

She laughs. "Yeah, right. We're getting front-row seats behind the glass so you can wave and blow kisses at Jasper during the game."

"I might actually have to kill you," I mutter. I pray that she's joking. She can't actually afford that, except she has a tendency to use her father's credit card, and he never seems to notice or care what she purchases.

Friday rolls around, and I'm donning a Greyson jersey. To be honest, I'm not sure whether it's Jasper's or his older brother Kyler's number. I asked the sales clerk, but she didn't have the faintest idea, and I had zero reception inside the store. The internet kept crashing, and I tried texting Charlotte, but the text didn't go through until I left the shop.

I contemplated buying both and returning one, but that would mean having the cash up front, and if I'm paying Charlotte back for the hockey tickets, then I'm already over budget for the month.

I could work extra shifts at the Mad Tea Shop, but I already asked for Friday off last minute, and at minimum wage, it'll take me a while to cover the cost of one jersey and a hockey ticket.

I walk to Charlotte's apartment after my classes are done, and I'm dressed for the game. I don't even have to head upstairs because she's waiting for me on the bottom step outside, talking to one of her neighbors.

And by talking, I mean flirting. She's twirling her red curls and laughing at something he says. I doubt it's that funny.

"I have to go," she says and gives him a little wave

before grabbing my arm and sauntering with me toward the subway.

"Who was that?" I ask, trying not to glance over my shoulder to see if he's watching us.

"Just Kingsley, my next-door neighbor," she says.

"Does Kingsley have a first name?"

Charlotte glances at me. "That's what you ask? Of all the questions one could think up, you ask if he has a first name?" She loosens her hold and glances over her shoulder at him.

She's interested, but she seems like she's playing the long game. The hard-to-get and staying just out of reach game, which I never quite understand with Charlotte. Because I've seen her with boys, and she definitely isn't that hard to catch.

"What should I have asked?"

"Too late," she says and laughs. "Come on." She grabs my hand and hurries down the stairs for the subway in a rush. There's definitely a train downstairs—I can hear the rumble as it comes to a halt—but it doesn't mean it's our train.

But I follow her anyway because I always seem to follow Charlotte's lead. Sometimes I think we're complete opposites, but we complement each other.

When I'm quiet, she's the loud one.

When I'm shy at a party, she has the tenacity to pull me out of my shell and make me mingle.

Sometimes I wonder what I offer her, and then I remember, I keep her from failing her classes. If it weren't for me reminding her we need to go home to sleep, she'd be up all night, partying. Every night.

But I love the girl like a sister.

While I do have a sister, Emerson, sometimes it feels like we're two worlds apart. She didn't even tell me that she was dating a hockey player! I had to find out on the news that she had gotten engaged.

Turns out, the entire ice arena had found out before I did.

I'm a little bitter over it, but I love Emerson. I just, honestly, sometimes don't like her very much. It's probably because I don't feel like I know her anymore. She went to Quantico to become an FBI Agent. She passed her tests with ease. I remember that because I joked about buying her drinks while I'm underage, and she grilled me about how that would be possible.

I neglected to mention the fake ID because if she is a federal agent, I don't need her confiscating my drinking pass.

And somehow, between her becoming a federal agent and her life, she's now dating a hockey player, and I don't know where she works. But it's not the agency. The newspaper ran a piece on her and Kyler Greyson, and it did not mention once that she worked for the bureau. It mentioned she did contract work. I don't even know what the heck that means. Contract work for whom?

I gave up on asking Emerson questions because she wasn't exactly forthcoming with the information, and when I called to ask about the engagement, she practically hung up on me.

We talked it out, at least a little, later that night, but we haven't really spoken much since. Typical Emerson, wrapped up in her own life.

I'm sure I'm in part to blame. It's not like I'm inviting her out on a Friday night to hang out or calling her, except on her birthday. We're not estranged; we're just two different people. One day, we'll cross paths again, and it'll all get fixed, but today isn't going to be that day.

Charlotte pulls me through the turnstiles and down to the platform as the incoming train, which happens to be ours, approaches.

"Do you have the tickets?" I ask, referring to the hockey tickets.

"In my phone. It's all digital nowadays, silly," Charlotte says with a laugh. She grips my hand as the throes of people empty and board the train. She wants to make sure that we don't get separated, and I'm all for it, especially since she has my hockey ticket.

"You didn't get a jersey," I say, gesturing at her ensemble. She's wearing a dark green sweater and black leggings. The girl can rock any outfit and look dynamite. It helps that she has the boobs to pull off anything.

I didn't get so lucky in that department, but that's what padded bras are for. I had hoped I'd outgrow those in high school, but now I'm a junior in college, and they're still giving me the full bust that I have.

She lets go of my hand and grabs the metal bar to hold on to when the train begins to move. There aren't any empty seats, and we're only a handful of stops away from the new ice arena that was built for the Ice Dragons.

"I can buy a jersey at the stadium," Charlotte says. She glances at the back of mine. "Which Greyson are you supporting?" She quirks a grin and glances me over.

"I don't know."

"You didn't look it up?" Her eyes widen, surprised that I had texted her but hadn't followed through with finding out the answer to my question.

I grimace. "Well, I mean, I already bought the jersey. If I'm wrong, I honestly don't want to know."

She tosses her head back and laughs, her hand gripping the metal bar, keeping her upright as the train jogs forward and shifts from side to side. "You are too much sometimes."

My stomach flops. I am the queen of anxiety. And Charlotte just managed to trigger my next episode. Thanks. "Should I look it up?" I ask and dig into my small purse that houses my cell phone, credit card, train ticket, and a few dollars in cash.

"No." Charlotte shakes her head. "Like you said, you're already wearing it. Kind of late now."

"But if I'm wrong, you could buy the right jersey, and we could switch?"

She snorts. "Absolutely not! I'm buying one for the Island Bruisers tonight."

"What?" My mouth drops. "You're going to support the other team?" Is she crazy? I thought we were friends.

"Opposites. I'm telling you, if you're rooting for the Ice Dragons, I have to support the Island Bruisers. That's how this friendship goes."

I tell myself that it doesn't matter. It's not like Jasper is going to see us at the game. We'll be nestled in with the crowd.

We arrive at the stadium, breeze through security, and Charlotte drags me to the shop where they sell jerseys. She buys herself the cheapest Island Bruisers jersey that she can find because while the girl has her daddy's credit card, she is trying to avoid him noticing the massive bill that will come at the end of the month.

She whispers something to the clerk, and he smiles and nods. I notice him ringing up two jerseys. What the hell?

"Those jerseys are buy one get one free," he tells us, handing me an identical Island Bruisers jersey.

I force a smile and mutter, "Thanks." I glare at Charlotte. No way is a jersey free at a professional hockey game. She's just trying to get away with murder.

"Do you need a bag?" he asks.

"No, we're going to wear them." She pulls hers over her head.

Does she think I'll fall for her little game? I purse my lips. Two can play at that. "Seriously, they have to give these away because no one wants them," I say, shoving the Island Bruisers jersey back at her.

"We should both wear the Bruisers jersey," Charlotte grins.

"Why?"

"I'll bet you the tickets to the game that if you wear the Bruisers jersey, Jasper will notice you."

I fold my arms across my chest and bite my bottom lip. "That's a terrible bet. If I lose, I can't afford both tickets, Char. I can barely afford the ticket and jersey that I paid for, and you just bought me this one."

She rolls her eyes. "Wear the Bruisers jersey, and I'll cover the cost of your ticket."

"That's crazy!"

Charlotte smiles and shrugs innocently. "I make more than you do. And I put it on Daddy's credit card, so we're fine."

"You shouldn't have done that, I will pay you for the ticket. Let me know what it costs, and I'll Venmo you the money."

"Wear the jersey," she says and points at the blue jersey in my hands.

I groan under my breath. "He's going to kill me."

"That's the point. I want him to notice you."

My stomach flutters, and I wince, pulling the jersey on over the Ice Dragons one I'm wearing.

We show our tickets to the attendant and are ushered down to the front row, seated just behind the glass.

"Holy crap, girl, you weren't kidding about front-row seats." I'm shocked. I really thought we'd be in the nosebleed section, which would have been fine for me.

I sit, and my foot taps restlessly.

What if Jasper sees me wearing the Island Bruisers jersey?

He will see me.

Charlotte grabs my hand. "Would you chill out? You're making me nervous."

I laugh. I swear, the girl doesn't even know what nervous means. She's always so calm and collected. Well, maybe calm doesn't describe Charlotte, but she always seems to have her shit together. I've never noticed her appear insecure or anxious.

I dig my phone out of my purse, and I'm surprised that I have decent reception. I snap a few photographs of us together in our Island Bruisers jerseys and post them to Instagram.

Charlotte is distracted on her own phone, and I type in Jasper Greyson, finding his Instagram profile.

It's not the first time I've stalked him online. I mean, it's just a harmless crush. After he swooped in and rescued me from that horrible date with Tripp, Jasper has certainly been on my mind.

But I should let it go. He's going to be my sister's brother-in-law. Which pretty much makes us family.

But he's hot and, from what I can tell, very single.

I scroll through the recent pictures, which are of him and the guys. There's even one of him and his niece, Bristol, which is sweet. They're both in skates on the ice.

The most recent picture is from a few minutes ago in the locker room, and he's shirtless. It already has over a thousand likes. He does have a good physique, and he clearly knows it.

Jasper Greyson isn't shy, certainly not about his body.

The man probably doesn't have any anxiety, either. Lucky bastard. I bite down on my tongue. I shouldn't be looking at his profile, but I can't help myself.

He has tons of followers, but he's only following less than one hundred accounts. I doubt that he'll follow me, but I follow his account and press the heart button by his photo.

It's unlikely that he'll even notice.

"Stalking your boyfriend?" Charlotte asks, glancing over my shoulder.

"No," I say and flip away from his profile.

"Liar." She laughs, taunting me. "You have to make him notice you. Right now, you're just another girl in the long line of women who want him. You have to stand out."

"And wearing the Bruisers jersey is going to do that?" I don't necessarily agree with her methods, but if it helps get him to notice me, maybe it's not such a bad plan.

"Let's take one more photo," Charlotte says. "Give me your phone."

I hand her my phone. She has long arms and manages to get a selfie of the two of us sporting our Island Bruisers jerseys. We're smiling and making silly faces. I assume that we're going to post it to Instagram with the other photos.

"Make it your profile picture," Charlotte says.

"What?" She's lost her mind. If I do that, everyone will think I'm an Island Bruisers fan. Not that I care, but my sister will see, and she'll probably disown me since her fiancé is an Ice Dragon.

"Well, that, or message the photo to him. You do have his cell phone number," she says cheekily.

"I never should have told you he gave me his number."

"Profile picture or text him." Charlotte is waiting for me to make a decision. She's always bitched about how I'm indecisive. Right now, both options seem terrible.

"Fine." I change my profile picture. It's unlikely he'll even notice that I followed his account or liked his most recent picture. That's the safer option.

The game finally starts, and I have no idea what's happening other than the Ice Dragons are in gold and black. Both teams fight for the puck, gliding across the ice.

The Ice Dragons have control, but not for long, when the Island Bruisers steal the puck. It goes back and forth, a constant battle between both teams with minimal scoring.

They're all trying to score, but both goalies seem to be doing an excellent job of keeping the puck away.

Jasper skates by the glass, his focus on the puck as he tries to get it away from the other team.

"Go, Jasper!" I squeal, not that I think he can actually hear me. The crowd is rowdy, and the other noise drowns me out.

Charlotte elbows me. "You're wearing a Bruisers jersey. You have to root for the other team."

"That wasn't part of the deal." I scowl at Charlotte.

"Should have been," she says with a wicked smirk.

I roll my eyes and stand when he comes near the

glass. Jasper is battling another player from the Island Bruisers team, Storm. He is fighting for the puck with his hockey stick when Storm strikes upward with his stick and hits Jasper in the face.

That's all it takes for Jasper to pound Storm into the glass. He's cursing, and they're taking blows at one another right in front of me.

I'm standing, shock evident as I watch the exchange.

Kyler is over instantly, and instead of pulling Jasper off the Island Bruisers player, he's right there with him. But it's not two against one. It's an entire team battling it out, fighting, and suddenly, I understand when they say a fight breaks out at a hockey game because, holy crap, not even the referee has control.

There are curses and punches being thrown, men shoved up against the glass, and somewhere between the beatings and the threats of violence, Jasper meets my stare.

"You're supporting them?" His jaw drops, and he lands a few more blows to Storm's chest. Storm doesn't just stand there and take it. He shoves Jasper against the glass, his back to me, knocking Jasper's helmet off.

"Jasper!" I scream.

The referee gains control, and Jasper Greyson and Knox Storm are sent to the penalty box. Jasper bends down, grabbing his helmet, but he doesn't turn around. He doesn't look at me. And I wonder if listening to Charlotte was the best idea.

FOUR

JASPER

"WHAT THE HELL WAS THAT?" Kyler asks as I'm finally delegated to the bench after a stint in the penalty box.

I'm not having my best game, and the fact that Emerson's little sister, Amber, is in the stands, wearing an Island Bruisers jersey, is killing me.

What the hell did I ever do to her?

Okay, it's probably not personal. But fuck me, she looked so excited watching me get the shit kicked out of me.

Some family we're becoming.

"Your girlfriend's sister has front-row seats," I mutter.

Kyler glances behind us at the private seats

where our players bring friends and family. "I don't see Amber."

"She's not sitting there," I grumble. "And she's wearing a fucking Bruisers jersey."

"Ouch," Kyler says with a smirk. "Might have to tattle on her to Em." He lets it roll off him like water, as if the news doesn't strike him as odd or hurtful.

It bothered him when Emerson wore an Island Bruisers jersey. Hell, it bothered the fuck out of him when she came sporting *his* Island Bruisers jersey with ridiculous drawings that the guys gave him as a go fuck yourself present.

"Where is she?" Kyler glances around the stands.

I nod in the direction of the goalie, trying my best to be discreet. "Front row, where I got into it with Knox."

"What the hell was that between you and Storm?" Kyler asks.

"Old shit," I say, not wanting to get into it with my older brother. There are some things that he doesn't know about the past, from when I was thirteen. I don't intend on drudging that shit up.

"Over a girl?" Kyler guesses.

"Do I look like I'm seeing anyone?" I glare at my brother to zip it.

"What are you going to do about Amber?" my brother asks.

I exhale a heavy breath. "Fuck if I know. Throw her one of my jerseys to put the fuck on over that monstrosity?"

"I dare you," Kyler says with a wicked grin and a glint in his eyes.

I've never chickened out over a dare before. I'm not about to start now.

I'm put back onto the ice a few minutes before the period ends, and I try to keep my concentration on the game. But every time I've got the puck, and I'm down near Amber, I glance up at her, unable to look away.

It costs me the puck and possibly a point.

I'm distracted.

She's the biggest distraction, and I should tell her not to come back and to stay away from the arena because her wearing *that* hideous ensemble is killing my mojo. But if she's an Island Bruisers fan, then all it's going to do is make her more tenacious to ensure that we lose.

The clock runs down, and the minute the period is over, I skate over toward the glass where she's seated.

Amber stands and gives me a nervous smile. "Hey," she says.

She ought to be nervous. She's been caught supporting the opposing team.

I remove my helmet and pull my jersey off. "You look ridiculous. Put this on," I say and toss it over the glass at Amber.

Amber stares at me but catches my jersey. Good, because I wouldn't want anyone else getting their hands on it.

She's either speechless or appalled by my suggestion.

Her friend beside her quirks a grin. "And if we say no?"

"We?" Who the fuck is this girl? They're wearing matching Island Bruisers jerseys in a sea of Ice Dragons around them. They must be friends.

Just wonderful.

Was it Amber's idea or her friend's, to support the Island Bruisers?

"Wear my fucking jersey, Amber."

"She's not your girlfriend," the redhead pipes up with a smile.

"She can speak for herself," I say, staring into Amber's blue gaze.

She sucks in a breath, and her cheeks are red. I can't tell if she's mad or nervous. I don't know Amber well enough to figure her out. I consider inviting her to the Blue Line, our local tap house where the team goes after a game to unwind, but I think better of it.

We don't invite fans of the opposing team, and if she is an Island Bruisers fan, I don't want her there. Not after the fight I got into during the game with Storm.

Tension is still heated amongst the players, and I don't want Amber making this difficult when we're supposed to celebrate. That's assuming that we win. The game isn't over yet, and the score is tied.

"Jasper!" Noah shouts for me to hurry off the ice. The rest of the team has gone to the locker room during intermission, and they're waiting on my ass. Coach Malone always likes to give a short speech, some insight on what he's seeing from the other team, and sometimes a bit of a pep talk or tongue-lashing, depending on the score.

"When I come out for the next period, I expect you to be wearing *my* jersey."

I skate off and head into the locker room with the guys.

"Lost the shirt off your back," Coach says as I head for my wooden locker. I grab another jersey and put it on over my pads, leaving my helmet on the bench.

"He's got a crush on a girl in the stands," Noah chimes.

I grumble under my breath. "It's not a crush." I don't have crushes. If I like a girl, I bang it out with her. Crush resolved.

My career is my focus. Hockey. Not girls.

Especially not girls who are fans of the Island Bruisers. Any other team, maybe I could look the other way.

"So, you just give your jersey to any girl you see in the stands supporting the opposing team?" Noah asks.

"He's just helping me out," Kyler says. His jersey is off, and he's wiping himself down with a clean towel. Some of the guys shower between intermission to cool off. "She's Em's little sister."

Noah doesn't say anything, but that look tells me that he knows me better than my own brother.

"Kyler is right," I say, jumping on his suggestion. "I don't want my older brother to look bad for the media. I mean, what if they find out Em's little sister is at the game wearing a Bruisers jersey? It would be horrible for the team and for his love life."

Kyler throws his sweat-soaked towel at me, but I catch it before it manages to hit me in the face.

"Jackass," I mutter.

"Talk about my love life again. I dare you," Kyler says, raising his eyebrows.

"That's enough!" Coach says, interrupting our brotherly feud. "Save it for the ice and the Bruisers, boys."

We only have a few minutes left, and I know that I shouldn't be checking my phone during intermission, but when I see a text from Amber pop up, I can't help but read it.

You expect me to wear your stinky jersey?

I laugh under my breath.

Wear it, or else I'll tell your sister you're an Island Bruisers fan.

Go ahead. I dare you.

"What's so funny?" Kyler asks when he glances over my shoulder at the text messages between Amber and me. "She's right. Your jersey probably smells disgusting."

"It was clean when I put it on."

"And you got the shit kicked out of you by Knox during the first period. There's blood and sweat on that thing. I wouldn't expect Em to wear it."

"You're full of shit." I elbow Kyler. "And don't girls like sweaty jerseys? Isn't that a turn-on?"

"Are you trying to turn on my fiancée's little sister?"

"That's enough talk, gather 'round," Malone says, and it's the first time that I'm grateful for the coach interrupting us.

We get suited up and back on the ice for the second period. I try to ignore the fact that Amber is in the stands, but when I skate near the goal and land eyes on her, she's wearing *my* jersey.

And I damn near feel proud that she's got my number on her and is supporting *the* team. The right team if you ask me.

I score four goals during the second period, and by the third, it's near impossible for them to catch us.

"I should give that hot piece of ass in the stands my jersey," Knox says as we fight over the puck. "If that's all it takes to get lucky."

"Stay away from her," I growl.

"Never knew you to chase tail," Knox says. "But then again, I guess you have to chase it since you're a virgin."

For the record, I'm not a virgin. But I also don't fuck just anyone with a pussy. I slam into him as we fight for the puck and shove him up against the glass.

This time, Amber isn't behind us, and I'm grateful because I slam my fist into Knox's jaw and pound the shit out of his chest.

"Leave Amber out of this," I say, slamming my fists into his chest. The hockey sticks fall onto the ice as we pound the shit out of one another.

"Oh, pretty girl has a name. Wonderful. She'll be my next score," Knox says.

"The fuck she will!" I'd fucking bite the bastard if I didn't have a mouthguard in and all the padding wasn't protecting him.

My fists don't feel like they're doing justice for the insults that he's flinging at Amber.

The referee throws both Knox and me out of the game for fighting. This time, it isn't even a short trip to the penalty box.

At least we're so far ahead it won't fuck up the game. But shit, Coach is going to be pissed at me.

I ice my knuckles and sit on the bench, watching the game from the locker room. Thankfully, there are televisions with the game on, but it's not the same as being with the team on the bench.

There are only two minutes left in the period, and we're winning by a landslide. I'm not worried about us losing the game. But I do feel like I let down the team.

There's another fight on the ice, and two more players are ejected from the game. Noah Reece with the Ice Dragons and Mack Conrad of the Island Bruisers.

Noah blows into the locker room, his helmet in his hands.

"You didn't have to keep me company," I say.

"They were talking shit about our women. I sure the fuck did," Noah quips.

I wasn't aware that Noah was dating anyone, but I don't pry.

"Are you dating that chick you gave your jersey to?" Noah asks.

"Amber? Not exactly." I smile and glance away.

"Are you going to invite her out for drinks tonight with the guys at Blue Line?" Noah asks.

Before I have time to answer, the game is over, and the team is headed into the locker room. Should I invite Amber?

I strip out of my clothes, shower, and then get dressed. My knuckles are a bit rough, and I've got a couple of bruises to the chest, but it could have been worse with all the punches thrown.

"Are you coming out with us tonight?" I ask Kyler,

already knowing the answer. He rarely comes out for celebratory drinks. He's usually at home with his daughter, Bristol, and his fiancée, Emerson.

"Not tonight," Kyler says, patting me on the shoulder. "Maybe when we get into the playoffs."

We finish up in the locker room, and a group of us heads to Blue Line for drinks. Noah, Owen, and I walk together.

Asher and his wife, Kate, are just behind us, and Parker mentioned that he'd catch up with us with Ava tonight after he grabs her from the wives' room.

I've never been invited to the elusive wives' room. None of the guys are allowed to attend. And it's by invitation only from one of the members.

Only serious girlfriends and wives can be invited. I heard it took a while for Emerson to get an invitation, but when she attends games, she joins the hockey wives upstairs. And she can't just invite a friend to join her—or her sister.

Not that I should be thinking about Amber. I shouldn't.

She should be the furthest thought from my mind. I glance at my phone. I'm not sure why, but I'm hoping that maybe she sent me another text.

We arrive out front of Blue Line, and Owen suggests a group shot outside the tap house. I'm in agreement because we should always celebrate a win.

Ava offers to take the pictures with my phone, and the guys all pack into the photo. She snaps a few pics and hands me back the phone. "I want copies."

"I'll text them to you," I promise. I find the best photo of us and post it on my Instagram page. My agent says it's good for my image. It makes me a household name to post candid shots. Makes the fans love me even more.

I think it's a bunch of horseshit, but I do it because I'm on a rookie contract, and I'd like a bigger payday when my contract comes due.

Kyler never has to worry about anything. He made some winning investments in cryptocurrency with our parents' life insurance policy. He bitches that it's cursed, but the man lives lavishly, so I don't see why he's griping. And he tells me that one day he will buy the Ice Dragons when he retires.

I'll believe it when I see it. It's a nice dream that he has, but there's a lot of work that goes into running a successful hockey team. If anyone could do it, Kyler Greyson has it in him, but he also has a big heart, and I'm not sure he'd have it in him to cut some of the guys and be ice cold when he needs to be.

We head inside Blue Line and right for the back VIP booth, which is reserved exclusively for us. We're regulars on game night, especially when we win. A few of us also show up when we lose, but it's mostly to drown out our sorrows with decent beer.

Thankfully, I'm twenty-one now, so I don't have to worry about the guys giving me shit when I can only drink soda because the owners and staff of the tap house know the team well enough to know who is under twenty-one.

We have a few underage guys, but they don't tend to frequent Blue Line with us. I know they go to a couple of other local bars and try to stay under the radar with their fake IDs because I've been invited out with them when I was twenty.

I don't need to fuck up my career over a couple of beers. That's one type of publicity that I don't need.

I let the guys with their wives have the booth, and I grab a seat on the stool at the end of the table. The waitress comes over, already knowing our usual, and ensures we don't need anything else before bringing us a round.

The guys are chatting and drinking, and I scroll through my phone, distracted, while I wait for another beer to come.

Owen and Noah are conversing about the game,

how we kicked the shit out of the Island Bruisers. That was fun.

I shouldn't even bother looking at my phone. There are no new texts from Amber, not that I expect her to send anything to me. It surprised me that she sent anything at all, and the snarkiness in her tone about my jersey being sweaty—heaven help me.

There aren't too many girls I've had my eye on lately. I've kept my head down, focused on the sport, and finally got the contract that I wanted. Being a rookie isn't half bad since they actually let me play, and I'm not benched most of the game.

Asher and Kate are making out in the back booth. You'd think, for a married couple, the heat between them would simmer, but after winning a game, they always seem cozy.

"Get a room, you two," I say and flip a bottle cap at them.

It bounces off the table and hits Asher in the arm. He ignores me, shoving his tongue down his wife's throat. Nothing distracts those two, not even if the fire alarm went off or if there was an all-out brawl in the bar.

My attention returns to my cell phone, and I can't help but notice that Amber Ryan liked my most recent post and followed me on Instagram. I click her profile, grab my beer, and take a swig, spitting it out the minute I get a better look at her picture.

"She's a fucking Bruisers fan," I mutter too loudly.

Owen pats me on the back and hands me a napkin. "Do we need to buy you a bib?"

"Shut it," I growl at him and flip through her pictures, shaking my head. She took quite a few at the arena, all of them in that stupid blue jersey.

Gripping the bottle, I take another swig of beer, seeing red as I glance up from my phone.

Her brunette hair, mixed with red highlights, shimmers as she steps into the bar.

"No fucking way."

And she's not wearing my jersey. She's wearing that damn Island Bruisers jersey again.

FIVE
AMBER

THE ICE DRAGONS jersey that Jasper tossed at me over the glass was a nice gesture, but it smelled like sweat, not to mention it was wet. Like, completely covered in sweat and even had a dab of blood here and there from the fight.

I could save it, maybe even sell it online, but wear it? No chance in hell was I putting that jersey on over my body.

Not until it had a nice, hot run through the washing machine.

Sure, a little bit of a man's scent is a good thing. It's primal. Sexual. Enticing.

No. This jersey stunk like he'd bathed in a swamp and battled a dragon afterward.

Gross.

I appreciate the gesture and the sentiment, although I think it's more to do with wanting my sister happy. I saw him and his brother talking before he tossed me the jersey.

But then Charlotte did the unthinkable and shoved it over my head when I wasn't paying attention.

I screamed like I walked in on someone being brutally murdered.

She laughed.

The minute the game ends, I yank his jersey off and ball it into my fists. What the hell am I supposed to do with it? If I bring it onto the subway, it'll stink up the whole rail car.

"Do you want to wait for the crowd to thin?" I ask.

"Yes, no sense in fighting the subway crowd." She stretches and stands, her gaze moving around the place.

I remain seated and glance through my phone, and my friend nudges me with her knees.

"Any more texts from the hottie?"

"Thankfully, no. I can't believe you texted him using my phone!" I'm still a bit peeved that she grabbed my phone and then used it against me to unlock it. Stupid face identification.

"I can't believe you fell for the oldest trick in the

book," Charlotte says. "It's obvious he likes you. He wouldn't have given you that nasty thing if he didn't." She gestures at the jersey in my hands.

"Thank you for at least agreeing it's nasty." I exhale a heavy sigh. "I should probably return it."

She plops down beside me on the chair when she catches me stalking his Instagram feed. I've been staring at it for a few minutes. She was bound to notice. A new image pops up with him and the guys. They're outside some bar, Blue Line, and it looks like he just took the picture.

"We're going there," Charlotte says and grabs my hand, practically dragging me out of my seat. The crowd has thinned from the seats, and if we wait too much longer, we'll get kicked out by security anyhow.

In my hands, I still have Jasper's sweaty jersey. Although, now, it doesn't seem quite as wet and gross. It still reeks, but there's a hint of Jasper's scent mingled with the dragon slayer sweat.

"I don't know," I say, my voice trembling. "What if he doesn't want to see me?"

"He gave you his jersey during the game. He wants to see you."

Charlotte makes a valid point, but that doesn't

stop the butterflies in my stomach or my hands from trembling.

"Wouldn't he have invited me if he wanted me to come?" I ask. She glances at her phone, grabbing GPS directions as we hurry out of the arena and onto the street.

It's dark outside and chilly. I'm half tempted to put the stinky jersey back on to keep warm, but instead, it remains in my grip with my trembling hands.

When we reach the Blue Line, I stand outside for a minute, my feet not working.

"Come on." Charlotte links her arm in mine.

"I can't do this," I say, shaking my head, self-doubt beginning to creep in.

"Why not?" she asks, turning around to face me.

"You and I are complete opposites. I hide behind my phone and my laptop. You go in there like a hurricane and get what you want. That isn't me."

Charlotte smiles, her shoulders seeming to relax. "So, just waltz in there, hand him back his disgusting jersey, and turn and walk away."

I can do that. "Okay," I say. "But you'll wait out here?"

Charlotte nods. "I'll wait at the bar and get us drinks."

"I can live with that," I say and step inside the bar. It's dark and crowded, and I'm glancing around, looking for Jasper. I could have been wrong. Maybe the picture he posted wasn't taken today. Wouldn't I feel like an idiot? Of course, he'd never have to know.

And that's when I meet his stare. He's at a table in the back, nearly hidden by the crowd. I suck in a nervous breath, try to remember to exhale and stalk across the bar.

"This is yours," I say, shoving the stinky jersey into his hands.

His brow is pinched, and he stands and pulls me aside, out of earshot of his buddies. I don't blame him. This probably isn't a conversation I'd want my friends to witness, either.

"What are you doing?" Jasper asks, his eyes wide.

"Giving you back your jersey." I shove it at him, but he doesn't take it.

"I gave it to you," he says, and I swear that he's steaming. His gaze moves over my body. "You can't wear *that* in here. Ice Dragon fans only."

I exhale a heavy laugh. "Okay." I put my purse on his table along with his jersey and reach for the hem of the Island Bruisers jersey that I'm wearing, pulling it up.

Jasper stops me before I even reach my stomach.

"What the hell are you doing?" he growls into my ear, his hands on mine, not letting me remove the jersey.

"Undressing."

His eyes are wide like two saucers. "In public?"

"I have something on underneath," I say.

He drops his hands and watches me slowly inch the Island Bruisers jersey over my head, removing it.

I stand in front of him in an Ice Dragons jersey with the name Greyson on the back. I still wasn't smart enough to take note of which brother's jersey I was wearing. I'd been so focused on watching Jasper that I hadn't even noticed his number. Some fan I am.

"Burn that monstrosity," Jasper says, nodding toward the blue jersey in my hands.

"You're not burning my jersey," I say.

"You only need one." Jasper stares at me, a smile tugging at the corners of his lips. He's pleased with the surprise that I had underneath my clothes. "Whose number are you wearing?"

I spin around and hear him scoff.

"My brother? Seriously, Amber?"

My cheeks burn, and I glance down at my hands. "It was a fifty-fifty shot when I bought it at the store."

"Give her credit for at least having something

other than the Bruisers jersey on underneath," his friend says.

"Amber, this is Noah," Jasper introduces us.

"Nice to meet you," I say, smiling weakly.

"Join us," Noah chimes. "Jasper has been staring at his phone for the past hour."

"We haven't been here an hour," Jasper snarls at Noah.

"Hot date?" I ask, pushing a strand of hair behind my ear. I glance back over my shoulder at Charlotte, who seems to have disappeared. She ditched me.

Jasper merely shakes his head no. He doesn't say a word.

The guys shift around, and I grab an empty stool, sitting beside Jasper. "Good game tonight," I say and push the dirty jersey he gave me back on the bar table in front of him.

Jasper leans closer, his lips brushing my ear. "You do know most girls would fawn over a player giving them the jersey off their back?"

"I'm not most girls," I say, staring at him. "And your jersey stinks." I pick it up and shove it in his face.

Noah laughs hard, wiping his eyes. "I like this girl. Where'd you find her?" Noah can't stop laughing, and I relax, the anxiety slowly slipping away as I grow comfortable around Jasper and his friends.

Jasper shoves the jersey out of his face, and I swear his eyes are watering.

"You know Emerson, Kyler's fiancée," Jasper says, glancing at his buddy. "This is her little sister, Amber."

"How'd you know where to find us? Ask around?" Noah asks.

"It's not like the Blue Line is a secret," Jasper says. "We come here after *every* win."

"Thanks, I wasn't aware, but now that I am, I might have to crash all your celebrations," I joke. There's a bucket of beers, and Jasper hands me one without thinking twice.

I pop the lid and take a sip, grimacing at the taste.

"Not your preference? I can bring the waitress over and order something else for you."

"It's fine," I say and try another sip, but it's pretty appalling. I've heard that beer is an acquired taste, but I have no intention of acquiring it anytime soon.

Jasper takes the beer from my hand. "I'll order you something else," he says with more insistence and gestures the waitress over. "What do you want? I'm buying?"

"I'll have a whiskey sour," I say.

"I'm going to need to see your ID," the waitress says.

I dig out my fake ID and hand it over to the waitress, hoping that Jasper doesn't notice the name on it isn't Amber Ryan.

She hands me back the ID, and I bury it in my purse. "Thanks."

"Anything else?" the waitress asks.

"Another bucket of beers. Keep them coming," Owen says. He has two empty beers in front of him, and he grabs a third.

Jasper leans closer as he whispers, "The man is a fish. I've seen him drink *a lot* and wake up pristine the next morning for practice."

"I wish I had that superpower," I say and laugh. I glance over my shoulder at Charlotte, who seems occupied at the bar with two men. She's laughing and twirling her hair, and I'm unsure if I should be rescuing her or letting her enjoy their company and the drinks.

Jasper turns and follows my gaze. "Your friend?"

"Yeah, she convinced me to—" I don't finish that sentence, and he turns to face me.

"You can't just leave me hanging," he says.

I nervously laugh and avert my stare, glancing

down at his hands in his lap, and he probably thinks I'm staring at his crotch.

Crap.

I glance up and inhale a sharp breath.

"Amber?" He's waiting for me to elaborate or explain why I was just caught staring at the bulge in his jeans. And it was an obvious bulge. Like, the man can hardly fit in his pants.

"She dared me to wear that stupid Bruisers jersey," I say.

"Dared you?" He's watching me, studying my face, and I can't quite read him. "Let me guess, you're the type to never back down from a dare."

I'm not sure that's true, but I leave off the part where she convinced me that it would get Jasper's attention, and she was right. It worked.

"I always loved playing truth or dare as a teenager," I say with a shrug. "I guess I never really outgrew it."

The waitress brings my whiskey sour to the table, and I graciously take a sip, although it's more like a gulp. Jasper makes me anxious—being in his presence, his scent, the fact that I can practically feel the heat off his body as his knee brushes against mine.

Unlike earlier, when the jersey smelled

disgusting, Jasper smells clean, like soap, but it's mixed with something earthy. *His scent.* I could gladly run my tongue along his body and kiss every inch of him.

The smirk on his face grows, and he reaches for his beer, bringing it back for another swig. "Truth or dare," he says.

I chuckle and take another sip of my drink. Unlike most places around campus, this bar doesn't water down its alcohol, and it's tasty with the sour mix, but it also helps me relax.

"Dare." Because if he asks me truth and wants to know if I have feelings for him, I can't voice it. Then again, he could dare me to kiss him, and maybe I shouldn't, but I want to, and it would give me a reason above all else without looking foolish.

He smirks. "Prank call my brother, Kyler."

"What?"

"I'll give you his number."

"He has my number. Remember, I met him at Tiffany's? I can't use my phone for the prank."

"What about your friend's phone?" Jasper points in Charlotte's direction.

"Fine. I'll commandeer her phone." I slide off the stool and strut across the bar, pretending not to be nervous. Charlotte will want an explanation, and I'm not sure she'll play along.

"Already done?" Charlotte asks when she notices me joining her at the bar. She pouts, looking disappointed as she glances past my shoulder at Jasper.

"Actually, I need your phone."

Charlotte doesn't just hand over her device. The corners of her lips turn upward. "Why?" she asks in a sweet singsong voice. She's prepared to tease me, and she doesn't even know what for.

"Just, can I borrow it?" I ask.

"Not until you tell me why you need it. You have your phone, right? Did you leave it at the arena?"

"Jasper and I are playing a game of truth or dare, and he wants me to prank call his older brother. Kyler has my number. He'll know it's me."

Her eyes light up. "I'm in." She glances back at the boys who were buying her drinks. "Sorry, I have to keep my friend company. It was nice meeting you both." She leads me back to the table with the hockey players, and Jasper is watching as we stalk up to the table.

"Are you in, or do you forfeit?" he asks.

"My girl never forfeits," Charlotte says. She digs

her phone out of her pocket. "I'll give you this, but you have to let me in on your little game."

"Truth or dare?" Jasper asks.

"I want to play," Charlotte says.

"Fine," I grumble and snatch her phone. Jasper gives me Kyler's phone number so that I don't have to look it up on my phone. I grab my drink from the table and finish the whiskey sour. "Get me another drink," I say to Charlotte.

"On it. After you make this call." She grabs a stool and pulls it around to sit beside me at the table.

I let out a shaky breath and hit the call button, waiting for Kyler to answer.

"Hello?" He doesn't sound sleepy, which is good. He probably just got home from the game.

"I can't believe you, Kyler Greyson. You stole my significant other."

"What?" he grumbles, and I can imagine the confused look on his face.

Jasper's grinning and gesturing for me to continue this charade. "Em is everything to me, and I saw what you did, asking her to marry you at the ice arena. Well, she can't. Because she's married to me!"

"Amber, is that you?" Kyler asks, and I immediately end the call.

"Shit!" I grumble and shove the phone back at Charlotte. "What if he calls back?"

"I'll answer it and tell him he's crazy, that no one called from this number," Charlotte says with a shrug.

My cell phone buzzes in my purse, and I glance at the name. "I'm not answering that!" I say and shove the phone at Jasper. "This is your doing."

"Hey, Bro, what's up?" Jasper accepts the call.

I can't hear what's being said from Kyler's side, and he can't put it on speakerphone because the bar is too noisy.

"No, you dialed me. I don't know where Amber is. I'm out with the guys celebrating. You should have come out tonight. It's been fun." Jasper frowns and pulls the phone back from his ear. "He hung up on me."

"That was too funny," Charlotte admits. "Okay, Amber's turn. Pick someone."

"She has to choose you. If three are playing, she can't pick the person who just gave her the dare," Jasper says.

I grumble and scowl at Charlotte. "Truth or dare."

"Dare."

"I dare you to get me that whiskey sour that I asked for."

Charlotte grins. "Well played. I pick you," she says at Jasper.

"Jasper."

"I'm Charlotte," she says, realizing they haven't introduced themselves to one another.

"I know," he says. "You've caused a bit of trouble tonight. I'll pick truth."

"She'll ask it," Charlotte says, pointing at me. "I've got to get the princess her drink." She saunters off to the bar.

"Do you think I'm getting my drink?" I laugh because I don't think she's planning on coming back anytime soon.

"Is that your question?" Jasper asks.

"No!"

"Then, no. I don't think she really wants to hang out with us. And I chose truth, so hit me with it."

"Do you have a girlfriend?" I ask, straight and right to the point. He hasn't had any pictures on Instagram with him and a girl, but that doesn't mean he's single. He could be keeping it private or making the ladies think he's available to help his status as an NHL player.

He sips his beer, his gaze never leaving mine. "I

do not. I focus on the game, and that doesn't make the ladies happy when I put them second."

"I can understand that," I say. "Your career is important to you. So, are you the kind of guy who prefers flings or friends with benefits?"

He laughs and shakes his head. "One question. My turn."

My eyes widen, and I exhale a nervous breath. "Okay." I glance over my shoulder at Charlotte, who is at the bar. She may actually be ordering me a drink, but she's not bringing it over quickly enough.

"Truth or dare?" Jasper asks.

"Truth," I say and stare at him, hoping this game isn't over before it's begun. I'm nervous and flustered. If I choose dare, I don't want him to ask me to do something else embarrassing, and with the last dare being a prank, the game isn't going quite in the direction that I had hoped. But we did just start.

He could be cautious?

"Do you like pussy?"

My eyes widen, and I think my mouth hits the floor. "Excuse me?"

Jasper quirks a wry grin. "Your sister mentioned something a while back before she and my brother were actually hooking up. Mentioned she had a sister who likes pussy. Do you?"

"I'm going to kill her," I mutter and glance over my shoulder at Charlotte.

I could really use that drink right now.

"It's okay. There's nothing to be embarrassed about." Jasper shrugs. "I mean, I've got friends who are gay. I swear it doesn't matter to me. I just want to know if we both like tits."

Tears prickle my eyes, but I'm filled with laughter, not sadness. "I do like a good set of boobs," I say, "and I've done some experimenting. I'm in college."

"Right." Jasper stares at me and finishes his bottle of beer. "Still not an answer."

"I've been with two girls."

"At the same time?" Jasper asks and reaches for another bottle of beer in the bucket. He pops off the top, his gaze never leaving my eyes.

"That's a second question," I say.

Jasper frowns. "No, I'm pretty sure it's part of the first question that you failed to answer."

"I'm still exploring my sexuality," I confess.

There's a smile on the corners of Jasper's lips. "Have you ever been with a man?"

"Again, that is another question." I point at him and laugh. "And you only answered one truth. That's all I'm doing."

Jasper nods with a wry grin. "So, you like pussy, but you also might like dick. But you don't know because you haven't gotten laid yet. Got it."

"I didn't say that," I counter.

"You kind of did, with your refusal to answer," Jasper says. He takes another swig of his beer and seems to relax beside me.

Charlotte finally comes back to the table, bringing me my whiskey sour and holding a martini for herself. I snatch my drink from her fingers and take a massive gulp.

"Glad to see we're having fun here," Charlotte chimes. "What'd I miss?"

"I just asked your friend if she likes pussy," Jasper says.

Charlotte coughs and glances from Jasper to me. "For the record, I've never dipped a toe into that pool." She takes a sip of her martini. "We're just friends." Charlotte wraps an arm around my shoulder.

I shrug her off, worried about what she'll tell Jasper because Charlotte knows everything about my love life and lack thereof. She's been telling me that I need to get laid by an older guy, someone who knows what he's doing and has experience.

Jasper isn't necessarily older, but I can't imagine

that he doesn't have girls throwing themselves at him all the time.

Charlotte senses the silence and doesn't let it last. "And what did my friend, Amber, tell you about her sex life?"

"Not much," Jasper says with a grin. "Two girls, but she wouldn't tell me if it was at the same time."

I elbow him in the ribs. "That is an entirely new question."

"I'm kind of with him on this one. It's part of the first question," Charlotte says.

"You are no help." I glare at my best friend, who is enjoying embarrassing the hell out of me.

Charlotte holds up her hands. "I'm not telling. It isn't my personal business to divulge. But you should know she has a track record of attracting crazy. So, if you have any interest in my friend, you're going to have to get my stamp of approval first."

"Crazy, huh? Well, I did meet that meth head," Jasper says. "You might be on to something, Charlotte."

"I swear if the two of you start colluding—"

"You'll what?" Charlotte asks with a sickly-sweet grin.

I grab her martini from her hands and down it.

"You brat." Charlotte laughs and playfully stomps off, heading to the bar for more drinks.

"Order me another whiskey sour!" I shout at her.

I don't have to look over my shoulder to know she's giving me the finger.

I finish the whiskey sour on the table and feel a nice buzz from the alcohol. The butterflies have gone to bed. "Truth or dare," I say, staring at Jasper.

"Dare."

SIX
JASPER

I STILL CAN'T GET the thought of Amber with two women out of my head. I shift uncomfortably on the barstool.

I'm doing everything in my power not to react to the fact that she likes pussy but also might like cock. And I really want to know if she has any interest in riding my cock.

But I can't just ask her that without seeming like a creeper. And while I don't know her friend, Charlotte, very well, she is right. From what I've seen, Amber isn't great with picking men.

At least that meth head, what was his name? He wasn't a healthy choice for her. And I'm curious about what other bad seeds she's dated, but that isn't at the top of my priority list for asking questions.

Besides, right now, it's my turn, and I haphazardly chose dare.

She's had two drinks. The girl definitely seems a little tipsy. I should end the game and send her home with her friend before she loses all her inhibitions.

But I want to see where this goes. For better or worse.

"Dare?" she repeats, and I swear she's plotting her revenge against me for making her prank call my older brother. Which, I might add, was hilarious. Too bad that he recognized her voice, or maybe he just assumed it was Amber because who the hell else would call and accuse him of cheating on Emerson?

It was a good guess if that's all it was.

I sip my beer and wait for her to throw me a dare.

"I dare you to kiss the prettiest girl in the room," Amber says.

Her cheeks are rosy, and she shifts on the barstool nervously. She gets fidgety when she's nervous. I've noticed that about her. It's cute and sweet.

Quite frankly, there isn't anyone other than Amber that I'd want to kiss in the bar. But she's also had a few drinks, and I'm not about to take advantage of her.

The waitress comes back to our table to check if we need any more drinks and grabs the empty glasses and beer bottles to take away.

"I'll have another whiskey sour," Amber says.

I wait until the waitress leaves before reaching my hand out to touch Amber's arm. "How'd you get here tonight?" I don't want her driving home. It wouldn't be safe for her.

"The subway," she says with a smile. Her shoulders are more relaxed, her body tilted in my direction, pointed at me. "Who are you going to kiss?" she asks.

Noah overhears her question and tosses an arm around my shoulder. "What's that?" he asks, joining in on the banter. Or maybe he's just trying to ruin my night of fun.

"We're just playing a little game. Aren't you and Owen talking?"

"I dared Jasper here to kiss the prettiest girl in the bar," she says.

Owen nudges the two in the back of the booth, and Kate climbs out. "I need to use the ladies' room. Ava, Amber, would you ladies join me?"

"Sure," Amber says and climbs off the stool. She

glances back at me, swaying slightly as she stands. "Your dare will wait until I get back."

"Of course," I say with a smile. I glance at Ava and Kate, wanting them to keep an eye on Amber.

They both nod in unison, seeming to understand my silent plea.

The minute the girls round the corner, the guys are on me. "You can't sleep with her," Owen says.

I run a hand through my hair. "Who said I was going to sleep with her?"

"It's bro code," Noah quips.

"Bro code?" I repeat. None of my hockey brothers have dated her. At least, I haven't seen them bring her around to any games or after-parties.

"She's family," Noah says. "Kyler is your brother, and you can't fuck his fiancée's little sister. That is a major violation of bro code."

"I wasn't going to fuck her."

"You can't date her, either," Owen chimes. "She's off-limits. Do you want a silly fling with a college girl to destroy the team?"

I hate that he's right.

"Do you both agree with them?" I ask my teammates Asher and Parker, who are married to great girls and have experience with women. Not that Owen and Noah don't get plenty of dates—they both have regular hookups and flings—but they've never slept with the same girl twice.

"That would be a major violation of bro code," Asher agrees.

Amber is pretty great, but she's also a virgin, and there's a lot of baggage that comes with that type of relationship. Commitment isn't something I have time for with regular games, practice, and focusing on my career.

But tonight has been fun, and I don't want to push that aside, either. Honestly, I haven't felt like this about anyone in a long time. Taking my jersey off at the end of the period to give to Amber, that was a big deal for me, and I'm still not even sure why I did it.

I felt compelled to make her want to care about the Ice Dragons and our team.

It was foolish and dumb. I glance down at my jersey on the table.

"What am I supposed to do?" I ask the guys.

"Remain her friend," Noah says. "You're likely to see her during the holidays. The last thing you want is for shit to turn awkward and having to explain it to Emerson or Kyler."

Fuck, I never even considered that it could get weird for us.

"Friends," I say and nod. I can do that, but it starts with having to friend zone Amber. Even if it's not what I want, it's for the best.

"And about that kiss that she keeps ragging on you to do," Noah quips. "Don't fall into it. It's a trap."

My jaw tightens. "What do you mean?"

"The prettiest girl in the bar?" Owen gestures. "If you kiss any other girl, she's going to hate your guts."

"I don't want to kiss any other girl," I counter. The only girl I want to kiss is Amber, and the guys are telling me not to get involved with her, and I hate that they might be right.

"Precisely, and if you kiss her, she's going to get the wrong idea," Owen says. "She'll want more than friends. She likes you, and you've made it clear that you're interested." He points at the jersey on the table, reminding me of what I've done.

"Just kiss her hand or cheek if she forces it," Noah says. "And maybe suggest that her friend take her home. Get her out of here before she takes things too far, and you're forced to break her heart."

I run my fingers through my hair. It's sage advice.

Not necessarily what I want, but I'd rather have Amber as my friend than her hating me for the rest of our lives. And if I have to see her on holidays or if

Kyler invites us all over for a party or get-together, I don't want shit to be awkward.

"Yeah, got it."

The girls hurry back to the table, and Amber sways a bit as she heads for her seat. "We should probably get you home," I say, glancing from Amber back toward her friend Charlotte, who has disappeared.

"You want to take me home?" Amber asks and giggles.

She's definitely bordering on drunk. "No, I want to take you back to your place."

Poor choice of words because she puts her hand on my chest and slowly lets it glide down to my stomach. My muscles instinctively flex under her touch. I grab her hand, stopping her before she lowers it any farther. I don't need her feeling my cock twitch in my jeans.

"Okay," Amber says.

She seems to have forgotten our little game of truth or dare, which is fine with me. "Do you want to text Charlotte?"

"She texted me in the bathroom. Told me she went home with some hottie at the bar. I reminded her to use protection."

"Come on," I say and help her gather her

belongings. She holds the hideous Island Bruisers jersey in her hands along with her purse while I grab my jersey from the game that she abandoned on the table.

"I'll see you guys tomorrow at practice," I say and leave cash on the table to cover the drinks for myself and Amber. I double-check to make sure I have my phone and house keys before walking with her outside.

"How far is the subway?" Amber asks, shivering. She pulls the Island Bruisers jersey from her hands and slips it on to keep warm.

I grumble in the process. Really? Does she have to torment me by wearing that ugly thing again?

I don't have a coat with me, and if I did, I'd drape it over her shoulders. Usually, I grab a cab back to the apartment on game night.

"Where do you live?" I ask.

"I have an apartment near NYU."

I exhale a heavy breath. "Roommate?"

"No, I'm in a studio," she says. "Do you want to come over, see my place?"

"You'll come back to my place." I don't know how much alcohol it takes for her to get sick, but I also don't want to risk leaving her unattended. Someone should stay with her.

I keep an arm wrapped around her waist, helping steady her. "Okay," Amber says and cuddles against me as we walk across the street. There's a hotel and a row of cabs lined up, waiting for guests, which makes it easy to snag a ride and not have to wait to call a cab.

It isn't long before I'm walking Amber inside my apartment. It's a luxurious two-bedroom, two-bathroom apartment. More than I need since I'm barely here with my rigorous hockey schedule.

The second bedroom is jammed with hockey gear, and while there's a mattress at the moment, it's leaning against the wall, unused. I don't have time or the energy tonight to clean the guest room and offer her the guest bed.

My bedroom is mostly decent, except the bed isn't made. She doesn't seem to notice or care. She plops down on the mattress and flings her shoes off. "Join me," she says, smiling with shut eyes as her head hits the pillow.

"Yeah, in a sec." I head into the bathroom to brush my teeth and change into something that could be construed as pajamas. I usually sleep naked, but that isn't an option with Amber staying under my roof.

I find a pair of boxers and a black T-shirt to wear to bed.

Amber grumbles as I step out of the bathroom, and she's removing the Island Bruisers jersey. "Too hot," she complains, tossing it at me.

"I'd be happy to burn it for you," I offer, catching the jersey in my hands.

She climbs under the covers. "You'd better not."

The girl has made herself at home in my bed, and I can't help but watch her from the bathroom doorframe. I don't have another bed that's set up to sleep on, and the sofa won't fit my long legs. I'll be cramped and uncomfortable.

I need a decent night's rest for practice tomorrow.

There's a chair in the corner of the room, and if I were a gentleman, I'd take the chair, fall asleep cramped, but deal with it during workouts in the morning to get myself in shape and fixed up.

I climb into bed beside Amber.

We're just friends.

Two friends can share a bed. Nothing has to happen between us.

She's out cold, and I reach for my phone, plug it in, and set my alarm. She doesn't budge an inch, and

I shuffle back on the bed, stretch out, and tug the covers over myself.

As long as she remains on her side of the bed, everything will be fine.

My alarm jars me awake, and I feel Amber stiffen as she hears it too. Her arm is wrapped around my waist, her body nestled up against my back.

It was rather sweet, but I can't be having these types of moments with her, not if we're going to keep things between us only as friends.

I don't say anything and untangle from her arms, sitting up in bed. I shut off the alarm, glancing at her over my shoulder.

"How'd you sleep?" I ask, noticing a text from Kyler. He sent it this morning.

"Good. Thanks for letting me crash here last night."

"It was nothing." I stand and stretch. "How's your head this morning? Do you need me to get you aspirin or anything?"

She bites down on her bottom lip, and her cheeks redden. "I'm good. I hope I didn't embarrass myself too much last night at the bar. I don't usually drink that much."

I gathered, but I don't say anything. "I've got to

leave for practice in thirty, but you're welcome to hang out. There's food in the fridge and—"

"No, that isn't necessary," Amber says and sits up in bed. She glances down, seemingly relieved that she's still in her clothes.

Does she not remember part of last night? I didn't think she'd been that intoxicated.

She glances around for her purse and grabs it on the nightstand, looking at her phone. "Did you get a text from your brother?"

I smile. "Yes, I haven't read it yet. I figured he's probably giving me shit about last night's prank."

"Open the message at the same time?" she quips.

There's a nervousness that's back in her voice that had disappeared sometime during our night out, between drinks and the little game that we played.

"Sure," I say.

We both open the text message from Kyler.

After practice, I want you to come over to the house. I'm proposing to Em and want to celebrate.

I glance at Amber, and her shoulders relax, the tension dissipating. I guess she was worried about the prank.

"Your brother invited me over this evening. He's proposing to my sister." There's a natural smile that adorns her face, the kind of pleasantness that shows me she's truly happy for Emerson, and she wants to share in that happiness with her.

"I was wondering when he was going to officially propose." He'd bought the ring and had been sitting on it for a few days. He hadn't mentioned it at practice and made me swear not to tell the guys on the team since they already thought that Kyler was engaged to Emerson.

"I guess I'll see you later tonight?" Amber says with a smile. She climbs out of bed, and I get a nice view of the purple lace panties covering her ass. The Ice Dragons jersey bunches up around her waist.

Sometime during the night, she decided to take off her leggings. She reaches for the clothes on the floor, and I head into the bathroom to shower and dress for practice.

By the time I get out of the shower, she's gone.

There's a text from Amber on my phone, and I open it.

See you tonight at Kyler's place. Should we bring something?

I laugh and answer her text while brushing my teeth.

Aside from ourselves?

She starts to type, and three dots indicate that

she's about to send me something. And then they disappear.

She's a tough one to crack. Not that I should. Noah and the guys were right. Hooking up with Amber would complicate things. Already, we're seeing each other again, this time with my brother and his fiancée tonight.

What if I had slept with her, and it was a disaster?

Not that I think it would be bad, but she seems a little nervous, and rushing it isn't the answer. Neither is jumping into bed together. We're about to be family.

She's just a friend.

A very beautiful friend.

Who's a girl.

I can keep it in my pants.

I don't have another choice, and banging it out with some other random chick isn't going to settle that problem because I'm slightly worried that I might moan her name or, at the very least, think about her.

Yeah, I've got it bad for Amber Ryan.

I have to figure out how to get over her. In the past, with girls who chased me, I'd give the cold shoulder to them and make it clear that I wasn't interested. But I don't want to hurt Amber or be a complete dick to her. She deserves better than that.

I grab a coffee on the way into practice, and as I'm heading inside, the cup of morning brew in my hand, my phone buzzes.

Amber sent me a text.

I should not feel this giddy or overzealous at receiving a text from some girl. But she's not just *some* girl. It's Amber Ryan.

No wonder my brother proposed the idea of a fake relationship with Emerson. I swear, there's something in the Ryan genetics that make the girls irresistible.

Not that I can tell Kyler.

I go to open the text, but my brother strolls up right behind me. "That better be decaf," he says, nodding toward my cup.

"Fuck, it was a late night. I need all the help I can get this morning."

"Whatever gets you through the day. But you are coming to my place later. Right?" Kyler asks. "I'm planning on doing the proposal, and I want you and her sister there to celebrate."

"Proposing again?" I chuckle, teasing my older brother. "Only you would have to propose twice after forcing her to say yes to you on the ice."

Kyler grits his teeth. "I didn't force her to do anything. And would you keep it down?" he growls at me. "No one else knows about the fake relationship shit. Not that it should matter. We are one hundred percent real now."

"Sure. Sure," I say and nod, patting him on the back. "Does your daughter know?"

"My little Bristol knows everything, and do you know what she told the hockey wives? That Emerson was faking it with me!" Kyler's face is red, and I can't keep from laughing.

"Why the hell were you telling your kid that shit?"

Kyler's jaw is tight, and his hands are balled into fists. He'd better not slug me during practice before we even get our gear on. "I didn't tell Bristol *that*. I explained our fake relationship to her."

"Why?" I ask, staring at my older brother. For a man with a family, who appears to have it all, he doesn't seem to have his shit together.

"Fuck you," Kyler says and grumbles, heading into the locker room.

My fingers itch to read her text message, but I can't. I shove my belongings into my wooden locker and change into workout clothes.

Kyler is beside me as we head into the weight room.

Silence seems to be our friend.

The other guys are bench pressing, and Kyler won't continue the conversation around them regarding Emerson. And I'm not about to bring up Amber.

I let it go. I don't need Kyler or Amber getting into my head while working out. There's too much at stake. My focus needs to be on hockey. We've got drills to run later, and I don't want to be distracted.

"Everything work out last night with that girl?" Owen asks. He's being elusive about Amber, since Kyler is in the room.

I work on some leg presses while the benches for lifting are currently full. Circuit training helps endurance during the game, although I prefer weights. But Coach makes us work on everything.

"What girl?" Kyler glances at me, grabbing a seat beside me on another leg press machine. His gaze tightens as he studies me.

Does he suspect that it might be Amber?

She was at the game, and he definitely saw her there, thanks to my dumb ass pointing her out.

"It was nothing. I made sure that she got a cab

home," I say, which is, in part, the truth. I did get her a cab. I just brought Amber back to my place. Nothing happened, but that's not open for discussion.

Owen doesn't elaborate. Perhaps he senses the tension. I certainly feel it brewing. I'm not looking forward to drills on the ice because I have a feeling Kyler will come after me, and he doesn't even know that I shared a bed with Amber.

But I think he suspects it's her.

The prank call probably tipped him off, or maybe it was when I answered her phone at the bar.

I could just be paranoid. Yes, I'm hoping that's all it is because the way he's looking at me, glaring, tells me that my brother knows I have the hots for Amber Ryan.

IT'S SATURDAY, which means I have the day off from school, but I do have to work the lunch shift at the Mad Tea House. Saturdays are always busy, but I let my boss know that I can't work a minute past six. Which barely gives me enough time to get ready and drive to visit my sister at her fiancé's place. I usually work from noon to five, but if Samantha doesn't show, I'd be required to cover her shift.

I had to look up the subway route to his place, which consists of changing trains a few times, and I'm hoping I make it by seven, assuming the trains are on time, which isn't a guarantee.

It's half-past three, and Jasper texts me back. I wasn't sure that I'd hear from him before tonight, especially after this morning.

I hurry to the bathroom for a quick break, and while I'm in there, I glance at the message from Jasper.

Do you want me to pick you up from your apartment?

We're not dating. Why is he offering to drive me to Kyler's?

I'm not sure that's a good idea. I'm at work right now. Can't talk.

The text that I sent him had been a simple *thanks for looking out for me last night.* It wasn't intimate or romantic. I tried to keep it platonic because, while I like him, jumping into bed with a guy while drunk isn't what I do.

I don't want Jasper to think that's who I am because it is the furthest from the truth as you can get.

Are you going to take three trains and make it on time tonight if you're at work?

I swear it's like he can read my mind, which I know is nonsense, but still. I sigh and text him back.

Probably not. I get off at six.

I wince at my response. Hopefully, he doesn't take that to mean anything other than I'm off work at six. But I already sent the text. It's too late to turn back now.

Text me your address. I'll be there 6:30. It'll be close, but we'll make it on time.

I send a quick text to Jasper with my address and wash my hands before heading out of the bathroom.

The afternoon is busy, and Saturdays are always swamped. Charlotte comes in to order her usual Mango Jasmine Green Tea.

If my boss wasn't helping the counter, I'd offer Charlotte her drink for free, but I can't with Maggie on shift today.

"How was your night?" Charlotte asks with a smile.

"I should be asking you that," I say, tilting my head at her while I ring up her drink. "You ditched me at Blue Line."

"You're welcome," Charlotte says with a wink. "I want details later. Are you free tonight?"

"No, I have this thing with my sister at seven." I don't want to elaborate because Charlotte only knows what the media does about Emerson and Kyler's relationship. I can't tell her, and I hate keeping secrets from my best friend.

"Sounds boring. If you get done early, text me."

Work seems to be nonstop, and at six, Samantha is a no-show. I don't know how she still has a job. Anytime Samantha has an evening shift on the weekend, she bails. Rumor is that she's Maggie's cousin, which makes sense as to why she hasn't gotten fired.

I don't get why she doesn't just schedule her for a different day. But Maggie works the evening by herself and insists that she has it on her own.

I hurry across campus to my apartment and change out of my work uniform into a sweater and leggings. I'm not sure what the attire is for tonight. I didn't think to ask Kyler, but it doesn't sound like we're going out.

I put on lipstick and eyeliner before grabbing my purse and phone. I head down to the elevator and hit the button repeatedly.

Jasper will be here any minute, and I neglected to give him my room number on purpose. I like him, but I don't want him mysteriously showing up at my door uninvited.

Not that I think that he would. He doesn't seem the type. But after the disaster with Tripp at the bar, I'm a little extra cautious around guys.

But Jasper isn't my date.

Him, picking me up, is because we're family. It's not because he's hitting on me or trying to hook up with me. He's given no indication of any interest other than that incident on the ice with the jersey.

I'm not sure that it was even flirting.

Jasper didn't want me to support the Island Bruisers. I get it. He's territorial when it comes to hockey. He wants his friends to support *his* team. I'm sure Kyler is the same way.

I hit the elevator button several times, and it finally arrives. The elevator is slow, but my phone isn't buzzing yet. Hopefully, Jasper isn't waiting for me. I'm not exactly on time anymore.

I head down to the lobby of our apartment and outside.

Jasper climbs out of the vehicle and gives me a wave, making sure that I see him.

In a matter of seconds, I climb into the passenger side. "Thanks for the ride," I say.

"No problem." His phone is geared up with GPS, and he pushes the green *go* button to begin the route to his brother's place.

"Nice ride," I say, not too surprised at the fancy digs.

"Right? I can't believe how many vehicles Kyler has when there's only one of him."

"This is his car?"

"One of many," he smirks.

I buckle up, and he pulls out into traffic, getting us there exactly at seven o'clock. The ride is quiet between us, and he has the radio on, which helps ease the tension.

Although, he doesn't appear tense. Jasper looks confident and relaxed.

My knee bounces the entire drive, and I glance out the window, taking in the sights. As we pull up to the estate, there's a large metal fence blocking the entrance. He punches in a passcode, and the gate opens, allowing us access inside.

"Fancy," I say.

"You haven't seen anything yet." Jasper grins, glancing at me. He puts the car in drive and pulls forward through the gate. There's a long driveway that runs to the front of the property. There are trees at every side, hedges that give off privacy, and a protective fence.

The house itself is huge, as if the property wasn't grandiose already.

I'm not used to such luxury, especially living in a studio.

He parks out front and steps out of the vehicle. I follow him up to the front entrance.

Jasper has a key and unlocks the front door. He gestures for me to step inside first, and I glance around the foyer. This is the first time that I've been to Kyler's home, and it is quite impressive. I knew he was a billionaire, but he lives the part in elegance and style.

I slip out of my shoes and remove my coat. I'd feel terrible if I so much as scuffed the wooden floors. The house looks pristine and immaculate, which is hard to imagine with his daughter running around.

Jasper takes his shoes off, too, leaving them by the door. He didn't bother with a coat, but he also didn't seem cold on the way over.

"Are they home?" I ask, glancing around. The house is quiet, and I'd expect a six-year-old to pounce the minute that we step inside. Not that she's a puppy, but she is quite enthusiastic and full of energy.

"They told us to meet them at seven," he says and glances at his watch. "We're right on time. We'll find them."

I don't know where anything is, and Jasper leads me down the hallway, where we can hear a little commotion. Kyler and Emerson are making out, oblivious that we just entered the house. And unlike where two people might be fooling around on the kitchen counter or shoved up against a wall, she's seated on his lap, and he's still on one knee.

When we're standing there for a solid minute, or at least it feels like that, Jasper clears his throat.

"Maybe we should come back," I suggest.

"Amber?" Emerson looks awestruck when she sees me and untangles from his embrace.

"It's good to see you again," Kyler says, shaking my hand. It's been a few days, and I almost reach out to hug him, but it feels a little too soon and informal.

Emerson's jaw is slack, and she glances from me to Jasper. "You're dating my sister?" I swear she could catch a few flies, and my stomach somersaults at her question.

What makes her think that?

Jasper is all smiles, and he glances at me before answering Emerson. "We're just friends. Your brother introduced us when he needed help picking out the ring at Tiffany's."

Emerson seems taken aback by the admission. I am, too, although I know we're not anything more than friends. And we technically met before Tiffany's, but I don't correct him.

"You're just friends?" Emerson repeats like she doesn't believe him. She's staring at me and then Jasper, waiting for confirmation.

Jasper nods. He looks far more relaxed than I feel. I smile, but I'm not sure my lips are even turning upward. This is awkward. Sharing a bed last night with him should not make me feel this unsettled. All we did was sleep!

"That's right, just friends," I affirm.

My sister turns around to face her fiancé, wrapped up in his embrace. "Why did you tell me Jasper was bringing his girlfriend?"

I choke on Emerson's words. "Girlfriend?" Thankfully, I'm not drinking anything, or I'd have spit it across the room.

"I wanted to surprise you with the proposal. And if I told you my brother and your sister were coming over, you'd be suspicious," Kyler says like it's the most usual thing in the world.

It would have been if I didn't drink myself silly last night and played a childish game of truth or dare with Jasper, which I don't regret. And that's the worst part because I shouldn't keep crushing on him.

Emerson seems to relax with his answer. "Well, you did a good job with the surprise." She turns around to face Jasper and me, and I try everything in my power to keep a reasonable distance between us, but if I shift slightly, he will brush against me.

Technically, I'd brush up against him. "Well, did you say yes?" I ask and glance at Emerson's hand. I need a distraction from the hot, single guy standing beside me. The one I've caught feelings for.

My sister shows me the ring on her finger. "I'm engaged!"

"Congratulations!" I squeal in delight and pull Emerson into my arms for a hug. I'm happy for her, especially now that the engagement is real, and she doesn't have to pretend to be in love with Kyler Greyson.

"I'm happy for you both," Jasper says, patting Kyler on the back. When I let go of my sister, he gives her a friendly hug. He glances around the room. "Something smells good."

"We just put a peach pie in the oven."

"You bake?" I ask, glancing at Kyler because I know my sister is terrible in the kitchen.

"The nanny does the cooking and baking around here," Emerson says. "She gave us a couple of peach pies during the summer, and we froze them."

"Sounds delicious." Jasper rubs his hands together.

"I have some dessert wine to celebrate," Emerson says, and she glances at me. "You can have a glass while you're here, but you'll have to stay a while. I don't want you tipsy trying to find your way to the subway."

"You don't have to take care of me, Em."

"I do. You're not twenty-one yet. One glass of wine. I'm not about to corrupt my little sister."

I don't have to glance at Jasper because I can feel his gaze burning me. "So, how old are you, little sister?" Jasper quips.

I exhale a heavy breath. "Is the pie done? I can take it out of the oven for you." Anything to avoid this conversation about my age because I don't want my sister to find out about me drinking at Blue Line or, worse, that I have a fake ID.

Kyler joins me over at the oven. The timer hasn't gone off yet. It reads fifteen minutes, and it's counting down. "It still has more time," he says.

He leans back against the cabinets, folding his arms across his chest, an amused grin on his face. He lowers his voice while Jasper is still reeling about me being under twenty-one.

"I know you prank-called me last night," Kyler says. There's a smug look on his face, proud that he figured it out. "I just can't ascertain as to why." He glances from me to his younger brother, Jasper.

My voice falters as I speak. "I don't know what you're talking about." I don't sound sure in my response, and I feel even less confident as I glance at Jasper, hoping that he might save me from this conversation. Because it just went from bad to worse for me.

Anxiety creeps into my stomach, setting the butterflies free. My fingers tremble, and I shove them into the corners of my pockets like I'm relaxed, but I feel anything but calm.

"I'm not upset, just curious," Kyler says, perhaps sensing my hesitation.

Although, I'm confident that anyone glancing at me can read that I'm not comfortable with this conversation.

Jasper strolls across the kitchen and meets my stare. His brow pinches as he steps forward, and I hope that he's going to rescue me from this onslaught of questions and looming drama that I don't want to face.

"You're in college. Let me guess, twenty?"

I press my lips together. "That's right," I say.

There's a knowing smirk on his face, but he doesn't tattle on me to Emerson. "We'll have to take you out when you turn twenty-one and celebrate," Jasper says.

"Of course," Emerson chimes and stalks across the kitchen, throwing her arm around my shoulder. "You'll have to try different cocktails and figure out what you like. I'll even hold your hair back for you."

"I'll pass on the vomiting." I elbow her in the ribs. "Some sister you are, letting me drink to excess."

"I'm a great sister," Emerson quips. "I'm letting you have a glass of wine with dessert."

"An actual glass, or are you giving me a sip?" I know the way my sister works. She makes it sound like she's doing me this grand gesture, but she'll give me the equivalent of a tasting you might get at a winery.

"You're twenty. When you become an adult like the rest of us, you can drink as much as you want." Emerson hugs me before shuffling over to Kyler. He wraps an arm around her waist, and I roll my eyes, more at Emerson than the two of them.

I'm happy for them, but I'm annoyed at her.

Jasper clears his throat, his gaze on me. "I remember having to wait until I was twenty-one to drink."

"You're full of shit," Kyler says. "I remember getting a couple of prank calls from you while you were trashed at some seedy bar down the street from your place."

Jasper rests a hand on his chest. "I would never do that."

"Bullshit," Kyler mutters with a laugh.

"Boys," Emerson says, glancing between them. "No fighting in the house. You save that for the ice."

"We're not fighting, babe," Kyler says and drops a kiss on Emerson's lips. "I'm just telling my little brother how it is."

"Little?" Jasper raises an eyebrow at Kyler.

I swear there's about to be a fight, and while it sounds in good spirits, knowing that they're two hockey players, it could easily turn into something fierce.

"I think the pie is ready," I say, glancing at the clock. It's counting down the last minute, and Emerson grabs the plates and forks while Kyler pulls the dessert from the oven and lets it cool for a few minutes.

"Where's the wine?" I ask while my sister grabs the wine glasses hanging in the kitchen.

"In the cellar. Do you want to take Jasper down there and help pick out a decent dessert wine?"

Jasper leads me out of the kitchen, and he seems to know his way around the house as he takes me down the stairs. The basement contains a workout room, and in the back, there's a door leading to the wine cellar.

The room is dimly lit, and he pulls on the overhead chain to cast a warm light over the chilled room. "Fancy," I say. The cellar looks old compared to the rest of the house, which is quite modern.

"I swear this is the only staple that's still original from the house," Jasper says. He glances at me and at the hundreds of bottles of wine around the room. "Do you know which one is a dessert wine?"

"You're asking me?" I laugh.

"Right. I forgot you're twenty," he jests, and I playfully snarl at him. "You can't tell my sister about the bar or the drinks or—"

"Or the fake ID," he adds. "I promise I won't. We all keep secrets from our siblings."

"What secrets do you keep from Kyler?" I ask and glance from him to the bottles of wine, reading the labels. Nothing screams dessert wine, but what am I supposed to look for?

I grab my phone from my back pocket.

"What are you doing?"

"Googling a dessert wine," I say and show him my phone.

"You could just text your sister," Jasper says. "She'll tell you what wine to grab while we're down here."

"You assume she knows, and do you really want her telling Kyler that you're incompetent in your knowledge of dessert wines?"

Jasper laughs, tossing his head back, his eyes watering. "Do you think I care?"

"Oh, well, in that case, I'll just text him."

"Wait," Jasper says, his hand coming to rest on mine, stilling my fingers from typing. I glance up from our hands to his face. He towers above me, staring down, and my stomach flutters while my insides tremble.

He makes me incredibly nervous. I wish I knew why. Is it because I have the biggest crush on him? Maybe it's because he's a famous NHL player, and I know he's out of my league. He's also handsome and available, which doesn't help my anxiety. Although, I'm not sure what he thinks of me, other than I'm Emerson's little sister.

And now he knows I'm twenty. Which means showing up at the bar might be a bit problematic next time unless he really can keep a secret.

He stares at me, the moment seeming to stretch on, and I exhale a soft breath. "Do I have something on my face?" I ask and wipe at my cheek.

His thumb strokes down on my skin, rubbing gently beneath my eye. On his thumb is an eyelash. "Make a wish," he whispers.

I wish that Jasper Greyson kisses me.

I purse my lips and softly blow on his finger, letting the eyelash fly away.

Jasper pulls back, ruining any chance of my wish coming true.

Damn.

It was silly thinking that making a wish on an eyelash might come true.

"So, what'd you wish for?" Jasper asks with a wide grin.

"That you'd pick a dessert wine already."

There's no way I'd tell him my wish. Nope. Zero chance.

Jasper grins and reaches for a bottle of Peach Moscato. "I think this one will pair well with peach pie."

"Do you have a thing for peach?" I tease, and he reaches for the light, pulling the chain and turning it off. The room is bathed in darkness, but the door is still perched open. I head out of the wine cellar and into the basement, glancing around the home gym.

"Do you guys ever work out together?" I ask.

"At every practice, but not here," Jasper says, pointing to the equipment. "If I want to work out, I use the gym at my apartment or during practice with the guys."

He lets me head up the stairs first, and I can't

help but wonder if he's checking out my ass on the way upstairs. I bite down on my bottom lip, trying to keep the smile at bay as we make our way back to the kitchen.

"Did you two get lost down there?" Emerson jokes.

The pie is out of the oven and already sliced and dished out onto plates. Bristol tears into the kitchen, smelling peach pie. She gives a brief wave to Jasper and stares at me curiously.

"Hi," I say, offering a smile.

"You don't look like Emmie," Bristol says. "I thought sisters always look alike."

"I see the resemblance," Jasper says. He grabs the corkscrew from the drawer, familiar with his brother's home, and opens the bottle, pouring us each a glass.

She grabs her plate of pie and carries it into the dining room.

"How much does your little sister get?" Jasper asks Emerson, toying with me.

"A taste," Emerson says. "I could be giving her grape juice with Bristol. Kyler, help me carry the dishes and drinks to the dining room, would you?"

I stay in the kitchen with Jasper while he pours each of them a heavy glass of wine. He gives me a taste in my glass and then hands me the bottle, leaning toward me. "Don't tell your sister," Jasper says and gives me a wink.

"Don't worry," I say. I turn my back and bring the bottle to my lips. If Emerson's going to give me shit about drinking alcohol and how much I can have in a glass, I'll just drink it straight from the bottle.

I dip my head back, letting the Peach Moscato slide down my throat, and damn, it's sweet and good. Jasper knows how to pick his wines or at least pair peach with peach. You can't really go wrong there.

"Don't make me carry you home," Jasper whispers, watching me with a smile. His brown eyes twinkle as he stares at me. That stare—the intensity of his gaze—brings the butterflies returning in full flight.

I bring the bottle back down and wipe my mouth with the back of my hand.

"Sexy," Jasper teases, and I shove the wine bottle at him just as Emerson hurries back into the kitchen.

"Do you need help carrying the rest into the dining room?" she asks, oblivious to the exchange between us. It's probably for the best because I'm not even sure what to make of it anymore.

One minute, he seems flirty. The next, we're clearly just friends. And then he's flirting again.

I could be reading into the flirting. It's not as though I have tons of experience with it. Jasper could be naturally a friendly guy who gets along well with women, and it comes across as flirting. Friendly doesn't equal flirting.

EIGHT
JASPER

DESSERT GOES WELL with Kyler and Emerson. I'm thrilled they're officially engaged, and my older brother is happy. I've never seen him quite so happy.

A small part of me is jealous because I want that feeling too. The happiness that the two of them share is genuine.

I drive Amber home after dessert and wine with my brother and his fiancée. Amber is quiet as we head to the car, and I open the passenger door for her.

She raises an eyebrow, surprised by my gesture, and opens her mouth to say something, and then shuts it. "Thanks," she finally admonishes before climbing into the front seat.

I hurry around to the driver's side. The air is

chilly, and I should have used AutoStart to warm up the vehicle, but I didn't think it'd be that uncomfortable.

"That was fun," I say, buckling myself into the driver's side. I wait for Amber to do the same before putting the car in drive and pulling away from the house.

"It was nice," Amber says, glancing out the side window and then at me. "Thank you for driving me here and then home. I could have taken the subway."

"Nonsense." I wasn't about to have her walk to the subway in the dark at night. That doesn't seem particularly safe, especially alone.

She adjusts the vents, and it takes a few minutes for the heat to blast through the car. There's a silence that envelopes us, and I can't tell if she's holding something back or what's going on in her head.

I clear my throat, not wanting to sit in silence for the thirty-five-minute drive to her apartment. "Do you go to a lot of hockey games?" I ask.

"No," Amber says, and I glance at her. She's smiling, glancing at me and then straight ahead at the road, like she's avoiding my stare when I look at her briefly.

"Your friend likes hockey, then?" I guess.

"Charlotte? Maybe, I don't know."

I laugh and shake my head. "Two girls who don't really care that much for hockey. Why did you both go and pay for front-row seats?"

She tips her head back like she's asking the universe to answer the question for her. "We thought it would be fun."

I don't push the question because I can sense her discomfort, and I have no inclination to make things more awkward. "Of course, that makes sense. Did you enjoy it?"

"Immensely," she says.

I catch a quick glance at her and see the smile on her face.

"We have another game tomorrow. You should come, but you can't wear that hideous Bruisers jersey."

"I would love to, but I don't think I can afford it," Amber says. "Actually, I know that I can't. But thanks for the invitation."

"I can get you tickets, for free, on one condition."

"What's that?" she asks, and her voice trembles slightly.

Do I make her nervous?

We're friends. There's no reason that she should feel nervous around me. "You have to wear my jersey," I say. "I want to look into the stands and see you supporting me."

"Do I have to wear your swamp-ass jersey?" Amber laughs.

"It didn't smell *that* bad."

"Oh, it did." She seems to relax when we're joking. "You threw me a sweaty, wet, stinky jersey and demanded that I wear it in front of everyone."

"Most girls would find that a turn-on," I counter.

"Yeah, I know." She laughs and pushes her hair behind her ear. "But I'm not most girls."

I noticed. That's probably why I can't stop thinking about her.

"For the record, I've washed it, and it's in the back seat." I point at the back row behind me. "Will you wear it to tomorrow's game if I get you tickets?" I ask.

"As long as the seats don't cost you anything. I don't want to get you into trouble."

"You won't. But do me a favor, leave your friend at home."

"You don't like Charlotte?" Amber asks, and now she's staring at me like I've grown two heads.

"She doesn't seem like a great influence, encouraging you to wear the Bruisers jersey instead of the Ice Dragons."

"I told you, it was a dare."

"And do you always accept every dare thrown at you?" I ask, trying to get to know Amber a little better.

"You don't?" she asks, turning the tables on me. She doesn't answer my question, at least not yet.

"Depends on who's doing the daring. I've been known to follow through on a few dares," I confess.

"Really? You don't seem the type," Amber says. "Always picking truth in our little game last night."

Did she forget that I chose dare? "That's not true." Although I hadn't followed through with the dare, but only because my teammates made it perfectly clear that if I kissed Amber, I'd be breaking bro code.

"Well, you didn't follow through with the dare," Amber says. She glances at me and then at the road. "It's okay. I'm not upset about it."

She doesn't sound happy, though, either, and unless I had kissed her, there was no other way around her dare that wouldn't have ended in disaster.

I don't know a lot about what women are thinking, but we were flirting, and she wanted me to kiss her. I could feel the heat between us. The sizzle of desire.

We round the corner, and I'm glad when her

campus is within sight. Another block, and we'll be at her place.

"You can pick up the tickets at will-call for tomorrow's game," I say.

"Tickets? I thought I couldn't bring a friend."

"Just not Charlotte."

"And if I do bring her?" The girl taunts me. I try to do one nice thing for her, and she's already planning on how to spoil it.

My jaw tightens. It's not that I dislike Charlotte. I met her at Blue Line, but that's where the bad feeling starts to sink in, and I can't let it go. Her friend ditched her for a guy. How was Amber supposed to get home? Walk to the subway alone, at night, well after midnight?

"I'll leave you one ticket at will-call," I say. "And when the game is over, you'll come with us to celebrate our win."

"And what if the Ice Dragons lose?" she asks. "What happens after those games?"

"You don't want to find out."

———

"You look nervous, bro," Kyler says as we're seated on the bench in the locker room before the game.

I don't tell him it's because I invited Amber to the game. I'm not nervous about Amber showing up. I'm more concerned that she might bring her little tyrant friend and be convinced to sport the enemy's jersey. Again.

It was bad enough that she wore an Island Bruisers jersey. No, the worst of it was that she had to wear Knox Storm's jersey. The jerk. He had to flaunt that she was wearing his number. He wouldn't have even noticed her in the stands if I hadn't made such a big deal out of it by removing my jersey and giving it to her to wear.

That had been my fault, and for the rest of the game, he'd given me shit, tossing slurs and innuendos at Amber, not that she heard any of them.

But it didn't matter to me whether she heard any of it or not. Knox Storm deserved getting his ass kicked, and I made sure to do that repeatedly. It also got me tossed out of the game during the last period.

A mistake that Coach Malone made clear I wasn't to do tonight.

No repeat performances, even if we did win the game.

"I'm fine," I grumble. I wish there were some way that I could see if she was in the stands if she showed up tonight.

I'll know the minute I step out and onto our bench because the private seats that we hold are directly behind the glass where we sit. The guys all get turns letting their family, friends, girlfriends, and whomever they want use the seats.

"You really sound fine," Kyler says.

Owen glances at Noah, exchanging a silent glance. "Is this about a girl?" They're attempting to be discreet in front of Kyler, but he doesn't miss a beat.

"What girl?" Kyler quips, staring at his buddies, and when they don't answer, he's glaring at me. "Are you finally seeing someone?"

I don't answer Kyler because while, yes, I'm seeing Amber, it isn't in the traditional sense of dating. We're not boyfriend and girlfriend. We're just friends. The guys pointed out the other night that it's all that it could ever be with her, and they're right.

"Do I look like I'm hooking up with anyone?" I answer his question with a question.

Kyler shrugs. "I don't go out to the bars with you guys after games. Wait, were you and Amber at the bar two nights ago? The prank call—"

Thankfully, Kyler gets interrupted when Coach Malone enters the locker room to give us a pep talk before the game. I've never been so happy to see Coach in my life.

When the game starts, we're introduced and head out of the locker room and onto the ice. Immediately, I see Amber in the stands. She's wearing my jersey, the one that I gave her, and I can't hide the smug grin on my face.

She waves, and I try not to acknowledge her when Kyler skates past me as we head for the bench. He notices Amber in the stands and my gaze on her.

She's just a friend.

I'm on the ice first with Kyler, Owen, Noah, Chase, and our goalie, Aiden. Kyler and I have always played well on the ice, given that, in our former years, we practiced together, we know each other's moves, and it's like a harmonious dance that we play, tossing the puck back and forth between us before he shoots it at Owen to make a score.

I want to be the one scoring, impressing Amber.

Fuck.

Where did that thought come from?

I glance at Amber in the stands, and she's cheering for Owen, clapping and smiling. I want her to do that because I scored a goal.

I've never been the jealous type.

There's never been a reason for me to be jealous. I've focused on my career instead of girls since high school.

I'm always happy when my teammates do well because we, as a team, do well. That's what's most important.

But I'm not feeling that way right now. There's a bitterness that consumes me, an internal rage that's crawling in my veins, itching to be unleashed.

I want Amber to scream my name, clap for me, and smile when she watches me score the next goal.

I should be happy for Noah, but I don't want her attention on him. My insides are on fire, and when I finally get the puck, I don't want to turn it over to Kyler, the center, even though he's open, and I have Storm and Conrad gaining on me.

Knox Storm uses his stick to trip me up, and Conrad steals the puck, returning it toward their goal.

"Your girlfriend is in the stands, and she's been screaming my name," Storm says.

I know he's trying to get to me. I should ignore him. He's always been a bit of an ass on the ice, but anytime he brings up Amber, I see red.

I slam Knox against the glass, my fist pounding into his chest, and he takes returns blow after blow to my abdomen.

The fight lasts a minute, maybe longer, before we're pulled apart.

"What the hell was that?" Kyler asks.

I don't answer my brother. He doesn't understand why I despise Knox. Storm and I are sent to the penalty box. Amber is seated behind the player's bench, across the ice rink, and can't see me. I'm relieved that I don't have to face her right now, especially after what Knox said.

NINE
AMBER

"I CAN'T BELIEVE you're making me wear a wig," Charlotte grumbles beside me.

"I got you a free ticket, shush." I glare at my bestie. We're both wearing Ice Dragons jerseys, although, more specifically, I'm wearing the one that Jasper gave me off his back the other day. At least he had the decency to wash it, and even though it's clean, it does give off a nice hint of Jasper.

I'm trying not to constantly sniff my jersey like a lunatic. Thankfully, the gagging swamp smell was removed in the washer.

"Yeah, but why doesn't your boyfriend like me?" Charlotte asks.

"He's not my boyfriend." I keep my focus on the game and have to admit, I'm disappointed that

Jasper is in the penalty box because I can't see him. At least if he weren't playing on the ice, he'd be on the bench in front of me.

Thankfully, the arena is loud, making it difficult for his teammates seated in front of the glass to overhear our conversation.

"Still didn't answer the question, why doesn't he like me?" Charlotte asked.

"I don't know. You encouraged me to wear the Bruisers jersey. Maybe he's holding that over your head."

Charlotte waves her hand dismissively. "We both wore the jersey. You're just as guilty as I am."

I glare at her. "You dared me to wear it."

"Yes, and I'm wearing this wig, so we're even. Okay?" The blonde wig looks pretty natural on her, with her pale and freckled complexion. She pulls it off well. "But I'm pretty sure your lover boy is going to notice who I am, wig or not."

"It's fine. I doubt he's paying us that much attention," I say, hoping that I'm right.

Jasper is released from the penalty box and back on the ice with Kyler and his teammates. The score is one to nothing with the Ice Dragons in the lead, but not for long.

Jasper is back in the game, and so is their opponent, Storm.

"Hey, isn't that the guy whose jerseys we bought?" I ask Charlotte.

"Yeah, think that's why they're fighting over us?" Charlotte asks, wiggling her eyebrows.

My best friend is crazy. "That's insane."

"But is it?" she asks, glancing at me. She shrugs, and then her attention returns to the hockey game.

The period is almost over, and when it ends, the guys all head to the locker room. The crowd around us stands and shuffles out of their seats, stretching, taking bathroom breaks, the usual. After a few minutes, one guy tries to squeeze by us in the front row, carrying three cups of beer. He manages to spill one on my shirt, soaking my Ice Dragons jersey.

"Sorry," he slurs and keeps walking.

"Seriously?" I stand, trying to wipe the remnants of beer from my clothes. "That's just great," I mutter. I'm not wearing anything but a bra under the jersey, and it's chilly in the arena. If that's not bad enough, now the beer has soaked through and is making me cold.

"Bathroom run," Charlotte suggests, and we hurry up the stairs for the bathroom. There's a long line, and we both promise everyone we're not cutting, just trying to get to the hand dryer, which doesn't work.

There are paper towels available, and I try to dry the soaked-through jersey, but it's still frigid and uncomfortable.

"You could get another jersey?" Charlotte quips as we head out of the bathroom, tossing the damp paper towels into the trash.

I'm gripping the front of my jersey, trying to keep the cold from biting my skin. The nearest booth that sells Ice Dragons merchandise has a line that wraps around the arena. We'll miss part of the game if we're standing in line.

"You could try over there," she says, pointing at the Island Bruisers merchandise.

I groan. I already have one of their jerseys that I'm never going to wear. "Seriously? Jasper will kill me."

Charlotte tilts her head, smiling. "Now, why is that? Because if you're not dating, I don't see the problem."

"We're friends, Char. It's like stabbing him in the back."

"He'll understand. If not, he'll bring you another jersey. Wouldn't that be great, two jerseys off his back? You can give me one when you're done with it."

I laugh at her candor. She walks me closer to the Island Bruisers little shop, which is empty of customers. We're at the Ice Dragons stadium, so it's not a surprise that the majority of the merchandise for sale is for Jasper's team. "Not happening. I can't do it."

"You either freeze in that soaking wet and disgusting smelling jersey, which reeks of beer or buy one of those jerseys so that you can watch your boyfriend play hockey."

"He's not my boyfriend," I grit between my teeth.

"Not with that attitude," Charlotte quips.

I stalk up to the stand. "What's the cheapest jersey that you have?" I ask.

"We have a rookie, Charlie Hayes, in his first year with the Island Bruisers. We have his jersey for sale."

"How much?" I ask. I pay with my credit card and quickly rush into the bathroom to change near the sinks since the stalls are all occupied, and the lines haven't diminished.

"Jasper is going to kill me," I mutter, sporting the blue Bruisers jersey as I head with Charlotte back to our seats.

"Maybe."

I glance at Charlotte. "Trade clothes with me. Give me your Ice Dragons jersey." Why the hell didn't I think of it when I was upstairs in the bathroom? The players start coming out of the locker room as the next period begins.

"No way in hell. This is going to be quite the show." Charlotte grins wickedly.

"I swear if you paid that loser to spill beer on me—"

"I didn't!" Charlotte chuckles. "But that would have been a great plan."

Jasper enters the player's bench and takes a seat. He glances back at us and frowns. "Seriously, Amber?"

I point at the guy six seats down the row at us. "He spilled beer on me!"

Kyler takes a seat next to his brother and glances back to see what the commotion is all about. "Damn, Amber. Never took you for a traitor."

My jaw drops. "I'm not. I'm supporting the Ice Dragons!"

"Really looks like it," Kyler says and shrugs it off.

"Your fiancée's sister is trouble," Jasper says a little too loudly. I wonder if he wants me to hear him.

"Not my problem. She can support whomever she wants. I know I'm on the winning team." Kyler smacks his brother on the back before he returns to the ice as the game starts.

Jasper, however, seems to be benched, at least for now. He stares ahead at the guys on the ice, his hands clasped together, and I realize there's a bag of ice on his knuckles. When he got into it with Storm, he probably bruised his hands.

When Kyler comes back, Parker Montgomery takes his place as center.

The more that I watch and focus on the game, the more I'm beginning to understand it.

Jasper tosses the bag of ice in the trash. I should be watching the game, but I'm spending more time watching Jasper than anything else, and the coach instructs Asher to come off the ice while Jasper takes his place as the right wing.

At least he'll get some more time to play. That has to be good.

The second period is a battle without a clear winner. When the Ice Dragons score, it's quickly followed up by a goal from the Island Bruisers. I make it clear to only cheer for the Ice Dragons, but with Kyler and Jasper on the ice, neither seem to notice me. And why should they? Their focus ought to be on the game.

When the second period finally ends, and the Ice Dragons are ahead only by one, I can feel the tension brewing amongst the team. The game is close. They head into the locker room, and I stand, making sure the same jerk who spilled beer on me doesn't get a second opportunity when he skirts by us for the aisle.

"Your boyfriend hasn't glanced at you once since you put on the rival's jersey," Charlotte says.

I wish I hadn't noticed, but it's been like Jasper has had a hockey stick shoved up his butt for the entire last period.

"He's not my boyfriend," I correct her.

"Well, it's clear that he wants you. At least it was when you were in the Ice Dragons jersey."

"Switch jerseys with me," I say, pointing at her jersey.

"And risk the wrath of the Ice Dragons? We are seated directly behind the team. No way in hell. Especially if there's a chance one of them is single," she says with a smirk. "Reece, what's his first name? He's kind of hot."

"Noah," I say and bite down on my bottom lip. He's nice-looking, but he's no Jasper Greyson. "He could have a girlfriend."

Charlotte is tapping away at her phone. "He

doesn't," she says, matter of fact, and shows me his Instagram profile photo. "Isn't he hot?"

She practically shoves the phone in my face, a little too close. I grab her wrist and pull it back slightly so I'm not staring cross-eyed at the phone. "Yeah, I don't see it."

"That's because you only have eyes for Jasper, who, I might add, is decent, but he's no Noah Reece."

"Ask him out if you're into him," I say. I doubt either of us has a chance with Jasper or Noah, but at least I won't be the only one getting my heart crushed and stepped on. Not that I wish that for her, but we're nobodies to the Ice Dragons, and I'm sure they have tons of other girls—hotter girls—chasing after them all the time.

Charlotte shakes her head. "No, he's going to ask me out tonight."

I don't know what she's scheming, but I can already imagine it has to do with something at Blue Line after the game. I'm not sure I'm up for drinks, especially if Jasper tattles on me with my fake ID.

Intermission is nearly over, and the team returns to the players' bench. I shouldn't be watching for Jasper, but when he finally comes out, he's got a jersey in his hands.

He approaches the glass, staring at me like I've

betrayed him.

I stand. I don't even know why or what compels me to, but it's like I need to be close to him, explain my side of the story, what happened.

"I blame you for my shitty performance on the ice. Wearing that—" he gestures to the jersey I have on, "is the biggest betrayal from a friend."

A friend?

I exhale a heavy breath, and I fog up a spot on the glass.

He's watching me, his eyes latched onto mine, gaze unwavering. There's commotion all around us, but I don't notice any of it. I reach my hand to the glass and draw a heart in the fog as I stare at him.

Jasper doesn't move. His brow pinches when he breaks my stare and sees what I've drawn on the glass, the heart between us.

He opens his mouth, and my stomach clutches, waiting for the words to find his lips. Noah grabs the jersey from Jasper's hands and tosses it over the glass at me. "Coach wants you on the ice," Noah says to Jasper.

I catch the jersey in my hands.

Jasper blinks and turns, the spell between us broken.

Noah watches his teammates skate onto the ice.

He's benched at the moment, which might give me the opportunity to find out what the hell is going on with Jasper.

"Put that jersey on before Jasper falls apart."

The gold jersey is clean and smells like Jasper. It's big, and so I throw it on over the other one that I'm wearing because I don't have anything on underneath except a bra to change clothes at my seat.

Noah grabs a seat on the bench in front of us, his back to us as he focuses on the game.

"Noah," I say, tapping the glass, trying to get his attention.

He glances over his shoulder at me and gives me a thumbs-up sign when he notices the Ice Dragons jersey.

Charlotte waves at Noah and smiles, but he gives a curt nod and turns back around when Montgomery, one of his teammates sitting beside him, elbows him in the side. They exchange a few words, but we're too far away to hear what's being said.

Jasper glances in my direction while on the ice, and the hockey player from the other team, Hayes, swings it like a golf club and smacks the stick up against Jasper's chin.

There are expletives from Jasper, and when the referees shrug it off, not having seen the play, Jasper waits until they're back on the ice playing and goes after Hayes. They're fighting over the puck, racing across the ice when Hayes begins to lose control and slide toward the wall. Jasper forces him into it hard. Stealing the puck, Jasper passes it to Kyler.

Knox Storm comes out of nowhere, slamming Jasper against the glass, throwing punch after punch, defending his teammate.

Conrad comes skating in from behind, ready to attack Jasper, when Kyler intervenes.

Kyler grabs Conrad by the jersey and yanks him around the ice and away from his little brother as they throw punches. The referees pull Kyler and Conrad apart but seem to be letting Storm and Jasper continue the fight.

Owen hurries over to Jasper, keeping the Island Bruisers from ganging up on Jasper; at least one-on-one, it's a fair fight. Two other Island Bruisers teammates come charging at Owen, and he blocks them from intercepting his Ice Dragons brother.

The referees finally pull Jasper and Knox apart, ejecting them from the game. They also eject Kyler and Conrad.

"Seriously?" Noah shouts.

TEN
JASPER

MY KNUCKLES HURT EARLIER, but the pain radiates under my chin, and as I sit on the bench in the locker room with a bag of ice on my chin, I see a smear of blood.

I wipe it away, but there's probably more where that came from.

I hadn't bothered to look in the mirror. I'm sure I'm quite the sight. Glancing at the overhead monitors, I can see the game on television, and at least I'm not the only player who got ejected.

"You look like shit," my brother says as he joins me in the locker room.

"Thanks," I say with a smile. At least I still have all my teeth.

He grabs a clean towel and tosses it at me.

"You've got blood," he gestures at my face. "Clean that mess up. The press wants an interview after the game."

"I'm not giving them shit," I say. They'll ask me about the fight. They don't give a damn about how I play, how many goals I've scored. It's always about the fight. The brutality of the sport.

"It's too bad we weren't twins," Kyler says with a grin.

"I know." My brother loves the spotlight. He thrives under it and has learned to use it to help his career.

Me? I'd prefer not to be noticed. I mean, I appreciate the rookie contract that I have, and when it's up, I'd like a bigger offer, but I don't like having to be interviewed and tossed questions, especially ones that have little to do with hockey.

In the last interview, the woman sports reporter asked me if I was dating anyone. Seriously? Like, what the fuck does that matter?

Turns out she was a puck bunny vying for our team after going through half the Wolverines and most of the Barbarians. No, thanks. I don't need to stick my dick into someone who's fucked two other NHL teams.

I glance at the monitor, watching the last few

seconds of the game. The Ice Dragons have the lead by one.

"This is painful," I say, watching and unable to do a damn thing to help our teammates.

Kyler strips out of his gear and sits beside me on the bench. He glances from the television screen and then back to me. "What's going on between you and Amber?"

"Nothing."

Kyler stares at me for a beat before nodding, accepting my answer as fact. "Okay, good."

We both resume our attention on the screen when the game ends, and it's clear that the Ice Dragons are the winner. I can finally breathe, exhaling a deep breath.

"Are you going to Blue Line tonight?" my brother asks me as the other players begin filing into the locker room.

"I was planning on it. Are you coming out tonight with us?" That would be the surprise of the century, Kyler taking a night off from fatherhood. I can't remember the last time he brought Emerson out for drinks with the team. It's been ages.

"Yeah, for a beer or two. Then I ought to get home."

"You could invite Emerson out to party?" I don't

understand why he always chooses to go home instead of out with the guys. "You have a nanny. Let her watch Bristol."

He grabs his phone and sends out a few texts. It's pretty rowdy in the locker room, and good luck making a phone call and the other person hearing a word that's being said.

I head to the shower, clean up, and get changed into a pair of jeans and a clean shirt. I wait for Noah and Owen to finish up before heading to Blue Line.

Kyler dries off after his shower and glances over at me as he dresses. "Two drinks. Then I have to get home."

"Is Emerson coming out?"

"I invited her," my brother answers cryptically.

"And?"

Kyler doesn't answer. He finishes getting dressed and sits on the bench, lacing up his sneakers. I finish getting my shoes on, and once my teammates are ready and done with the press, we head to Blue Line.

Our reserved table is open in the back, and we all pile into our seats. Kyler sits across from me, and I'm on the end, as usual.

Owen and Noah always joke that I have the best seat to check out the ladies and hit on them. I grab a beer from the bucket and pop the cap off, taking a swig. The cold bottle feels good on my knuckles. I had forgotten how battered they'd gotten during the game when my chin stung.

The ice helped numb that up pretty quickly.

Kyler grabs a beer for himself and sits back with a smug smile. "M&M, you came!" he shouts and waves her over.

I can't help but look. M&M? I turn toward the door, and Emerson strolls into the bar. She looks dynamite, wearing Kyler's jersey and black leggings.

My stomach flops, and she strides over to the table, planting her lips on Kyler's. He pulls her against him, their mouths dueling as his fingers tangle in her hair.

I glance away, take another swig of my beer, and my eyes nearly pop out of my head when I spot Charlotte and Amber stepping into the bar.

Amber, who is twenty years old and has no business being at Blue Line, saunters up to the bar to put in an order.

I climb off my stool. "I'll be back," I mutter under my breath, hoping the guys don't ask any questions. Kyler, at least, is enthralled in Emerson. I don't bother glancing over my shoulder at Noah and Owen. They'd stop me from making the biggest mistake of my life.

I stroll up to the bar, bottle of beer in hand, standing beside Amber, turning to face her. She smiles, and I glance down, seeing her wearing my jersey. My heart swells, but it shouldn't.

I shouldn't have even given a crap when she wore that dumbass rookie Charlie Hayes' jersey earlier. But it had eaten me up inside, torn me apart limb by limb.

"I'll have—" She opens her mouth and holds out her ID.

I shove her hand down on the bar and push it back against her chest. "She stays sober tonight," I say. "Don't give her anything with alcohol."

"What are you—" Amber says, and I shift lightly, letting her see past me. Her sister is with my brother. "Fuckety Fuck," Amber grumbles.

"I'm sure they won't stay long." I block her view or, more importantly, block their view of her. I'm protecting her, but I'm not even certain why I'm doing it. She's twenty. She shouldn't be inside Blue Line. They card when entering, but she must have shown him her fake ID to get in, just like she did the other night, for drinks.

"You're not ratting me out to my sister?" Amber asks, and she tilts her head slightly, a curious expression on her face.

"What fun is that?" I say with a shrug. "I'd rather watch you squirm." My gaze moves over her body a little too long.

She shifts on her feet and glances away, forcing a smile and pushing a strand of hair behind her ear. Amber glances at me, and I can feel her nerves bouncing off her, hitting me like little sparks of electricity.

Amber doesn't say a word. I've never known her to be quiet, but it's not like I know her all that well, either. We've spent a little time together, nothing unreasonable for two friends.

Is that what we are, friends?

"So, what's your type?" I ask, catching her stare before glancing around the room. "I could be your wingman, help you get any guy in here you want."

Why the hell am I offering to help her get laid?

I take a swig of my beer, needing to mentally plant two feet on the floor. Drinking isn't going to help that, but it will keep my mouth shut while I swallow the alcohol instead of talking too much.

"I don't—that's not really how I work," Amber says.

"Right. You mentioned girls," I say, forcing a smile. Of course, she likes girls. At least her turning me down doesn't hurt as bad, knowing she doesn't like dick.

Amber's cheeks redden. "I like both, for the record, not that it matters. But I don't do hookups."

Charlotte pops her head in from behind Amber. She's wearing a blonde wig, and it looks fairly natural, except it's her friend, and I recognize her face. I told her not to bring Charlotte and what does she do? Brings her to the game. Why did I think she'd listen to me?

"You again," I mutter, glaring at Charlotte, the girl who is ruining my chances for—what, exactly? Amber is off-limits, although my cock doesn't like to think so.

"She's a virgin," Charlotte chimes.

My tongue darts out to the side of my lip as I take in the information that her friend has shared with me. I figured as much based on what she'd told me a few nights ago, but I've just had my suspicions confirmed.

Amber's eyes widen, and she smacks her friend's arm. "You brat!"

Charlotte laughs and kisses Amber's cheek. I can't help but feel my cock stir, imagining the two girls tangled in the bedsheets.

"Get lost," Amber says and shoves Charlotte away. "I'll find my own ride home."

"I just bet you will," Charlotte says with a wink. She turns to face me. "Take good care of her."

Charlotte disappears amongst the crowd, and Amber glances down, shoving her face into her hands. "That was humiliating."

I consider asking her 'what,' but that'd make her relive it. "Everyone has a first time," I say with a shrug.

"Not me," she mutters into her hands.

Virgin territory.

I should leave well enough alone. It's not like I haven't dipped my stick in the honey pot, but I know better than to get involved with a virgin. They tend to be clingy and overly emotional. The game is my priority, my first love.

I like sex—what hot-blooded male doesn't—but I don't need a girl to be writing me love letters every day or drawing our initials in hearts on her schoolwork.

"You will," I say and rest my hand on her arm.

She pries her face from her hands and glances up at me cautiously. "You're not making fun of me?" she asks, surprised.

"Why would I?"

"Because I'm a twenty-year-old—" She doesn't finish the sentence.

"It's not a big deal. I mean, you've been kissed before. Right?"

And when she doesn't answer me, I realize how innocent and inexperienced Amber is, and I want to help her, but I shouldn't.

"No," Amber says and reaches for my bottle of beer.

I relinquish it, letting her take a swig. She grimaces from the taste but doesn't spit it out. My mind immediately goes where it shouldn't, wondering if she'd spit or swallow—I clear my throat and reach for the beer bottle. "You've had enough."

"We're friends, right?" Amber asks, and I nod.

"Yes, I'd consider us friends." I haven't told Emerson that her underage little sister is at the bar. I think that means we have a solid foundation of friendship, or at the very least, I'm enjoying her company, and I don't want her to leave.

"Will you teach me how to kiss? I mean, what if I'm terrible at it, and no boy ever wants to kiss me again?"

"Wait. You've been with two girls, and you never kissed either of them?" I run a hand through my hair. To say I'm at a loss for words is an understatement.

Her cheeks redden, and for a minute, I think she's about to tell me that she's punked me. That she's either not a virgin or hasn't been with girls. I'm not sure which I'd rather hear. Honestly, it doesn't matter. I don't care about her past. I care that she's honest with me.

"Kissing was off-limits. It was more exploratory." Amber's face is flushed.

I take another swig of my beer, which is now very near empty. "Exploratory. How?" I want to get her to open up to me. I'm unsure why I'm continuing down this line of questioning, but I want to hear more.

She crinkles her nose when she smiles. "You're not going to make me spell it out for you."

"Tongue? Fingers? Toys?" I ask, trying to gauge what she's done.

"I will answer that if you order me a stiff drink," Amber says and gestures toward the bartender.

"Can't do that," I say. And boy, do I ever want to get her tipsy and hear every dirty detail about her experimentation phase in college because I'm a guy, and my cock is as interested as I am.

"Then I can't answer you," Amber says shyly. "But I've never kissed a guy or a girl. And the other stuff was okay but not great. So, I guess you could say I was curious."

"And now you're curious about guys?" I ask.

"I've never really had a guy into me," Amber says. "The ones I crushed on, it was unrequited."

I press my lips together and think about her statement for a minute. Amber is young, innocent, and naïve. She's probably had tons of guys interested and was just unaware because of her lack of experience.

She lets out a shaky breath. "Will you be my first kiss?"

"No," I say, and I hate myself for turning her down. "It should be with someone you like, not just a friend."

I'm pretty sure she does like me, and I feel like a complete ass for turning her down, but I can't do this with Emerson's sister. Kyler would never forgive me for breaking Amber's young heart.

"I dare you to kiss me," she says, staring up at me, hopeful.

"We're not playing truth or dare," I say. I learned my lesson with that game the last time. Mostly because she dared me to kiss the prettiest girl in the room, and that would have been a setup for disaster.

Knowing she hasn't had her first kiss, I don't want to be the guy taking it from her at a bar.

She deserves to be wined, dined, and then taken home and dropped off with a goodnight kiss. I'm not that man. I know my dick, and we'd both want more from her.

"But we could? I thought you never backed down on a dare," Amber says.

She's right, I don't, but I didn't agree to this pop-up game of truth or dare that she's decided to spring on me. "We're not knee-deep in a game of truth or dare," I repeat.

"You never followed through on the last dare," she counters, pinning me with her stare. "I dare you to kiss the prettiest girl in the room."

I exhale a heavy sigh. "You don't want me to do that, Amber."

Her brow pinches, and she purses her lips. Is she worried that it's because I think there's someone prettier than her in here? Because there isn't anyone else. I have eyes only on Amber Ryan.

My fingers graze the jersey that she's wearing. My jersey. I grab the hem, tugging her closer against me. "Why did you change into a Bruisers jersey today?"

"Some dipshit spilled beer on me between

periods," Amber mutters. "I'd have bought another Ice Dragons jersey, but the line was too long."

"You just like riling me up," I say, staring at her, trying to figure her out. Amber is a mystery. Even with all of her cards out on the table, I still can't figure her out.

"Do you want to get out of here?" she asks. "Doesn't seem like my sister and your brother are leaving anytime soon."

Normally, when a girl asks me if I want to get out of there, it implies going back to her place or taking her to mine for a romp.

But that's not what I have in mind for Amber.

ELEVEN
AMBER

"IT'S BEAUTIFUL," I say, staring across the city as we stand on the roof of his apartment complex. There's a flower garden, with string lights giving off a romantic vibe and a speckling of stars across the night sky. The city makes it hard to see too many stars, but it's still quite beautiful.

Does he bring all the girls he dates up here before inviting them back to his place?

I shiver, and Jasper notices. Removing his leather jacket, he drapes it over my shoulders.

"You're going to freeze," I say, glancing at him as he comes to stand beside me.

"I'm plenty warm."

It's late, well past midnight, and I should

probably call it a night, but I don't want the night to end. It's only just gotten started with Jasper.

"Do you have a game tomorrow?" I ask.

"Practice day. What about you? Early classes?" he asks.

"Not too early." I have class at nine in the morning, but I don't want him to send me off to bed so that I get enough sleep. I'm not a kid.

There are two outdoor chairs on the roof, and he pulls me to sit in his lap, his arms around my waist.

I exhale a nervous breath.

Is he going to kiss me?

I told him that I wanted him to be my first kiss, that I wanted to know how to properly kiss a boy, and while he didn't necessarily agree to it, tonight has been a blur of lines being crossed.

Why take me to see the city and the stars at his place if he wasn't interested in me? Why lead me on?

Unless this is what he does with all his friends? Doubtful. There's no way that he's bringing his teammates up here, pulling them on his lap to sit with him.

I tense, and he reaches for the lapels of his jacket, tugging them closer together to help keep me warm. "You're shivering." He finds the zipper at the bottom and zips the jacket around me.

I am shivering, but it's not from the cold. It's chilly outside, but my nerves are making me tremble.

At least he can't seem to tell the difference. I should be grateful, but my stomach is somersaulting.

"You make me nervous," I whisper, hoping that if I voice my anxiety, it'll cease to have power over me.

Jasper quirks a grin. "You don't have to be nervous around me. We're just friends."

I exhale a short breath, but it's loud enough that he raises an eyebrow, waiting for me to speak. "I dare you to kiss the prettiest girl on the roof," I say.

The smile grows on his face, and he pushes the long strands of my hair behind my ears, pulling it back into a ponytail. He fists my hair, holding my head up, my eyes meeting his, keeping me entirely in place and at his mercy.

Dare I say that I like the way it feels, giving him control over me. He lets his fingers caress my head, my hair, and then he leans in, his breath teasing my lips before he leans closer to my ear. "Babe, you were the prettiest girl at the bar, but I won't kiss you."

The air feels snatched from my lungs, and I'm grateful that I'm seated, even if it's on Jasper's lap, because otherwise, I'd have lost my balance. The room spins, and I'm trying everything in my power to catch my breath.

What am I doing?

Why do I keep throwing myself at him when he's clearly not interested? Sure, he thinks I'm attractive, but there are tons of other attractive women he's more interested in, and they aren't me.

I should stand and move off his lap. The red alarm bells in my mind are going off, warning me that sitting on his lap is dangerous right now.

But I can't bring myself to move, not even an inch. I'm frozen. My breathing comes out raspy and fast, nervous and panicky.

"Of course, you won't," I say and take several deep breaths before rocking my hips against his as I try to stand, but his hands on my hips won't let me get up.

And now what I feel isn't just his hands, but something else nestled under my ass as it pokes me.

My eyes widen, and I glance back at Jasper. "The prettiest girl at the bar doesn't do it for you? Well, I'm sure whomever you're fantasizing about, you can call her or use your hand." I untangle from his grasp, and he lets me go.

I hurry down the stairwell to the first floor and

head outside, grabbing a cab. There's one pulling up just as I step outside.

"Amber Ryan?" the driver asks as I open the back door.

"That's me," I say.

Jasper must have called for a cab. Rather than chase after me, he's sending me home. Well, at least I know where his priorities lie.

When I get home, I fall right into bed, but I don't get to sleep for long. Two hours and twenty minutes, to be exact.

The fire alarm goes off, and thankfully, I chose to sleep in a T-shirt and flannel pajama pants. I grab my purse, phone, and keys. It's probably a false alarm. Drills are a semi-regular occurrence, but they've never been in the middle of the night.

I touch the door handle and head into the hallway. There's a haze of smoke, and the hallway is warmer than it should be, like fire is covering the building.

I'm not the only one in the hallway. A few more neighbors start to see what the fuss is about, and when we realize it's not a false alarm, we knock on the doors, making our way for the stairwell, trying to wake everyone up.

Finally stepping foot outside, in the distance, the

sound of a fire engine wails upon its arrival. Flames light the night sky. The roof is consumed by fire, and the top floor near the west side of the building is completely gone. At least two apartments have been destroyed, possibly more. It's impossible to tell from here.

We move across the street, watching as the fire department arrives and hooks up their hose. They send a team in, searching for residents.

Another fire engine and ambulance arrive. I glance at my watch. It's half past four in the morning.

Charlotte lives in another apartment complex. I dial her, but it goes straight to voicemail. I'm not even sure she's home. She might have slept over with some guy she met at Blue Line.

I send Charlotte a brief text.

Apartment fire. I'm fine. Text me when you get this.

I'm sure she'll hear about it when she gets up or sees the destruction on her way to class tomorrow at seven.

I didn't even bother with shoes in my haste to leave, but it's probably for the best. I could have been stuck, trapped inside.

The fire roars, flames kicking up higher as more

of the building becomes charred, and the fire rages down another floor.

My floor.

I glance at my phone.

I ring Emerson, but she doesn't answer. I hang up and try her again. Maybe she didn't answer it quickly enough? No doubt she got in late. Her phone is probably set to silent.

I have Kyler's number, and I grimace, trying him next.

"Hello?" he grumbles, half asleep.

"I need to talk to my sister."

"Amber, is that you?" Kyler asks. "Are you all right?" He sounds more alert, awake when he realizes that I'm calling and something must be wrong because I never reach out to him.

"I need to talk to Emerson."

"What's wrong, Amber?" my sister asks, finally answering the phone.

"There's been a fire at my apartment," I say, my voice shaky. "I'm fine, but I need a place to stay for the night."

She invites me to their place, and they insist I take a cab at this hour. I don't argue. I call for a ride and wait down the block, away from the chaos. The police are arriving, having people move back, out of the way, and away from danger.

The firefighters no longer appear to be trying to salvage the building so much as protect the apartment complex beside it and keep the fire from raging out of control onto another building.

But they are shooting water hoses, and smoke towers above before more flames brighten the night.

I can't watch, and I'm grateful when the cab arrives and takes me far from campus.

The gate opens promptly before I have time to buzz it, along with the front door.

Kyler is awake, waiting for me when I arrive.

"I'm sorry to have woken you," I say.

He glances at my bare feet and frowns as he stands at the entrance to the front door.

"I didn't have time to put on shoes."

"I imagine not," Kyler says. "Come on, I'll show you up to the guest room. Tomorrow, Em can take you shopping and get you some new clothes and shoes."

I press my lips together and nod. I don't want new clothes. I like my belongings, but even if they survived the fire, they're not going to be accessible immediately. Even if I wear my pajamas to class, I can't show up barefoot.

"Thank you," I say. I follow Kyler upstairs, and I try to be as quiet as possible.

The bedroom door on the left swings open, and Emerson steps out, pulling me in for a hug. "I'm glad you're all right."

"Thanks." I force a smile. I am all right, but I don't feel it.

They lead me into the guest bedroom down the hallway, and I shut the door and collapse on the bed.

TWELVE
JASPER

MY CELL PHONE is obnoxiously loud this morning. I grumble and reach for the phone. "What?" I say, recognizing the caller ID.

"Oh good, you're awake," Noah chimes.

"Couldn't it wait until practice?" I mutter. Whatever he wants, the answer is going to be no. No favors. No coffee runs. Just plain no.

I'm extra grumpy this morning after whatever it is that happened between Amber and me.

"Your girlfriend, she goes to NYU."

It's a statement, not a question. "I don't have a girlfriend. Where are you going with this, Noah?" I rub the sleep from my eyes and sit up in bed.

"Amber, the chick you've been pining after, did

you see it on the news? One of the apartments near campus burned to the ground."

That wakes my ass right up. I jump out of bed and flip on the television.

"What channel?"

"All of them," Noah says. "They've already recovered three bodies."

My stomach drops like it might fall out, and I find one of the local channels that has smoke remnants still charring in the background, and an apartment complex is a pile of rubble and ash.

"Did they say the address?" I ask.

And just as I ask Noah, it pulls up on the bottom of the screen.

"That's Amber's building." I throw on a pair of jeans and a T-shirt and head out the door. I hang up on Noah, needing to call Amber.

She doesn't answer.

I glance at my watch. It's nine o'clock. Could she be in class this morning? Maybe she's with Charlotte?

Although I don't know where her friend lives.

I try calling her again.

No answer.

I send her a text.

Are you alive? You're not answering your phone, and there was a fire in your building last night? Call me.

Obviously, if she's not alive, she couldn't answer my text. But in a panic, I sent the first thought that popped out of my head.

I grab a cab and head straight to her apartment. I'm not sure what I expect to find, but I need answers. Maybe they can tell me who died in the fire because the news refuses to give out that information until next of kin has been notified.

I'm nauseous just thinking about next of kin. Is that Emerson? Would she find out first or someone else? I've never heard much about Emerson's parents, and Amber has never mentioned her mom or dad.

I hardly know anything about Amber, and that hurts even worse.

Barricades are put up a block from her apartment, and the cabbie drops me off as close as he can get. I hand over cash, including tip, and hurry the rest of the way on foot.

There's a trailer parked in the middle of the street and a whiteboard on the side with apartment numbers of people accounted for.

I don't know Amber's apartment number. I never

went inside her place. I snap a few photographs, trying to make sense of the information.

"Can I help you?" a woman asks, glancing me over.

"My girlfriend..." I pause. That's not quite the right word. Although she is a girl and a friend. "...she lives here."

"What's her name?"

"Amber Ryan," I say and exhale a breath.

"Apartment number?" she asks.

I shake my head. "We just started—"

She doesn't smile, her expression is somber, and she reaches into the trailer and retrieves a clipboard. "Her name is Amber Ryan?" the woman repeats.

I nod. "That's correct."

"She's unaccounted for," the woman says.

"What does that mean?" I shake my head in dismay. "The news, they said there were at least three bodies pulled from the fire." I don't want to imagine she might be one of those bodies.

"There were quite a few residents who escaped the fire and left with friends nearby on campus, or family picked them up. We tried to get everyone to give us their information, but some residents left before we showed up."

"She got out," I repeat. I have to believe it. Amber is a fighter.

"We don't know. We have twenty-six residents unaccounted for. It's also possible some might not have been at their apartment last night," the woman says.

Amber was here. I sent her home, and if anything happened to her, I'll never forgive myself.

The remnants are blocked off with caution tape like it's a crime scene, and I stumble back to the subway. I don't bother calling a cab. I need the cold air on my face to numb me.

I try Amber again. No answer. I'm not sure if she's ignoring me or if something happened to her. But I'd like to think she wouldn't ignore me, especially since her apartment burned down. She has to know that I'd be worried.

I don't have Charlotte's number. There's no way for me to reach her. And I don't know what classes Amber is taking, so I can't exactly stalk outside the classroom. NYU has a large campus, which isn't going to make it any easier for me to find her.

I head down to the subway, grab the train, and let my mind wander. If she's in class, she wouldn't answer my texts or phone calls. She might not even see them for a little while.

It's been over an hour since I called her this morning.

I can't take waiting. Wondering. Worrying. It's too painful.

I change trains at the station and follow the map, having to switch again in order to get to my brother's house. It would have been simpler to take a cab to Kyler's place. I'm not sure that he's even home, but I need someone to talk to, and maybe Emerson has heard something, or I'm going to worry her to death.

I don't see another option.

It takes a while for me to get to Kyler's house, mostly because the trains don't run on time. But when I finally get to his place, the sky has grown cloudy and dark. It feels like rain, which seems fitting.

I'm granted entrance inside the main gates. I have the access code and walk up the driveway to the front doors.

What am I going to say?

What if Emerson doesn't know?

I knock at the front door, and while I have a key, I don't feel right just stepping inside uninvited.

Kyler opens the door, glancing me over, frowning. He looks about as tired as I feel.

"Did you hear about the fire at NYU?" I ask,

unsure how to broach the subject with Kyler. Starting off the story with your new sister-in-law— or rather sister-in-law to be—might be dead, is a bit drastic.

Kyler sighs and nods. "Yeah, we found out about it. Amber's still asleep upstairs." He points toward the staircase.

"She's here?" The air seems to rush out of my lungs, and I'm momentarily lightheaded, even dizzy.

"She called her sister last night, and when she didn't answer, she rang me to let us know what happened. She grabbed a cab and stayed over. She and Em are going clothes and shoe shopping when she wakes up." He glances at his watch and shrugs. "I imagine she'll be up in a little bit."

"I'm relieved," I say and try and screw my head back on because Kyler is looking at me strangely.

"Yeah, we all are. Do you still have that spare room?" my brother asks.

I nod. It's got a ton of crap in it, but the bedroom itself didn't just disappear. "Yeah, why?"

"Em and I are engaged. We're in this perfect little bubble, and I'm concerned that bringing her sister in to live with us might—"

"Might burst your bubble?" I laugh and fold my arms across my chest. I can see where he's coming from. He's just finally established the relationship between himself and Emerson. Adding another person into the living situation could certainly affect the dynamics.

"Amber is great. I was thinking you talked about having a roommate, and since you're hardly ever at your place between games and practice, you might consider inviting her to move in with you."

"Hard pass," I say. "Besides, isn't there other campus housing she can rent?"

Kyler shrugs. "I don't know. I'm grabbing a coffee. Do you want one?" he asks, heading for the kitchen.

"I'm good. I'll be a minute," I say and quietly head up the stairs. If Amber is still asleep, then she hasn't seen the frantic texts and phone calls that I sent her. And she doesn't ever need to see them.

I know my brother's house fairly well, which room is his, his daughter's, and even where the nanny occasionally sleeps. There are still several guest rooms at the end of the hallway, and I take a gamble, quietly pushing the door open.

The lights are off, the curtains shut, and Amber is snoring softly on the bed, her head on the pillow, her hair fanned out beside her.

I try not to stare, but it's hard not to watch her sleep. She's beautiful.

I glance around the darkened room and spot her phone beside the bed. Of course, she put it near the bed. I am as quiet as possible, tiptoeing toward her and reaching for her phone.

She mumbles in her sleep and rolls from her back onto her side, facing me.

Waiting to make sure that she doesn't open her eyes, I give it a few seconds before unplugging her phone and glancing at the screen. It's locked.

I turn it toward her face, trying to use face ID, when it lights up like the sun shining on her face.

Her eyes open, and I yank the phone down, not even glancing to see if it worked.

"Jasper?" Her brow pinches, and she rubs the sleep from her eyes. She pulls the blanket tighter around herself. "What are you doing in my bedroom?"

THIRTEEN
AMBER

I'D HEARD THE CREAK, the floorboards groan, but I was sure it wasn't in my room. Hell, I'm not in my own room.

The memories of last night come flooding back, and I don't want to wake up. I want to sleep, be basked in another world of sweet dreams and fantasies that are warm and comforting. Not the cold, harsh reality that my apartment caught fire last night, and I'm crashing at my sister's fiancé's home.

But when I open my eyes, because I swear someone opened the curtains, I come face-to-face with Jasper.

Technically, he's hovering above my bed, and I'm lying with my head on the softest pillow imaginable, but he's staring at me unapologetically.

"Jasper, what are you doing in my bedroom?" I don't want to give him a free show of any kind, so I pull the blanket higher. Although I am wearing a T-shirt, I don't have my pajama bottoms on anymore. I was hot under the covers, and sometime during the early hours of the morning, I shucked them off to the floor.

"How about we talk over breakfast? Get dressed, and I'm buying."

I exhale a sigh. "Fine. Get out," I say and point at the door.

He hurries out of my bedroom and shuts the door. I wait a minute to make sure that he doesn't barrel back inside before climbing out of bed. I grab my flannel pajama bottoms from the floor and slip them back on.

I suppose I'm dressed. It's not like I have other clothes. I didn't pack for a trip. This isn't a vacation.

I reach for my phone on the bedside table and realize it's gone.

"Jasper!" I growl and thrust open the bedroom door. He's standing in the hallway, glancing at my phone. "What the hell are you doing?"

"Nothing," he says. He shoves the phone in my hand and hurries down the stairs.

What the hell has gotten into him? I glance at my

phone. Nothing weird or suspicious, but it is unlocked.

Wait. Did he use my face while I was sleeping to unlock my phone? Could he have seen me put my passcode in at the bar?

I head down the stairs after him, barefoot, and follow into the kitchen.

"I'm going to take Amber out to breakfast. Mind if I borrow your car?" Jasper asks his brother.

"Sure, and get her some clothes and shoes when you're out. Em mentioned that her shoes won't fit her sister and mine will be too big."

It's like I'm not even standing in the kitchen with the two of them talking around me.

"Shopping first, breakfast second. Got it," Jasper says.

"Breakfast first," I say, folding my arms across my chest. "I'm famished."

"Never argue with a woman," Kyler says.

Jasper leads me to the garage, and he grabs the keys to the Porsche. I climb into the front seat in my comfy pajamas. Although, it's a little chilly once he opens the garage, and a cold gust of wind assaults me. I shut the door and buckle my seatbelt.

"I know a cute little diner across town if that works for you," Jasper says.

"Are you buying?" I ask, glancing at him.

"My brother is," he says and shows me Kyler's credit card.

"Did you seriously steal that from Kyler?" My jaw drops, and I glance back at the garage door to the house, waiting for it to open and for him to yell at his younger brother for stealing from him.

"Nope, he gave it to me for emergencies, and seeing as how you only have the clothes on your back and no shoes, I'd consider this an emergency."

"I don't want a handout, Jasper. And it's your brother's money."

"Emerson was planning on taking you shopping today—"

"Yes, and I planned on paying for everything I buy."

Jasper nods, pulling out of the driveway. "Okay, then you have renter's insurance, and you plan on turning in the receipts for reimbursement," he guesses.

"That's a thing?" I shake my head. "No one mentioned getting insurance for the apartment."

Jasper remains quiet as he pulls up to the front gate, punches in the code, and it opens for him.

We drive in silence until he finally pulls up out front of a diner. He gets lucky because someone just pulled out, and there's a space in front of the restaurant. The place looks decent from the outside, and my stomach grumbles.

"Wait here," he says, and I stare at him like he has grown two heads.

"Um, why?"

He shuts the engine off, gets out of the car, and hurries around to my door, opening it.

"Okay, you can unbuckle your seatbelt," Jasper says with a laugh. He almost looks nervous with his boyish grin adorning his face.

I unsnap the buckle, and before I can step my feet onto the ground, he lifts me into his arms. "What are you doing?" I shriek with laughter.

"You don't have shoes on, and I'm not risking you catching tetanus or hepatitis or something on the sidewalk."

I wrap my arms around his neck as he carries me into the diner and finds us a booth. He gently places me down to sit at the edge, and I swivel around to face the table.

"I don't think you can get tetanus or hepatitis from bare feet," I say, smiling.

"Well, you could get frostbite."

"Sure, if it were twenty degrees colder. Not that

I'm complaining. I've never had a man carry me around."

Jasper scoots into the booth seat across from me as the waitress brings us both a menu.

"I'll have coffee, extra cream, and sugar."

"Coffee, black." Jasper smiles at the waitress, who is old enough to be our grandmother. But the woman jots everything down and makes her way back behind the counter. "Let me guess, you prefer your coffee not to taste like actual coffee."

He's poking fun, and I don't mind it. I'm happy for the distraction, especially after last night and this morning.

I bite down on my bottom lip, remembering the feel of sitting on his lap, and open the menu, attempting a distraction.

"What's good here?" I ask, and the room feels warm, a bit stuffy even. I hadn't noticed it earlier, but I was outside being carried in by the hottest NHL player in the league.

"Everything," Jasper says. "But my favorites are the crispy waffles with cherries, chocolate chips, almond slivers, and whipped cream."

I shake my head, smiling as I glance up at him. If I ate the way he did, I'd be twice my weight, but he also works out a lot, and he plays hockey, which has to burn a ton of calories.

My gaze travels down his torso, imagining what it would feel like to press my fingers, my palms, over his warm skin.

"You're staring," Jasper says.

And I blink rapidly, glancing back up at his eyes.

He's grinning, and he sits back, stretching, the smile never leaving his face. His eyes shine, the brown looking more like warm chocolate under the harsh restaurant lighting, yet somehow, he always looks good.

"What's on the agenda for today, I mean, other than taking you shopping?"

"You don't have to go with me," I say. I can't imagine that he wants to go shopping with me. He's just doing it because, well, I'm not even sure why he agreed to it. Emerson was supposed to join me, but she probably got busy. I don't need a chaperone.

The waitress brings our two cups of coffee along with a small bowl of single-serve creamers and different varieties of sugar and sugar substitutes.

"Shopping?" Jasper laughs. "It's what I live for."

I roll my eyes and grab a packet of sugar, tossing it at him. "Liar."

Jasper is leaning forward when the sugar packet

hits his chest and falls to the table. He grabs a creamer and holds it in his right hand.

"I thought you take yours black."

"Oh, I do," he says with a smirk and gently squeezes the sides of the plastic container of creamer. The lid presses forward but doesn't quite pop off.

"I swear, Jasper, if you spray that at me—" I warn him. The container is pointed directly at me.

"You'll what?" he asks with a sly grin. "What will you do?"

"I'll wear your rival's jersey to the next game I attend," I threaten.

He pushes a little too hard, and the creamer explodes across the table, hitting me in the face. He laughs, but it seems displaced. Perhaps he's embarrassed or nervous? I've never really known Jasper to be either of those things.

His eyes are wide, and he glances around. Is he worried that anyone saw him?

The waitress comes to the table. "That was cute," she says and places a half dozen extra napkins next to me.

I dab at the creamer, wiping up the mess that he made.

"Thanks," I say to the waitress, and she gives a nod.

"Are you ready to put in your order?"

"We need a few more minutes," Jasper says, and his face is turning fifteen different shades of red.

Oh hell, he's embarrassed. It's actually kind of cute, except for the part where he sprayed me with cream.

"You really enjoy it when I wear the Island Bruisers jersey to the game," I say, staring at him.

His gaze tightens. "You've already done it twice. I think you can leave the rival team's jersey at home." He winces when he hears his own words. Home. As in, the place that burned down last night. "Shit, I'm sorry." Jasper glances up at me and reaches for my hand on the table.

"It's fine," I say. "Just one more thing for me to replace, right?" I force a smile, and he glares at me.

"You're not buying another Island Bruisers jersey. Are you trying to tell me you're in love with them or something?"

Not them.

I wince, and his brow pinches. "I swear if you're dating Knox Storm or Charlie Hayes," he growls.

"That's cute. You getting all jealous," I say and scrunch my nose with a smile, teasing him.

"Especially when you know I don't have a chance in hell with a professional hockey player."

Jasper clears his throat and glances at the menu.

He doesn't even deny it.

"Are you ready to order?" he asks.

What I want isn't on the menu. *Him.*

FOURTEEN
JASPER

AFTER BREAKFAST, we stop to buy her shoes first because she insists that I can't carry her around to every store. That's where she's wrong. I could, quite easily, carry her around. There have been a couple of people who stopped and stared. I've ignored every one of them.

A few snapped photos, but I'm sure it's because they're not used to seeing a guy carry a cute girl around in her pajamas.

I wasn't wearing a jersey. It's unlikely I was recognized.

Kyler tells me that I'm in denial when it comes to my image and the fact that every time I step outside my apartment, someone could recognize me.

I'm not like my older brother, who is constantly

getting bombarded by the media and requests for autographs when I go out. At the game, when I'm recognizable in my jersey, sure, the fans flock for an autograph, but they do for any of the players on the team.

We cruise through two stores, and her first purchase is a pair of fashionable boots, along with a set of black and pink polka-dot socks to rock with her pajamas. The girl makes everything look hot.

She hasn't let me use my brother's credit card, except for breakfast, where she insisted that I should pay because I sprayed her with cream.

Yeah, that's not the only cream I'd like to see on her face.

I push my feelings and the growing hard-on for her aside by thinking about anything else.

It doesn't really work.

To be honest, the more I push her away, the more that I want her. It's probably the whole forbidden romance vibe, and once we bang it out, we'll both be over it.

Which worries me more because I can't have an awkward encounter with her after we bang it out since we are likely to see each other. For starters, at Kyler and Emerson's wedding.

My only other option is to heed Noah's advice

and friend zone her. I've done a fairly good job at making sure that we stay platonic, but every time she gives me those doe eyes or that explosive smile, I want to fuck her and show her what it's like to be worshipped by a man.

"Almost done in there?" I ask. She's in the dressing room for the umpteenth time, trying on a dress, which surprises me, since I always see her in jeans, leggings, and a jersey or sweater.

"Don't laugh, okay? I need your opinion." She slowly opens the door and steps out.

My cock twitches the moment she steps foot out of the dressing room. The dress is a deep blue, and the neckline falls incredibly low while pushing her tits together, giving an ample view of her cleavage.

She rocks the dress. It puts other dresses to shame. But her wearing that for some other guy makes my stomach flop. I don't want her going out with Charlotte in *that* dress, pretending to be twenty-one, drinking, partying, having fun, and getting hit on by multiple guys.

"It's slutty," I say. I regret every word that comes from my mouth because she looks hot as sin, and even more so because I hate the word. I clear my throat. "You'll give off the wrong impression unless you're trying to tell every guy at the bar that you're DTF."

"DTF?" she repeats.

"Down to fuck," I say.

Her eyes widen, and she covers her tits, hurrying back into the changing room.

I'm the biggest asshole on the planet. I can't have Amber Ryan, but I don't want anyone else to have her, either.

She doesn't say another word, leaves the dress on the rack near the dressing room, and grabs a couple of pairs of jeans, leggings, and sweaters. Wordlessly, she stalks up to the register.

"Do you need to try any of that on?" I ask.

"Nope." Her answer is cold, calculated, and decisive.

I pull out my brother's credit card, his black Amex when the cashier begins to ring up all the items.

"Put that away," Amber says. "I can pay for my own clothes." She nudges me aside, using her credit card on the register terminal.

I open my mouth to argue, but the cashier is staring at us, and I swear she's about to bite my head off next if I intervene. When she finishes, she asks the sales clerk to take the tags off and if she can use the dressing room to change clothes.

Amber takes her bags with her into the dressing room, and I grab the dress abandoned on the rack that I so eloquently told her made her look like she was willing to get laid. I'm a monster.

I bring it to the cash register while she's changing.

"Are you sure?" the sales lady asks. "You seemed pretty gung-ho on your girlfriend not wearing it."

"She's not my girlfriend," I say and gesture for her to ring the purchase up.

She saunters out of the dressing room, her pajamas presumably shoved into one of her shopping bags. Instead, she has on black leggings and an oversized maroon sweater that falls past her ass—an ass that she shouldn't hide. I silently pray she doesn't still hate me for my earlier remark.

"Where to?" I ask.

She glances at my hands, holding one of the department store bags. "Did I forget something at the register?" she asks.

"Nope, I just did a little shopping for me."

She smiles, her eyes lighting up. "What'd you buy?" She peers at my bag, but there's tissue paper on top, hiding the surprise inside.

"I'll tell you on one condition—nope, never mind."

"What?" Her mouth drops. "You can't leave me hanging like that, Jasp. Give it to me."

Oh, I'd like to give it to her all right, but not like she thinks. I bite down on my tongue and keep the shopping bag out of her reach as she tries to grab it from my hands.

"I let you see that silly dress on me. What'd you buy that's so embarrassing? Was it underwear?" Amber laughs, and it's natural and real. There's nothing fake about her, ever. I love that about her, how she can be so carefree, even after what happened this morning.

"It's not underwear or lingerie," I say.

Her eyes light up. "Oh, that would have been good! I wouldn't have thought you'd wear women's lingerie." She nudges me and heads for the door. She opens it before I get there and gestures for me to step out first.

I don't argue with her, although I like to hold a door open for a lady. It's at least a small form of chivalry that shouldn't be dead.

"For the record, I don't wear women's lingerie," I say, leaning closer, not wanting anyone to overhear our conversation because it's way too embarrassing out of context.

"See, I'll never know that until you show me," Amber says with a straight face, her eyes glancing up at me. "Show me what's in the bag, or show me your panties." The smile reaches her lips from ear to ear.

"Nice try," I chide. "Not happening. This precious gift is mine."

"Wait. So, it's a gift?" Amber doesn't miss anything. "Is it for your brother? My sister? Me?" The last one comes out a bit squeaky, like she's just throwing it out there and doesn't believe it could be for her.

"I'm not at liberty to discuss."

I keep walking, heading back toward the Porsche, and she's right beside me, hurrying to match my strides. I slow down, realizing that I'm nearly a foot taller, and she seems to be jogging to keep up.

"That's an interesting use of terminology," Amber says. I can't tell if she talks more when she's nervous or just really wants to know what I have in the bag. "Is it for a girl?"

"What is this, twenty questions?"

"Yes!" she says and snaps her fingers. "Let me

guess it in twenty questions, and if I get it right, I get to see what it is. If I'm wrong, then I'll leave it alone."

Yeah, I doubt that.

"Fine," I grumble. This had better be worth it. "Yes."

"Yes, to the twenty questions, or yes, it's for a girl?" she quips. We approach the car, and I hit the unlock button on the key fob.

I make sure to pop the trunk and drop my bag in there, where she can't reach it, and look through the contents while I'm driving.

"That's another question," I warn her. "Yes, to the girl."

Her eyes widen, and she purses her lips. Amber drops her bags into the trunk beside mine and hurries into the car. The air has gotten chilly with the sun hiding behind the clouds. I didn't bring a coat, but she had enough forethought to buy warm clothes, at least, while at the store.

"Girl. Okay, next question. Are you dating anyone?"

It's not the first time she has asked me that question, but maybe she thinks that changed over the past couple of days. "No." That's the only answer that she gets, yes or no.

"Okay. Is the gift for family?"

I wince as I try to think of exactly what Amber is to me. We're not family yet. "No," I say.

"That took you a while to answer. Not family, but you weren't sure. Oh, is it for my sister, Emerson? She's going to be family, but not quite yet."

She is too damn astute.

This time, I answer quicker, "No."

"Okay, not for family. Not for my sister. It's for a girl, so it can't be any of your teammates."

"Is that a question?" I ask, knowing it's not but trying to veer her off course.

"Is it for someone who enjoys hockey?"

I laugh. "Yes." I think she enjoys hockey, she's been to two games, so I'm going with yes. That was a total cop-out question on her part. She could have asked me something better, juicier. I should be relieved that she didn't include herself in the line of questioning. "You have fourteen questions left."

"Is it for me?"

That's the question that I don't want to answer. I glance in the side mirror, wait for traffic to clear, and slam on the gas.

"Well?" She's waiting for my answer.

I'm not about to lie to her. Avoid, maybe, but not lie. "Yes," I finally say.

"Can I open it?"

"No."

"Why not?" Amber whines, and I swear she sounds a lot like Bristol when my niece doesn't get her way.

"Yes or no."

She grumbles under her breath. "Are you planning on giving me the gift?"

My hands white knuckle the steering wheel. "Yes."

"When?"

"Yes or no," I repeat. "And you wasted two questions with your why and when."

"Those don't count because you didn't answer."

At least this time, there's not a question in there. She huffs and folds her arms across her chest. She doesn't seem mad, just annoyed with me. "Fine, next question. Are you going to give it to me today?"

I glance at her. Probably not, but I have to answer yes or no. "No."

"Tomorrow?" she asks.

"No."

She rests her head back on the seat. "On a holiday?" she guesses.

"No."

"It's for me, but you don't plan to ever give it to me. What gives, Jasper?"

"That's another wasted question," I say, trying to hide the smile on my face. She's asked fifteen questions so far, and she's far from guessing the gift.

"Okay, so not for a holiday. Oh, my birthday. Do you plan on giving it to me for my birthday?" Her eyes light up like maybe she figured it out.

Except, I don't know when her birthday is. So, I shake my head. "No."

"This game is tough," she says with a laugh. "I still have like ten questions, right?"

"Four left."

"That's it? Okay, I really need to buckle down." She rubs her hands together as she contemplates her next question. "Is it something that you would give someone in public?"

I'm confused by her question. "Yes?" I'm not quite confident in my own answer. Why wouldn't I gift it to her in public? But then again, why would I?

She presses her lips together. "Then it's not lingerie for me," she says cheekily. "And no, Jasper, that's not a question."

"I wouldn't know your size," I whisper, and the car is feeling quite suffocating.

"Okay, so it can't be clothes because you don't know my size. But the shopping bag is from the same store where we just bought clothes. Is it a cover? Did you buy me something from a different store and ask the clerk to put it in one of their bags?"

"That's two questions. No, and no. You're on your last question," I say. "Make it count." I'm glad that I'm keeping her distracted, but I'm not sure how much longer she'll be smiling as we head closer to the NYU campus.

She takes note of the direction that we're heading, away from Kyler's place and across town from my apartment. "Where are we going?"

I smirk, grateful that at least her last question was wasted on something unrelated to the dress. I will give it to her. I just need the right opportunity.

"That's twenty questions, and I'll give you the last one. We're heading to your apartment. We need to let them know that you're safe. They have you unaccounted for after the fire, and they're trying to identify remains."

"Oh." She exhales a soft breath, and her shoulders slump. Reality seems to hit her as she grows quiet.

"It'll be okay," I say and reach for her hand. "You don't have to do this alone."

We drive as far as we can and walk the additional block on foot. The perimeter is roped off, not letting people drive through the street. The command post from earlier is still parked out front of what used to be the apartment building.

Amber's hands are shaking, and I give one of them a squeeze before pulling her closer, wrapping an arm around her waist. I'd never been so worried as I was this morning—frantic, unable to get ahold of her.

She approaches the person in charge, answers some questions, and fills out a questionnaire for the local emergency management team, Red Cross, and the school.

I give her some space as she sits on the edge of the curb, the clipboard in hand. "Umm." Amber gestures me over.

"Sure, what is it?"

"They need a location that I'm staying in—I don't plan on being at your brother's place for long, but can you give me his address?"

"Use mine," I say.

"What?" She stares at me, confused.

I force a smile. "I don't know his address without looking at my phone. I left it in the car. Just use mine." I recant my apartment address to her, and she scribbles it down.

"Thanks."

When she finishes the forms, she asks them

about additional housing options, and they give her a phone number to contact through the school. She makes a few calls on the way back to the car, but every apartment within a five-mile radius is unavailable. The dorms are full, having already housed several residents who were displaced from the fire.

She hangs up and grimaces. "It's fine. I'll get a place farther from campus and commute on the train." I open the car door for her. She looks lost, tangled in her thoughts, like a web that she can't break free from.

My brother's words play through my head, reminding me that I should invite Amber to stay as a roommate. I'm not exactly near NYU's campus, but it would make housing affordable, having a roommate. And while I don't need the cash that she'd contribute to the bills, I like being around her. I wouldn't need an excuse to see her, and I'd be helping her out of a tough situation.

"I'd be happy to have you as a roommate," I say, staring at her.

"You're just saying that because you feel bad for me." Amber slides her feet into the car and grabs the seatbelt. I shut the door and hurry around to the driver's side.

I climb in and turn on the car, and it doesn't take long for the heat to kick in. The engine is still a little warm from our last drive.

"I don't feel bad for you. I was looking for a roommate before I got drafted in the NHL Entry Draft."

"I won't cramp your space?" Amber asks. "I mean, we'll have to have some type of code, you know, in case you want to bring a girl back for fun times."

"Fun times? You mean like video games and booze?" I know that's not what she's referring to, but it's fun to watch her squirm.

"Netflix and chill."

"You mean you don't just sit and watch a movie and share popcorn together?" The smile doesn't leave my face as I head toward my apartment. I have a bit of cleaning up to do to the guest room, but Amber can help or, at the very least, make fun of me while I make the room presentable.

"Maybe? I've never actually Netflix and chilled with anyone," she quips. "Remember, virgin over here?"

I try not to laugh or get ridiculously turned on by her honesty. It's refreshing. "You probably shouldn't make it a habit of telling single guys you're a virgin. They may think that means your DTF."

"Oh, well, in that case, Jasper, I'm a virgin."

I swear she's trying to give me a heart attack. Every time the word 'virgin' leaves her lips, my cock stirs. It's like the magic word that turns the damn thing on, quite literally. And there is no off switch when it comes to Amber.

FIFTEEN
AMBER

WE ARRIVE at Jasper's home, which he insists that I can move into, but I'm not sure that's the best plan. I mean, the hot hockey player whom I've had a major crush on and secretly been stalking online wants me to live with him?

Charlotte would tell me, *hell yeah, move in with him.* But I haven't texted her yet. Maybe I should. She might even knock some sense into me.

But I can't live with Charlotte. She has a one-bedroom apartment, and unless I want to sleep on the couch indefinitely, that isn't going to work. She also likes to bring guys home, and I'm not keen on waking up in the middle of the night to see them naked and heading to the bathroom.

"I need to text Kyler, let him know we'll be back

for dinner, and I'll return the Porsche tonight." Jasper rattles off a text in the hallway as we walk to the elevator.

I'm impressed that there are elevators and a doorman. The place already appears swanky, and I'm wondering how I'm going to afford even half the rent. That's a discussion we need to have pronto.

"Yeah, sure," I say, and he heads for the elevator, hitting the button for the twenty-fourth floor. I'm familiar with the building. I've been inside once when I was a little more than tipsy, and he let me have his bed. The other time was last night when he took me to the rooftop and showed me the city at night.

He hits send and grumbles. "No signal." It takes a minute for the message to go through once we're enclosed in the elevator.

"Did you mention to him that you asked me to live with you?" I smirk, teasing him.

"I thought I'd bring it up over dinner tonight."

I'm not sure if he's joking or not. The elevator dings, and he gestures for me to step out. "This is us."

I step out, and he attempts to send the text again. This time, it goes through. He grabs the key from his pocket and unlocks the front door. "Ladies first," he says, and I glance at him and shake my head, smiling.

"You won't be saying that after we live together —as friends," I clarify, although I'm not sure why I bother to add that tidbit. He knows that's all we are. Jasper has made sure that we stay parked in the friends' zone, and I'm blocked in, unable to get out.

He lets me inside his place and flips the light switch as soon as I enter, shutting the door behind me. I place the purchases that I made inside, near the door. He carries his secretive bag with him around the house, toying with me.

There's a full-sized kitchen and a counter for eating, with stools. The dining room has been converted into a game area with an air hockey table. Why am I not surprised?

"That converts into table tennis too," Jasper says, "if you play."

"I've dabbled. Sounds fun."

He leads me farther into the apartment, which feels cozy but more like a house in that it's much roomier than my studio apartment. "The living room." He gestures to the leather sofa and huge television attached to the wall.

"Wow."

"Yeah, seventy-five inches. Doesn't get much bigger and still fit in this place." He beams.

I press my lips together and refrain from making some torrid joke comparing the size to a man's cock. It's on the tip of my tongue, but I can't bring myself to do it.

My nervousness seems to be reappearing, and I ball my hands into fists and then fold them across my chest.

Jasper doesn't seem to notice my discomfort, or he acts like it doesn't exist. "The bedrooms," he says and gestures for me to follow. "My room." He points and opens the door for a few seconds, long enough for me to get a quick glimpse. He shoves the mysterious bag inside his bedroom by the door.

The bed is made, but there are a few clothes spilled out of his overflowing laundry basket on the floor.

Are they clean or dirty? It's not the first time I've seen his bedroom, but my head hit the pillow the last time, and the rest is a bit of a blur.

"And your room, which we need to tidy up, or at least, I need to tidy up, and you can sit and watch television or keep me company," Jasper says.

"I can help," I say.

"You might regret that offer." Jasper opens the

bedroom door to the guest room. Inside, there are piles of books stacked from the floor to my waist and the table tennis table resting against the mattress vertically against the wall.

There's a dresser in the corner, the only piece of furniture that is actually in a decent place and doesn't seem like it needs moving.

In the middle of the floor is a huge, black bag that could seriously contain a human. "What the hell is in there?" I ask and point at the oversize duffel.

"Work stuff."

"Work? Where the hell do you moonlight that involves dead bodies?"

Jasper chuckles. "The NHL, and while there are a few rivals I'd like to see dead," he stalks past me and bends down, unzipping the black duffel, "sorry to disappoint, but no dead bodies. Just extra hockey equipment."

I feel dumb. Of course, Jasper works for the NHL. That's his profession. He's a hockey player. "What's your gear doing here? Don't you keep it, like, at the stadium?"

"The team has an equipment manager who handles everything, but I've got gear from before I joined the NHL. I can't just throw it out."

"You could donate it," I suggest. "Or sign it and

give it to charity if you're not using it. I imagine it would go for quite a bit of money at a charity auction."

He smiles warmly. "You give me too much credit." He grabs the duffel and lugs the massive bag, throwing it into the coat closet, which is now overstuffed with three coats, two pairs of shoes, and a huge hockey bag.

"What do you want to do with all the books?" I ask, glancing them over. There's a pile of textbooks. He had gone to college at some point. Jasper never mentioned being a student, although I don't imagine that he'd be enrolled anymore, with the NHL keeping his schedule busy.

"Those," he says and lets out a sigh, "we can donate."

"Are you sure? We might be able to sell these back to the school where you bought them. They all look pristine."

"That's because I never opened them," Jasper says. "I debated with college or the NHL Entry Draft. You can see which one won. Don't get me wrong, I have absolutely no regrets other than spending money on those giant paperweights."

"You could sell them back to the bookstore," I say.

"And get twenty bucks on a three-hundred-dollar

book? No, thanks. I'd rather donate it. Let some college kid get a nice surprise when they're shopping at the thrift store."

"If you do that, you might want to drop it off at a thrift store near the campus that you attended. Unless it isn't in New York?"

I don't know much about Jasper or his past. What I know is based on our short conversations together and his social media profile, which seems like he parties and has a lot of fun with his teammates.

How much of that is real?

"We can drop it off near NYU," Jasper says.

A smile plasters my face when I realize that we could have gone to NYU at the same time, maybe even been classmates. "What were you planning to study?"

"I'm going to sound like a nerd."

"That's what you're worried about? Tell me; you know I'm going to school for microbiology."

He shakes his head and laughs, his hair falling across his eyes. "Right, I forgot. Bigger nerd." He points at me and smiles.

"And?" I'm waiting for him to elaborate. He likes this game of teasing me, not giving me anything real in terms of answers. The truth is that I don't mind it, either. I relax when I'm around him, especially when he's joking around and playful, like two friends who've known each other their whole lives.

"Twenty questions?" He grins at me.

"No!" I laugh and smack his arm. "Just tell me."

"Okay, how about you ask a question, I answer it? And vice versa. Back and forth."

"So, like truth or dare without the dare?" I ask.

"I wasn't thinking of it as a game, but yeah, if that's what you want to call it." He grabs a handful of bags to put the textbooks in, but he can't fit too many, or the bags will tear far before he'll have trouble lifting the bag.

"You asked your question. I'll answer. I enrolled at NYU to study literature."

"Nerd," I say, teasing him. I help pile the textbooks into several different bags.

"My turn," Jasper says. While I put the textbooks into the plastic bags, he goes through the pile of fiction books, deciding which to donate and which to put onto a bookshelf in his bedroom. "What's the real reason you wore the Island Brewers jersey during the second period of yesterday's game?"

That's his question?

"I told you, and I meant it. Some jerkwad spilled beer on the jersey that you gave me. It was wet, and the ice arena is cold. It wasn't a great combination. I wanted to buy an Ice Dragons jersey with your number on it, but the line was crazy long. Besides, it got your attention," I say with a shy smile.

"You always steal my attention during a game," he mutters.

"My turn. What's in the bag that you bought for me?"

Jasper grins and rolls his eyes. "You can't let it go. Do you not like surprises?"

I press my lips together as I finish with the stack of textbooks. "I like some surprises, but I also get nervous when I don't know what the surprise is." There's no way that he hasn't seen my nervousness and anxiety kick in.

"That's fair," Jasper says.

"And? You didn't answer what was in the bag."

Jasper inhales sharply, his breath catching in his throat. "You noticed my avoidance of the question. How about we each get one that we don't have to answer?"

I can live with that. "Fine. Okay, next question—"

"It's my turn," Jasper says.

"No, it's most certainly not. You asked if I don't like surprises. Ergo, your question. The next one, I ask."

He grumbles under his breath. "Hit me with it."

"Have you ever thought about me, not as a sister, as like—" I pause, trying to ask without saying the actual words.

"You mean romantically?" Jasper is careful in his confirmation of the question.

I should say yes, that's what I meant, but it isn't. And this could be my only chance to lay all our cards on the table.

"Sexually."

Jasper stands and dusts his hands on his pants. He's looking anywhere but at me. "That's enough of that game," he says and skirts out of the bedroom, past me, and over the bags of books.

I curse under my breath and pinch the bridge of my nose. I went too far.

SIXTEEN
JASPER

I CAN'T BELIEVE Amber's question. Okay, maybe I shouldn't be so surprised since she still enjoys games like truth or dare and twenty questions. But I did instigate this little truth-telling game, so she's not entirely to blame.

I should lie to her, tell her that I don't see her as anything other than a little sister. That she's cute but too young and immature to ever be with someone like me. If I say the right thing to leave a small scar, she'll move on. She might hate me, but at least we can both put this unresolved sexual tension to bed.

Well, not literally to bed.

I don't know how I'm going to manage to live with Amber and watch her date other guys. But that's a problem for another day. Right now, she asked if I've ever thought about her sexually.

My response?

I ran away.

I'm a fucking coward when it comes to Amber.

If I told her the truth—that I think about her all the fucking time—when I shower, I masturbate to the thought of her giving me head; when I try to fall asleep at night, I rub one out, imagining her pussy like a vice on my cock.

And the dreams, they're even more real. I can smell her scent, the sweet lilac and lavender body wash that makes my cock twitch when she's around. Just one whiff, and I get a hard-on.

But that's too much to divulge, and if she's going to live with me, there have to be boundaries and ground rules.

For starters, no sex.

At least not with each other. And if I have a say in the matter, I'd prefer her to remain a virgin because I don't want anyone else getting frisky with Amber, either. I bite down on my bottom lip.

I can't fucking tell her not to date. She's twenty. Single. She's bound to find men to go out with, or women for that matter. I don't know. I just don't want her bringing any of them home. Not that I'm keen on her fucking them anyplace else and then sneaking into the apartment in the morning or late at night.

I groan and head for the kitchen when I hear her soft patter of footsteps following me.

"Jasper?" Amber's voice is soft and sweet, like honey.

But if I indulge in what I want, I'm bound to get stung. Noah was right, she's off-limits, and that's if we weren't living together.

She's my new roommate.

I can't be fantasizing about bending her over in the shower or fucking her on the kitchen counter.

"I'm fine. I just needed some water." I grab the pitcher in the fridge with filtered water and a glass, pouring myself something to drink. "Do you want some?" I ask.

"Any chance you have something stronger?" Amber asks with a laugh. It's the nervous laugh, the one that escapes when she's uncomfortable and anxious. I've seen the ticks. The smallest things that others might not notice about her, I see. Her foot bounces. She fiddles with her fingers in her lap. Sometimes she even chews on her bottom lip.

There's a beauty in her nervousness, not that I'd ever tell her that. It'd probably only make her more anxious.

"Sure. Show me where the glasses are?" Amber asks.

I give her a quick tour of the kitchen, what dishes go where, and then retrieve a glass for her to have a cup of water.

"Thanks." She's forcing a smile, and her cheeks are overly flushed.

I'm betting she's wishing that she didn't ask that question five minutes ago. Maybe I can pretend it never happened? Does that make me an asshole for avoiding answering whether I've thought about her sexually?

Of course, I've thought about her sexually. I've thought about her naked too. And I've thought about what it feels like to fuck her on the ice with the entire arena watching and cheering us on.

They're just fantasies.

They can't happen. Certainly, not the last one. And maybe it's okay to keep those fantasies to myself to give myself something to enjoy when I need to unwind. I've never been interested in the puck bunnies—the girls who chase after hockey players to fuck, like we're a notch on their bedposts.

No, thank you. I don't need to stick my dipstick where my brothers have been, and I consider all of my teammates my brothers, not just Kyler.

Amber's phone buzzes, and she pulls it from her purse, glancing at the message on the screen. "It's your favorite person, Charlotte," she says and sends a quick response.

I can only imagine what those two are conjuring up next.

"Tell her the blonde hair doesn't fool me. I know she was at the game with you."

"The wig was my idea," Amber quips. "Contrary to what you might think, I don't have a lot of close friends. Besides, without her, I wouldn't have gotten the nerve to show up at Blue Line again."

"Well, anytime the guys are there, you're welcome to join us. I can't promise Kyler won't bring Emerson, though, so that's something you two will have to work out."

Amber blushes. "You mean you won't keep covering for me?"

"I'd cover for you, but I'm pretty sure that you keep it up, and you'll get caught. Kyler or Emerson will notice you."

She sighs and takes a sip of water. "I don't want to get on Em's bad side. I've been there, and it's not pretty." Her phone buzzes, but this time it's not a text. Charlotte is calling her.

"You can take it in my room," I offer, trying to give

her some privacy while I finish clearing out the guest room so that it can officially become hers.

"Thanks," she says and smiles weakly, sauntering down the hallway. I shouldn't turn around. I shouldn't steal one more glance, but I have to, and I wonder if she knows that I'm watching her, pining over her, fantasizing about her.

I keep hearing Noah's words in my head.

Bro-code.

But it's more than just bro-code now that we're roommates. Hooking up with Amber would not be wise. It'd make things messy and complicated, and for a few minutes of undeniable pleasure, it's not worth the risk.

Because undoubtedly, it will fail. Whether it's in a few weeks, months, or years, I will always put hockey first, and she'll be disappointed, and her resentment will turn to hate. I don't want to put Amber through that kind of pain.

I like her too much to hurt her, and I do want her in my life as a friend, first and foremost.

It takes a couple of hours, but I'm nearly done and putting the bed frame back together when I hear my bedroom door squeak open.

She had talked with Charlotte for a while before silence enveloped the apartment.

Amber emerges from my bedroom. She looks like she just woke from a nap. Her cheeks are rosy, and her hair is tousled. The look is good on her, but she could make anything sexy.

"Sorry, I fell asleep on your bed."

I'm not sorry. Tonight, my sheets will smell like her. "That's fine," I say. "How'd you sleep?"

"Better than last night." She quips a faint smile and glances at her watch. "You've got most of it done."

"Yeah, just have to finish this frame and then drop the box spring and mattress on it. Do you want to text your sister and let her know we'll be leaving soon?"

"Sure," Amber says and yawns. She looks absolutely adorable half-asleep.

We finish with the mattress, and the guest room is presentable. Amber will have plenty of room to put the few things that she acquired today in the empty dresser. Surprisingly, the drawers were already empty. The rest of the room, however, had been a disaster.

"Do you want to grab your bags and put your stuff away?" I ask and exhale a breath.

The bag with the dress that I bought her. I'd forgotten about it. About the fact that I shoved it into my bedroom, the same room she'd been occupying alone for quite some time.

I meet her stare, but she doesn't say a word. If she knows the dress is in the bag, she hasn't even given the slightest hint. She's also no longer asking what's inside, but maybe she succumbed to the fact that I was going to make her wait.

But for how long?

And why the hell did I think it was a good idea to buy *that* dress? I don't want any other man ogling her in it.

My pants tighten, and I grumble as I head for the kitchen. I open the fridge. I'll need to restock if Amber is going to be living here, not that she can't buy her own groceries, but I also don't want her thinking that I live on takeout. Because I don't. Well, not usually.

My body is a temple.

Do you know that bullshit? Well, as an athlete, I believe it. The food that I put into me provides me with nutrients and keeps me ready for game day. If I snack on crappy foods all day, I don't have the same endurance for a game.

"I'm ready," Amber chimes as she waltzes into the kitchen. "But we should talk."

"About?" I glance at her over my shoulder, shut

the fridge, and spin around her to face her. Usually, those words aren't ones that I like to hear.

"The rent."

"Right," I say with a nod. "What did you pay for your place?" I know without a doubt that my apartment is going to be well outside of her budget. It's disgusting how much property is in New York City, and I don't expect her to contribute half when I know her income isn't anywhere close to mine. She's in college and working, I think, part-time. We haven't really broached that subject recently, either.

"I was paying $2,850 in rent."

"Can you continue to afford that?" I ask, getting right to the point. My rent is upward of $14,000 for a two-bedroom, two-bathroom in Manhattan. I'm not about to ask her to split the mortgage. She makes less than a tenth of what I make in a year, and I'm signed for a three-year contract.

"Yeah, I can swing it." She forces a smile, and I get the impression that she's probably struggling to pay her bills. Unless she comes from money, and I've seen no indication of that from Amber or Emerson, I can't imagine how she can afford to make rent working part-time.

"Pay me half your rent, $1,400, and that should

be fair and equitable. Plus, I've got the utilities covered."

"You don't have to—"

"I know, but I want to," I say. "You're going to be replacing your wardrobe, textbooks, and whatnot."

Amber groans. "Don't remind me."

"Any chance one of those books you could use?" I ask, pointing at the piles of bags in the hallway. I should take them down to the car and donate them, but I doubt there's enough room in the Porsche for all of it.

"Nada," Amber says. "It's fine. I'll use my good looks and charm to convince the teachers to give me A's."

"Yeah, I don't think that works in college, but maybe if you show them your boobs."

She smacks my arm, throwing her head back and laughing. "Half my teachers are women."

"Doesn't mean they don't appreciate a nice set of tits when they see them."

Her cheeks burn, and she grabs one of the bags I plan on sending to a thrift shop. "Just leave it. I'll call someone to pick all that crap up."

"We can drop it off on the way to dinner," Amber says. "At least some of it."

"That's the opposite direction, and it's fine. I'll

text a friend. He'll have it gone by the time we get home."

"Seriously?" She looks at me like I've grown two heads. "What kind of friend makes things disappear from your apartment?"

Grinning, I stare at her, tilting my head. "Are you sure you want to know?"

She snorts and shakes her head. "Not really. I don't need to be an accomplice to any crimes."

"One of my friends lives in the building, and he works near the thrift shop. If I pay him a hundred bucks, he'll be ecstatic to take the bags down there for me."

"I'll do it for a hundred bucks," Amber quips.

"Do you have a car?" I've never seen her drive in the city, but it's possible she could have a vehicle parked somewhere.

"I'll lug the bags on the subway." The smile on her face grows. "Imagine all the looks of me dragging three bags down the stairs and onto the subway station platform."

"With the weight of those bags, someone is bound to think there's a body in one of them."

"A jagged, sharp, book corners body," she quips.

I grab the keys to the Porsche and the apartment keys. There's a spare in the drawer, and I grab it on its lonesome keyring. "The key to your new home," I say, handing her the spare.

"I really thought when I'd move in with a guy, it wouldn't be like this, with us." Amber blushes.

I lead her out into the hallway, down the elevator, and to the car.

"Can I drive?" she quips, wagging her eyebrows at me.

I don't know whether she has a driver's license or not, but I don't think my brother would appreciate me handing over the keys to his Porsche to my roommate.

"How about you ask Kyler, when you see him at dinner, if you can borrow the car?" I open the passenger side door for her and gesture for her to climb inside.

"It was worth a shot," she says, smiling weakly as she steps down into the car.

I shut the door and hurry around to let myself in, start the engine, and we head toward my brother's place for dinner.

"Are you going to tell them, or am I?" Amber asks.

"Tell them what?"

"That we're living together." The way that she says it makes it sound almost scandalous.

I bite down on my bottom lip, glancing at her. "We're just roommates," I remind her.

"I know that. We could play with them and tell them we're seeing each other."

"No," I snap, putting a pin in her idea before it gets wildly out of control. "We're not doing that with Kyler. You can tell Emerson whatever you want, but I'm not telling him I'm banging his fiancée's sister."

She has no idea that Kyler asked me to have Amber move in with me, and I wasn't on board initially with the idea.

But it's grown on me today, having her around, realizing that she needs someplace to stay, and I want her as a roommate.

Amber grins, staring at me. "I dare you to do it."

LIVING with Jasper has been easier than I imagined, probably because I see him far less than I see my own sister. Well, that's not exactly true.

We run into each other on occasion. But with his early morning practices and game nights staying out until late, we run different schedules.

I have school and three shifts a week at Mad Tea House. I've picked up an extra shift to make sure I have enough to cover my portion of the rent, which I know isn't anything close to what Jasper actually pays, but my rent has been depleting my savings account.

Jasper won't let me pay a cent more, and I honestly can barely make ends meet as it is with having to replace what I lost in the fire, including my laptop, which cost nearly as much as my rent check.

My phone buzzes, and it's Charlotte, letting me know that she's outside. I head down to the elevator to greet her. She's standing outside in the cold when I step onto the sidewalk.

"You can come inside," I say, throwing my arms around her for a hug.

We haven't caught up since the fire. I've been working like crazy, trying to catch up with my studies. I missed a couple of days after the fire. One of those days was easily excused. The other two were because I didn't feel like catching the subway to go to class. It was raining and dreary.

Lame excuse, I know. I did the reading and assignments that were posted online for the class.

"You did well for yourself," Charlotte says. "Is the boyfriend home?"

"He's not my boyfriend, and yeah, this place is amazing. Come on up. Besides, it's freezing out," I say. Charlotte isn't shivering, but I am, wearing a sweater and jeans. I'm going to need to buy a winter coat soon, but I've been putting it off, waiting for my next paycheck to cover the cost.

We head inside, and I lead her to the elevator and then to the enormous two-bedroom apartment.

"Holy crap," she says when I let her inside. "So, this is how the rich live."

"I'm not rich," I counter. But she's right. This place is spectacular, especially compared to my previous living arrangements. Her one-bedroom place isn't much better than what I had, a little bigger kitchen, but that's it.

"No, but he is. I googled the starting salary for an NHL player and holy mackerel! It's nearly a million dollars a season."

"No way." I don't believe her. She pulls it up on her phone, tapping away until she shows me the three-quarter of a million-dollar figure on the search page.

I don't want to look. I feel like it's an invasion of his privacy, a boundary that I shouldn't cross. But she shoves the phone in my face, making it impossible for me not to look.

"Good for him," I say. At least I don't feel that bad paying my tiny portion. I'd love to pay him more since we're splitting the place and living together as roommates, but I can't come anywhere close to affording this swanky space.

"Good for you," Charlotte quips. "Can you introduce me to one of his single friends? Noah is hot."

I grab two hard lemonades from the fridge and lead Charlotte into the living room. "I don't really know his friends," I admit. "I mean, other than our interaction at the bar." I grab a seat on the sofa beside my bestie. There's an empty chair opposite and the television across from us. I don't bother turning it on. I have enough entertainment with Charlotte visiting.

"You two don't hang out? And will Jasper care if you're stealing his liquor?"

"It's mine, and let's not tell him I picked it up. We need to finish the twelve-pack before he gets home."

"Or hide it under your bed." Charlotte laughs, shaking her head. "Are you seriously worried he's going to be mad when he finds out? He's not your dad. I mean, unless you like it when you call him Daddy."

I grab the throw pillow from the sofa and shuck it at her. "You're terrible, and we're practically the same age."

"Except he can legally drink," Charlotte says.

What's her point? In a few months, I'll be old enough to drink legally too. So will Charlotte.

She rolls her eyes and leans back, getting comfortable on the sofa. "Gosh, I'm so jealous you have it all, Amber. The digs. A hot boyfriend. Plus, he's in the NHL. That's like an extra check mark of awesomeness."

"Don't be jealous. My apartment burned down," I remind her.

She purses her lips. "But it's better that it did. I mean, make lemons out of lemonade."

"I think you mean make lemonade out of lemons," I correct her.

She takes another swig of her hard lemonade. "Make alcohol out of lemons. That's the winner." Charlotte stands and glances around. "Give me the tour."

"Oh, right. Sure." I'm a terrible hostess. I'm used to my studio apartment, where you pretty much see everything with one foot inside the place. I lead her around the apartment, pointing out the kitchen and living room, which she already saw. "This is the game room," I say, gesturing to the air hockey table in the middle of what would ordinarily be a dining room.

"Bachelor pad." Charlotte coughs under her breath.

I elbow her to shut up. Thankfully, Jasper isn't around to be insulted. But I don't like her picking on his place because it's mine now too.

"Show me where the magic happens."

"What?" I ask.

"His bedroom." She waggles her eyebrows.

"I'll show you my bedroom, but no magic. No action. No excitement except sleep."

"Sleep can be fun. After riding him cowgirl style," Charlotte says. She doesn't seem to know when to shut herself off.

I yank open the bedroom door. The room is plain, practical. There's a desk by the window that Jasper insisted on buying for me to study. The dresser is against the wall, and the bed is at the opposite end.

"And his room?" she asks, after glancing in at my mundane space.

"Off-limits," Jasper says, coming up from behind.

"I didn't hear you come in," I say. My hand is wrapped around the can of hard lemonade, and he glances at it but doesn't say anything.

"Hi! I'm Charlotte." My redheaded friend beams like he hasn't already seen her at the hockey games and met her at the bar.

"I know who you are." Jasper's eyes tighten. "Don't you have class?" he asks me.

"Finished up for the day. I already did my homework, too," I say.

Charlotte mouths *Daddy* behind his back as she

heads out of the hallway. "I can go if I'm interrupting something."

"You just got here. Don't be ridiculous," I say. "I was going to make dinner soon, Jasper. Are you staying in tonight?"

He had a game yesterday, which means today was just working out, practicing, the usual—whatever the hell it is that professional hockey players do on a day when they don't compete.

"Seems like I am," he says, nodding at my drink. "Someone needs a chaperone."

"You're only a few months older than I am," I counter. "And I'm not going out anywhere."

"Drinking and cooking could also be construed as a crime if you burn the apartment down," Jasper says.

Charlotte silently watches us, tossing back the rest of her hard lemonade. There's a smirk on her face. She's enjoying this banter a little too much.

"I didn't start the fire at my apartment complex."

"No, but you did set off the fire alarm here twice," Jasper says.

Charlotte can't contain her silence any longer. "Is that why you always order takeout or eat on campus at the cafeteria?"

Did Charlotte just try to burn me? "Traitor!" I

scowl at her and turn to Jasper. "For the record, the fire alarm is just overly sensitive."

"Should I give it a tissue to keep it from crying?" he quips. His eyes sparkle, and I want to wipe that smug grin off his face.

"No, but you could take the batteries out of it," I say.

"Zero chance in hell that's happening. I'll cook dinner," Jasper says and gestures for Charlotte and me to head away from the kitchen. I'm not even in the kitchen, just standing in the hallway, but I get the hint and plop down on the plush sofa with my friend.

"What are you making us?" Charlotte asks from the couch, a cheerful grin on her face.

"That depends. Do you burn down kitchens and set off smoke alarms?" Jasper asks Charlotte. "You do seem like the type, given your desire to convince my roommate to wear the rival's jersey at every game she's attended."

"Two games," I say, holding up two fingers at him. "And you haven't invited me back to see you play."

"I had a string of away games," Jasper says. "Home now."

"Missed anything?" Charlotte chimes.

"Other than my own bed?" Jasper asks.

At the mention of his bed, my cheeks warm, remembering when I took a nap on his mattress. Hell, I slept under his covers the first night that we met. Although I was trashed, and he was a perfect gentleman.

Sometimes I wish he hadn't been, and maybe then this unresolved sexual tension between us would be, well, resolved.

"You missed me," I say. "Worrying about whether I burned down your apartment making dinner."

"I left you takeout menus," Jasper quips. "And cash, but I see you left that untouched."

Charlotte leans in closer, eyes wide, and whispers to me, "He left you money?"

"And I didn't touch it. We're roommates. It wouldn't be appropriate." My whispering needs a bit of practice because Jasper glances up at me from the kitchen.

"What part of feeding yourself and not destroying our home wouldn't be appropriate?" Jasper asks. He's genuine in his question, and he breaks eye contact to bend down and grab a cutting board from the cabinet.

"It's your money. I'm not going to spend it." Just like when I told him that I wasn't going to let him, or his brother, pay for my clothes or shoes after the fire.

"She's honest," Charlotte quips. "But if you want someone to take your money—" She holds out her palm, willing to take whatever cash he's offering, which happens to be none for her.

"Oh, I'm sure there are plenty of girls out there for that," Jasper says. He smiles at me as he starts chopping up the vegetables, and I stretch out on the sofa, invading Charlotte's space.

She gets the hint and shuffles to the empty chair, making sure that when the time comes for Jasper to join us, he's forced to sit on the sofa with me.

That wasn't my plan, I swear. I just wanted to stretch my legs. But it isn't long before he's got dinner in the oven and the timer set.

He opens the fridge and grabs a beer. "Do you girls want another drink?" he offers.

"Yes!" we both say in unison.

Jasper brings two more hard lemonades over to the living room and a bottle of beer for himself. "You should buy the bottles of hard lemonade," he says. "They don't have such a metallic taste."

"Maybe I like the metallic taste," I quip. "And the ease of opening it." I shift around, sitting up so that Jasper has room on the sofa beside me, and pop the top when he sits.

He clanks my can with his bottle. "Cheers."

Charlotte holds her drink up in unison, giving us an air version clank rather than getting up from her chair. I commend her for taking the empty chair.

After a minute, Jasper places his beer on the coffee table beside the couch.

"You can put your feet back up," Jasper says, and I raise an eyebrow, curious. I shift back slightly, moving my legs to the couch but keeping them bent, making sure not to encroach on his space. This is still his house, and while I shouldn't feel like an outsider—I pay rent—it still feels like his place, and I'm just a guest.

Not that he ever makes me feel that way. On the contrary, he does everything imaginable to make me feel welcome. He put out fresh towels and even texted me from the hotel that he was at that they had cute tiny shampoos and asked if I wanted him to steal any from housekeeping's cart when he walked by.

For the record, I said no.

I can afford to buy my own shampoo, body wash, and a new toothbrush. And while he has someone bring him groceries because he's too busy to go shopping, there's a store a couple of blocks away that I walk to from the apartment to do my own shopping.

I keep my knees bent, my feet right beside his legs, but I don't rest my body on his. That's a line that we haven't crossed, and I don't think that he wants my feet, clad in knee-high pink and black polka dot socks, on his lap.

"Aren't you glad you moved in with a roommate who happens to be an amazing chef?" Jasper boasts.

"Amazing? I've yet to taste any of your meals." He's always out at a game, practice, or traveling for the team. I press my toes into his leg, nudging him. "How do I know you're not trying to poison me? Lure me into your beautiful abode where you steal my weeks' worth of clothes, shiny new laptop, textbooks, and smother me with a pillow in my sleep?"

He gently grabs my legs, pulling them down onto his lap. "Are you sure you're not a drama major?" he quips.

Jasper pins me with his stare, and I feel the air knocked out of my lungs from the intensity of his gaze. His fingers move to my feet. I'm not sure if he's about to tickle me or give me a foot massage.

"I should probably go. I'll grab dinner on the way home." Charlotte stands, and she interrupts the moment, shattering it like glass.

Jasper sits up straighter, his hands hovering over my feet, but he no longer pays me the same attention that he did. He reaches for his beer on the coffee table and takes a swig.

The man never strikes me as nervous, which makes me more concerned that he could be regretting the heated gaze we shared.

It was nothing.

Just a look.

"You're welcome to stay," Jasper says. He takes another sip of his beer. "Dinner is on. I made enough for three."

"Well, when you put it like that." Charlotte plops back down on the chair.

I take a sip of my second hard lemonade, which tastes even better than the first.

Charlotte is smirking, and that grin has me concerned because she always seems to cause trouble when she's scheming. "So, tell me, have you two kissed yet?"

When the words leave her lips, the hard lemonade leaves mine, spitting it out and right at Jasper, spraying him mercilessly. I curse under my breath, and I'm certain my cheeks are crimson. There is no mistaking my humiliation for what it is or hiding from it.

He takes his shirt, lifts it to wipe his face, and then removes it completely from his torso, tossing it at me.

It lands on my face and falls to my lap. I wasn't expecting him to disrobe in front of me or Charlotte.

"I'm not putting this on," I say, pointing at the sprayed hard lemonade on his T-shirt. The last time he took off his shirt and tossed me it to wear, it was his sweaty jersey.

It sits in my lap as he runs his fingers over my feet delicately, trailing a path from the top of my foot to the bottom.

And that's when he tickles me. His fingers dance with a featherlight touch over my insole, and I'm squirming on the sofa, attempting to break free, but he doesn't let me.

"Your punishment," he says with a sly grin.

"For what?" I shriek with laughter, and he continues to torment me as I try to move my feet away. He pulls me farther down on the sofa, straddling me, tickling my stomach, and making me squirm under his touch.

The only escape is to retaliate, and I attempt to tickle his hips. He squirms just a bit, enough to rock his center over mine, and it feels deliciously good.

"Charlotte, help me!" I squeal between fits of laughter.

I glance at her, and she's sipping her drink,

watching the show that we're putting on for her. "I am helping you," she says with a wink and stands.

"Where are you going?" I shout.

"To get myself lost in the kitchen," Charlotte says.

"It's just you and me," Jasper says, staring down at me.

I'm gasping as he momentarily stops tickling me, letting me breathe. Staring down at me, his brown eyes are a darker hue, and his breathing is thick and heavy.

He shifts, and I feel his cock twitch against me.

I want him to kiss me, but if I move up, if I reach for him, he'll push me away like he's been doing all along. I know he wants me. I can *feel* that he wants me.

Jasper clears his throat and climbs off the couch. "I should grab a clean shirt and check on dinner."

Charlotte steps aside as I glance at her in the kitchen. "Dinner still has fifteen minutes on the timer," she says. With his back to me, as he heads down the hallway for his bedroom, she mouths something unintelligible.

I shrug, unable to read her lips, and gesture her closer.

She tries again as he emerges from his bedroom, and when I can't figure out what she's silently mouthing, she gives up. Charlotte grabs another hard lemonade from the fridge. "Do you need another, Amber?" she asks.

"I'm good." Two is definitely my limit tonight if I want to keep things from getting any more awkward between us as roommates. My feelings for Jasper need to be buried.

"Are you free tomorrow night?" Charlotte quips, bringing her hard lemonade with her as she crashes on the sofa beside me.

"I don't have anything planned," I say. "Why?" I can already see the cogs going in her head, and it makes my stomach bubble.

"There's a party on campus, and I want you to come with me."

"There's always a party on campus," I say.

"Trust me, there will be," she lowers her voice to keep Jasper from hearing us, "hockey players."

"What?" he barks. Her version of whispering is about as bad as my version. "Who the hell from the team is going to a frat party?"

"College hockey," Charlotte emphasizes. "I figured with the unresolved sexual tension around here, if she has a thing for hockey guys, maybe she could hook up with one on campus."

"I don't have a thing for hockey guys," I say.

The only guy I have a crush on is standing twenty feet away. Sure, he happens to play hockey, but my feelings are for him. It doesn't hurt that he has a rocking body, abs to die for, and a mind that is just as sexy as the rest of him.

Damn, I'm way too invested in Jasper Greyson. Maybe I should heed Charlotte's suggestion and go out and meet some new guys.

Jasper is silent. I watch him as he removes the plates from the cabinet and then digs into the fridge, preparing something to keep busy.

"Do you need any help?" I ask.

"You've done enough," Jasper mutters.

Charlotte and I meet each other's stares. *Jealous,* she mouths, and she's right. But why?

We're just friends. Jasper has made sure that's all that happens between us. Even after he tossed me the jersey, he's turned down every advance that I've ever made, and while it hasn't been that many, it's more times than I wish to recount.

I can pick Charlotte's brain later when Jasper isn't within earshot. I grab my phone from the table and text her.

Why is he jealous?

I let her see the text and refrain from sending it. There's no need to have a record of our conversation or her phone to buzz for him to wonder what's going on between us.

She grabs my phone and erases the text, answering me.

He wants to get in your pants.

I yank the phone back from her and erase the message as quickly as possible. "What are you two conspiring about?" Jasper quips, glancing over his shoulder at us.

"Nothing. I was just showing her some photos on my phone." It's a little white lie, but I am passing my phone to Charlotte, so at least it's believable.

Charlotte has a smug smirk on her face—an *I told you so* look—that says way more than necessary.

I'm in denial. No way that Jasper Greyson has feelings for me. I click away, showing her another message that I type.

No way. He sees me as a sister.

She grabs the phone, laughing as she erases the message.

"What kind of photos?" he asks. He's standing at the counter chopping vegetables and preparing a salad in a large wooden bowl. He pauses and stares at me, his lips parted, but he doesn't say anything further.

There's something very domesticated about his behavior, and I try not to stare at him.

"The racy kind!" Charlotte quips, and I smack her shoulder.

"And she's showing them to you?" Jasper frowns like he's trying to make sense of my behavior, as if I would show my best friend naked pictures.

"She's not naked," Charlotte says, and I'm sure my face has turned the color of an overripened tomato. "Just lingerie, and I'm helping her pick the best photos for a dating site."

"What?" The knife he's using to cut up the vegetables for salad clanks to the floor.

"Are you okay?" I ask, standing to make sure that he didn't butcher himself.

"Fine," he mutters and bends down, retrieving the metal instrument from the ground. He picks it up. "I still have all my toes. You can sit back down." He turns on the sink and washes the knife with soap and water.

I ignore him and finish the rest of my drink. "Let me help," I say, coming into the kitchen. Unlike my studio, where the kitchen barely fits one person, his kitchen easily accommodates two people. Heck, his living room could host a comfortable party; even with only four places to sit, there's plenty of mingling room.

Charlotte stands, slowly approaching the kitchen. "I feel like I should offer now, or I'm a terrible guest." She's smiling and watching the two of us as she props herself at the kitchen counter on one of the stools.

Jasper has already set the counter bar where we eat with plates, silverware, and napkins. "One of you can grab drinks for dinner," he suggests.

"I'm on it," I say and retrieve three glasses.

"I'm good. I have my drink here." Charlotte lifts her hard lemonade to indicate that she doesn't need anything else to drink.

He runs a hand through his hair before returning to dicing up the vegetables, tossing the chopped cucumbers into the wooden bowl with the fresh lettuce and carrots already mixed in.

"I'll just get my appetite ready," Charlotte says and then pins Jasper with her gaze. "Are you dating anyone?"

"Excuse me?" He clears his throat and glares from her to me as if I put her up to this line of questioning. I didn't. This is one hundred percent Charlotte being overly eager to see me get laid. Well, not literally see me, just hear about it from me.

"You two are roommates. Obviously, you aren't bumping uglies," she jokes. "Are you dating anyone?"

"I'm not interested," he says curtly as if to imply there is no interest between him and Charlotte. He makes that clear quite quickly, and I don't want it to mean anything else, like he harbors feelings for someone else—me.

Wishful thinking.

"No! I'm not asking for me," Charlotte says and puts her drink on the counter, holding her hands up. "I just mean that you're roommates. Have you two talked about the inevitable? When one of you brings someone home, and there is a scrunchie or tie on the doorknob?"

"We're not in college. We have our own bedrooms," Jasper says, and his voice is thick and raspy. "I don't think a tie or scrunchie is necessary. Do you?" He holds the knife in his hand and points it in my direction, his gaze meeting mine.

"I'm good with discretion as long as I don't walk in on you sleeping with some chick on the couch or air hockey table."

Jasper grins. "Did Kyler tell you about that?"

"What?" Thankfully, this time I don't have a

drink in my mouth, or someone would have gotten a second sprayed shirt.

He's laughing. "It's a joke. Relax. I will keep my festivities in the bedroom or the shower. Anywhere with a locked door."

"Duly noted," I say and plop my butt down on the stool next to Charlotte. She's grinning, and I elbow her. She's asked him enough questions to humiliate me for the rest of my life. I don't trust what else she'll ask over dinner.

EIGHTEEN
JASPER

DINNER WITH AMBER and Charlotte is interesting. Her friend is growing on me. Not in the 'I want to bed her' way, more along the lines of I can see why Amber keeps her around.

Where Charlotte is wild, and without abandon, Amber is quiet and reserved.

They are complete opposites, yet somehow complement each other. Charlotte also won't stop herself from saying whatever comes to mind. It's a bit refreshing but also horribly annoying when she's trying to set the two of us up.

I'm not blind to the attraction and the chemistry between Amber and me.

But I'm trying to be a better man by not acting on it, and if bro code alone wasn't reason enough before, then the fact we're roommates is an even bigger reason to abstain from having sex with Amber Ryan.

Okay, not just sex.

Kissing.

Fondling.

Hell, even tickling her and feeling her squirm under my body cannot happen again.

My dick is still twitchy, and I've done everything imaginable to try to put distance between us. I don't want her to see me as cold or distant. I do like her, I like spending time with her, but it can't be as anything more than friends.

We cannot jeopardize our friendship.

We finish dinner, and the girls clear the dishes and prepare some type of interesting fruit parfait for dessert. It actually tastes a million times better than it looks. Of course, the kitchen is a disaster, with whipped cream on the ceiling, floor, and all over Amber.

Has she ever used an electric beater before?

It's a cute look on her, and it takes all of my willpower not to drag my finger across her bottom lip or her cheek. I want to taste it. Taste her. But I refrain.

"I should go," Charlotte says, glancing at her watch. "If I leave now, I can make the next train."

Amber is wiping up what she can reach of the whipped cream splatter with a rag.

"Assuming it's on time," I say and glance at Amber. "Leave the ceiling. I'll get that when I come back." I look back to Charlotte. "How about I walk you to the subway station?" I'm not keen on her walking alone at night. It's nearly nine o'clock, and while the neighborhood is decent, I'd feel better knowing that she made it to the subway.

"I can text Amber when I get home."

"You'll do that too," I say. "I'm walking you."

"Okay, but for the record, you're not my type." Charlotte makes her position clear, and I'm relieved that she's not going to hit on me, that her little angle of questioning earlier was entirely for her friend's benefit.

"Good, because you're not mine, either." I grab my coat and keys. "I'll be back in a few," I say to Amber.

She nods, her back to me as she wipes the outside of the fridge, smearing the whipped cream on the stainless steel. Yeah, that's going to make a bigger mess. I'll deal with it when I get back. At least she's trying. I give her kudos for that.

We head down to the elevator, and the minute we step inside, she folds her arms across her chest, and her eyes narrow as she stares me down. "So, what's your deal?"

Okay, I wasn't expecting the next inquisition when I suggested walking her to the train. Me being nice is probably going to backfire on me, at least when it comes to Charlotte.

"My deal?" I repeat with a laugh. "You're the one encouraging your friend to wear the Island Bruisers jersey to our games."

Charlotte grins. "Yes, I did." She's smug and proud of her little accomplishment like she knew it would get under my skin.

Dammit.

"You're not dating anyone. Are you into Amber?" Charlotte asks the difficult questions. The girl doesn't avoid them like I'd prefer to.

"I'm focused on my career," I say because stating that *I date my job* would sound weird, but that's pretty much the only action that I see lately—on the ice or with a one-night stand.

"That's a lame answer. I'll bet you get plenty of offers from girls at the bar. What are they called, the girls who follow hockey players around, chase after them?"

"Puck bunnies?" I supply.

She snaps her fingers. "For the record, Amber is not one of them," Charlotte says.

I never got the impression that she was. She hasn't even so much as glanced at any of my teammates. "I know. And what about you? What's your deal?" I ask. "You play the overbearing big sister with her pretty well, but you do know that she has a sister already, don't you?"

"Emerson?" Charlotte shrugs. "I've never met her."

Interesting. I try not to overanalyze what that might mean. The only reason I know Amber's sister is through my brother. It's not like Amber introduced me to Emerson.

We step out of the elevator and head outside. The air is chilly and damp. The street is glistening with a fresh coat of rain that has recently fallen, but it's not currently raining.

I walk alongside her by the curb, escorting her a couple of blocks toward the subway. While the streetlamps are on and a few people pass us while walking, it's still pretty isolated.

"It was nice getting to know you," Charlotte says as she points at the entrance to the subway station. "Thanks for letting me crash dinner with you and your not girlfriend." There's a smile on her face, and I shake my head.

"Why can't you believe that we're just friends?"

"Oh, I believe it, but I don't think you do." Charlotte smiles and waves, hurrying down the stairs to the platform, leaving me standing there for a solid minute before I turn and head back to the apartment.

It's a brisk walk, and I shove my hands into my pockets and hurry back to the building. The elevator is waiting for me, and I take it back up to our apartment.

Our apartment.

It still feels like a foreign concept in the grand scheme of things, but it's not solely mine anymore. And I never thought I'd be open to a female roommate, especially one I'm not sleeping with.

I shove those thoughts aside as I open up the front door and step inside.

Amber is balancing on her tiptoes, standing on the kitchen counter with a rag as she wipes the ceiling clean. The problem is that the whipped cream isn't only over the kitchen counter. It's also in the middle of the kitchen on the ceiling, and she can't reach that from her position. She grabs the rag and whips it across the ceiling while holding the edge, trying to smack the whipped cream clean.

I never realized how short she is, and it's quite endearing.

I stalk across the kitchen. "Didn't I tell you to leave it until I get back?"

She reaches a little too far forward, losing her balance as I catch her on her way down, holding her in my arms, not letting her go.

Amber gasps. The sweet, innocent sound that spills past her lips almost sounds sexual, although I know it isn't meant to be—the gasp of shock and fear as she finds herself falling, but luckily, I'm right there to catch her. Since she didn't take much of a running leap, there is not enough force for her to knock me back.

I'm steady on my feet, my arms around her waist, and I don't let go.

"Sorry," she says, quick to apologize. Her arms are wrapped around my neck, and I should put her feet down on the floor, but I'm keeping her pressed against me, enjoying the intimate moment between us.

I want to steal every second that I can, and it'll never feel like enough.

She tilts her head down as I have her nestled

between me and the counter. I prop her on the edge and, with one hand, push her hair out of her face.

I crave her more than the air that I breathe.

She is the night sky, speckled with stars.

Brilliant and beautiful.

She doesn't even have the faintest idea of what she already means to me. It's not about lust or sex. The desire is already there. It's been there since the moment I first laid eyes on her. The problem is bigger than a small crush or a moment of longing shared between two friends.

I think that I'm falling in love with her.

I want to kiss her. Taste her. Enrapture her lips with mine and carry her into my bedroom. I still smell her scent on my bed. The first night that she stayed over, it lingered for days until I was forced to wash my sheets.

Now her scent is everywhere. The lavender and lilac carry through the house. It's nestled in my shirt from her proximity, on my pillow from when she took a nap in my bed when I cleaned out the guestroom, and it continues to taunt me, like an addiction that I cannot rid myself of, nor do I want to.

She is slowly becoming an obsession. Spending time with her. Stealing a touch without it being construed as something more because it can't be more.

We're roommates. Friends.

I can't risk it with her.

But inside, I'm screaming for her to kiss me, to let me undress her, take her to bed, and show her what it's like to be worshipped and ravished. If only she'd ask me again to be her first, to dare me to show her what it's like to kiss, to touch, to explore one another, I don't think that I could say no.

There's a wall that I need to put up to protect her and myself. It stands brick by brick, the mortar crumbling with every second that we stare into each other's gaze, and I know she feels exactly the same way.

Amber smiles and leans her forehead against mine. She opens her mouth, but before she can say anything, a dollop of whipped cream falls from the ceiling right onto my nose.

"I think I missed a spot," she quips.

Amber reaches out with her hand for my face, and I grab her wrist, stopping her. With my grip around her wrist, she still manages to tap my nose with her index finger, getting the white fluff off my face.

Before I know it, she's putting her finger into my

mouth, between my lips, and I'm sucking off the whipped cream, curling my tongue around her finger, wishing it were her lips and mouth on mine.

Her phone buzzes from the counter behind her, and I step back as she hops down from the countertop and hurries around the other side to reach for it. She glances at the text and then at me as I stare at her, the counter between us making us feel miles apart. "Charlotte made it home safe."

I can't believe her friend just cock blocked me from halfway across town.

"ARE YOU SURE ABOUT THIS?" I ask Charlotte, glancing at my reflection in her full-length mirror at her apartment. I didn't have any sexy clothes, as she blatantly put it, and we are planning on attending a campus party that I don't even have any interest in attending.

"You look dynamite." Charlotte flashes me her biggest grin.

I'm in a short, black skirt which isn't going to keep me warm tonight. The long-sleeved ensemble is cute but a little tight, showing off my bust.

"You need to wear these too," she says, shoving her fuck-me boots into my hands.

We're within half a size for shoes, so I shove

some toilet paper in the toes to keep them from being too loose.

"You should totally hook up with an NYU hockey player tonight."

I grumble under my breath. "I'm not hooking up with anyone." I shoot her a look and then glance at my reflection again. I've put a touch more makeup on than usual, accenting my eyes with thick eyeliner and my lips with a natural red.

Damn, I do look hot.

"Because you're hung up on Jasper?" Charlotte quips. She grabs my phone and snaps a picture of me. "Send this to him, and I'll bet you he'll show up at the party."

"I'm not texting him a photo." I shove my phone into my purse. "He's busy tonight. Plans." I don't elaborate. He has the night off, and he's in town. I'm not actually sure what he has planned, but he mentioned seeing the guys.

"Plans with a girl?"

"Friends. Leave it alone," I warn Charlotte.

"I know you two are friends. I'm trying to get you a little more action."

I had meant that he was with friends, but I leave it be. "Party. Let's go." I'd rather mingle at a party and get ditched by Charlotte when she finds herself a hottie to hook up with for the night. At least then, I can have a few drinks, dance, flirt, and call it a night.

For the record, I don't plan on hooking up with anyone tonight. Not even a little tonsil hockey.

We arrive at the party, and within twenty minutes, Charlotte has already ditched me. I should be furious, but I'm used to her flaking on me when there's a hot guy who catches her attention. The girl is like a magnet to them.

I'm leaning against a wall, drink in hand, keeping to myself. I don't really feel like mingling. I thought going out would be fun and a good idea, but now I'm regretting the decision.

"Hey, I think we have statistics together," Atlas says.

He's well known on campus as one of the star athletes for NYU's hockey team. The fact that he even notices me is shocking.

I glance around, making sure that Atlas isn't talking to someone else because that would be far more likely. We've never said two words to each other in class, but he's right. We are in statistics together.

And I despise that class.

"Yep," I say and take a sip of punch, which offers

quite a bite. No clue what alcohol they dumped in, but it's more alcohol than punch.

I'm not overly chatty. Atlas is nice-looking and has a decent body. I mean, he is an athlete. But I feel awkward and force a smile. Which, unfortunately, he seems to think means that I'm interested.

In his defense, he's probably never met a girl who wasn't interested in him.

"You're chatty," he jokes and smiles warmly at me. "Let me guess, you came here with a friend, and she ditched you for a guy?" Before I can answer, he points at the corner toward a couple making out. "My friend, and he ditched me."

I don't actually know where Charlotte ended up. Probably in a bathroom with one of the hockey players. If she becomes, as Jasper referred to it, *a puck bunny*, I don't know what I'll do. She'll need an intervention for sure, but we're not there yet. I'm not sure if the guy she's hooking up with is even a hockey player.

"Some friends we have," I say, and he nods. He's got a red solo cup in his hand with punch. He taps my cup.

"Cheers."

I'm not sure that's something worth drinking to,

but I don't comment on it. I keep that thought to myself.

"Does your friend drag you to a lot of parties and ditch you?" I ask. I'm trying to keep the conversation going, but I don't really feel it. He seems nice, but there isn't the spark, the chemistry, that I feel around Jasper.

And I hate myself for thinking about *him* right now when this perfectly nice guy is trying to vie for my attention or at least keep me company until he meets someone else more charming.

"Do you want to know a secret?" Atlas asks, and before I can tell him I don't really care that much, he leans in. "He's one of my teammates, Reid."

The name doesn't ring a bell, and I haven't been to any of our school's hockey games, so I can't say that I recognize him, either. "Oh," I say, as if that's supposed to mean something because it doesn't.

"Reid Clayton." He stares at me and realizes I'm clueless as to who he's yammering on about. "The star of the hockey team—oh, never mind, not a hockey fan?" he guesses.

"I've been to a couple of Ice Dragons games." I leave off the part where I'm rooming with Jasper Greyson, one of the NHL players.

"Wait, you're an Ice Dragons fan?" He looks

slightly displeased by the news. "You wore my brother's jersey to one of his games. I thought you were an Island Bruisers fan."

My stomach tumbles, and I can't help but take a small step backward, like he's invaded my space and my privacy. I bump into the wall behind me. I'm sure that Atlas hasn't been stalking me. We're in class together, and he probably just recognized me at a game, but his comment is still off-putting.

"His games? Your brother is—" I can't even remember whose jersey I bought the first or the second time, and both were burned in the apartment fire. That's one loss that I don't really care much about.

"Knox Storm," Atlas says with a grin and leans closer, putting his arm around me. "I could give you a private tour of the ice arena, take you out on the rink, and we could—"

"If that's supposed to be a pickup line, you are so far from the goal." I shrug him off and head for the door.

"Seriously?" he shouts at me over the music pumping, chasing after me. He grabs my shoulder, spinning me around to face him.

"Listen, I'm sure you're a nice guy, but I'm not interested." I don't want to be here. I'm sure there are plenty of other girls who fall for his ridiculous lines and his good looks, but that's not me.

"Everyone is interested. There's not a soul in this school who wouldn't beg for a chance with me. Come on, *Ice Queen*."

"Ice Queen?" My mouth drops as I stare at him, shocked. "You don't know anything about me." I shouldn't have come, and worse, I'm going to have to face Atlas in statistics class on Monday. At least I have the weekend to try to forget this conversation and night ever happened.

I hurry outside, my legs freezing in the short black miniskirt, and it's a decent walk to the subway. I ring Jasper, wanting to talk to someone in the darkness while I'm heading for the subway station to go home.

"What's up? Hold on a sec," Jasper answers, and there's noise in the background. After a second, it's quiet, like he went outside or took the call in another room. "Everything okay?"

"Yeah," I say with a heavy sigh. "I just, I'm kind of far from the subway, and I wanted someone to talk to until I get to the station. Is that okay?"

"Are you alone?"

I laugh and sniffle from the cold. My heart hurts a little, too, but I'm not crying, at least not outwardly. "Yeah, that's why I called. Is it okay? Are you busy?"

"Where are you? I'll come to get you," Jasper says. "Are you on campus?"

"I'm just walking back from a party. It's fine. By the time you get here, I'll be at the platform."

"How long a walk is it?" Jasper asks.

"Half an hour if I wore boots that fit and a skirt that isn't quite so short." I have to take smaller steps, and while I'm gripping the phone with one hand, I'm also trying to keep my skirt from flying up and revealing what's underneath. Note, it's my black lace panties. In hindsight, I should have opted for something less sexy.

He clears his throat. "Send me your location."

I glance at my phone and stop walking long enough to give him my whereabouts. "Tracking me now, are you?" I joke, trying to make light of the situation. Slowly, I'm walking, my feet tingling from the cold, my legs numb.

"I'm picking you up."

"Jasper, that isn't necessary."

"Stay on the phone with me until you see the Porsche." There's noise in the background once again, and the phone is muffled as Jasper says something to someone, I presume his brother.

"You have your brother's car?" I ask.

"Borrowing it," he says, and the silence follows him as I assume he's heading out of whatever building he's in. Bar. Club. His brother's house, which is unlikely since I could be home by the time he'd pick me up. Well, it would be close. "Just keep talking to me," Jasper says.

"Umm, yeah, sure." It's the first time I don't know what to talk about. I don't feel like rambling. My teeth are chattering, and I'm regretting wearing this ridiculous skirt when it's cold enough to snow.

"Where's Charlotte?" Jasper asks, keeping the conversation going. His voice sounds more distant, and I hear the rev of a car engine.

I'm hoping he'll be here soon, but I know it's going to take a little while. So far, the sidewalk is abandoned. I haven't seen anyone since the party, and the streetlamps flicker overhead as I pick up my pace.

My feet are growing cold and numb from the chill outside. So much for Charlotte's boots keeping my feet warm.

"Charlotte? She is probably sleeping with some guy she met. I don't know, she disappeared at the party and ditched me. Typical Char."

I swear that I hear him growl at my answer.

"It's fine. I'm used to being her wingman. I just couldn't take any more of the guy who was hitting on me."

"Hitting on you?" His responses are short. Curt. Rough.

"It's nothing." I don't really want to talk about it with Jasper, or anyone, for that matter. I don't know what Atlas was thinking. Why bring up his brother at all? Did he honestly think that having Knox Storm as a brother would impress me? Because it doesn't. And calling me *Ice Queen*? What the hell was that about? Because I wouldn't give him a blow job or fuck him?

"You're dodging my question," Jasper says.

"Can we talk about something other than the party?" I wince at my tone, not wanting to snap at him. None of this is his fault. "Sorry."

"Don't be," he says, his voice calm and collected. "I'm almost there. I've got the heat on in the car for you."

"If you put the air conditioning on, I think I'd have to murder you, Jasper."

"A woman with a vengeance," he teases. There's a lightness to his tone, and I see a Porsche at the next light, his blinker on, waiting to turn down the street where I'm walking.

The chilly air tickles my skin, and I shiver, wrapping my arms around myself.

As soon as the traffic light changes, Jasper rounds the corner, and the roar of his engine approaches as he hits the gas before coming to an abrupt halt.

He pulls across the empty road and idles the vehicle. I hurry to the passenger door, yank it open, and climb inside. The welcome blast of heat is refreshing against my tingling skin.

Jasper doesn't move. His gaze rakes over me.

"I should have brought a blanket," he says, taking in a long look as he does another once over, making sure to get a nice glance at my bare legs.

Any other guy, and I'd make a snide remark about his lingering stare, but instead, it heats me to the core, and I exhale a nervous breath.

"Nice car," I say, trying to direct his attention away from my body without actually telling him not to look. Because the truth is that I don't mind his attention, I like it.

"Yeah, I borrowed Kyler's car. I can drop you off at home before returning it to him."

He runs a hand through his hair, shakes his head like he's trying to get focused, and pulls back out onto the road.

The silence stretches between us for only a few seconds. "I don't feel like going home," I admit, changing a glance in his direction. "Can I hang out with you guys tonight, or is it like, no girls?" I don't want to crash his night if it's like a guys' night out thing with the team.

"There are always girls, even when we don't invite them," Jasper quips. "Unless we're hanging out at someone's house or something. Sure, you can come." He glances at me, his gaze on my short skirt, before returning his attention to the road.

"Thanks for picking me up," I say, fiddling with my hands in my lap. The butterflies are always there around him, but they're tamed, and my desire for him is insurmountable. It's probably the rum punch from the party letting me act out of want, and I'm okay with that. If this is what it takes to make it known how I feel about him, so be it.

I reach across the car, resting my hand on his thigh.

He's wearing jeans. They're tight, and he's warm as I stroke my fingers against his pants. I'm cautious not to just go right for his cock, which I want, but I caress his leg, my fingers moving inward toward his inner thigh.

Jasper's breathing deepens. Each breath grows

louder as his lips part, and I swear the car begins to fog from the heat between us.

"Amber, what are you doing?"

I smile, staring at him. "I thought it was kind of obvious?" I shift slightly, letting my legs part, and my skirt rides up just a bit higher. I want him to chance a glance in my direction and see my heat, my lace panties, and find his control wavering.

His voice catches in his throat. "We're roommates," Jasper says, and I watch as all control melts away, and he pulls over to the side of the road and puts the engine in park. "Get over here," he growls.

Willfully, I unbuckle and climb across the center console. Jasper pushes his seat back as I come to straddle his lap. I can feel his heat pushing against his zipper jeans, poking me as I tease him with my hips.

His hands grab my ass from under my skirt, spreading my cheeks, his finger dipping between my panties, and he tears them to shreds, ripping them off.

I gasp at his eagerness, and already, we're both breathless, staring at each other. My fingers tangle in his hair, pulling him closer as I lean down to kiss him.

Our lips haven't so much as touched, and he's staring up at me with heavy lids and grinding into my hips.

My mouth parts, and he leans forward, kissing my neck as I hang my head, eyes falling shut.

"Just feel it," he whispers into my ear, licking and nibbling the lobe as my body turns to jelly from his touch.

Jasper grinds into me, thrusting his pants-clad hips, pushing his clothed cock against my core. I tremble in his arms, and he sucks and kisses my neck while his fingers hold my ass, bare hands over my skin as he holds me tight against him.

I rock my hips in tandem with his.

"I want—" I gasp, unsure what I want other than him. I'm rocking against him, my insides warm and toasty, like a molten river of lava flowing through me.

He presses his lips over mine as I feel the wave, the heat, my core clenching down, wishing it was his cock buried deep inside of me.

I thrust my tongue inside his mouth, drinking him, tasting him, devouring the orgasm as it rips through me, and his fingernails dig into my ass.

My wetness seeps onto his jeans, and I'm pulling him tighter and harder, heart pounding against my chest as I finally come up for air, gasping and panting.

"Wow," I pant, trying to regain some composure. He's still rock-hard beneath me.

I shift my hips and reach for his zipper, but he stills me, covering his hands with mine. "Your first time isn't going to be in a car," he says.

"What about my first blow job?" I ask, licking my lips as I shuffle back to my side of the car, facing him as I reach for his zipper.

He growls and covers his face with his hands. "I don't think I can last if you keep talking like that, *babe*. And this isn't my car." His gaze flickers, and I can see the concern on his face. If the car gets returned to his brother with stains from our rendezvous, we're both fucked.

"I'll swallow," I say, letting my finger dance on his zipper.

He rests his hands over mine, his eyes dark with desire. He keeps a firm hold over my hand on his crotch, not letting me unzip his jeans.

"You don't want this?" I ask.

"Fuck, I do," Jasper says. "You have no idea how much I want you—"

I don't want him to finish the sentence because I hear the proverbial *but* coming, and I can't take whatever he plans on saying and accept it. I crawl on all fours, covering his lips, pushing my tongue inside his mouth, my fingers at the nape of his neck, holding him to me. "I want you." I make my intentions clear. There's no mistaking my desire for anything less than what it is, need.

"You've been drinking," he says and presses a soft kiss to my lips before pulling back. He moans against my lips, stealing one more kiss. "You taste like rum punch."

Damn, he's good. A little too good.

"I had a drink," I say, leaving off the fact that it was more than one, but I'm not drunk. Slightly tipsy, yes, but I know what I want. I've always wanted Jasper, but that hasn't changed and isn't about to when I'm one hundred percent sober in the morning.

"Your first time isn't going to be in a car, drunk, with your roommate."

He gently guides me back to my seat, and I take his hand, sliding it up under my skirt, letting his fingers dance between my legs and explore where I'm soaked because of him. "Are you sure about that?" I ask.

TWENTY
JASPER

I HAVE A LOT OF WILLPOWER.

It's something that I've had to instill as an athlete, especially playing hockey. Drinking, sex, drugs. It can all be tempting at some point, either through peer pressure or the need to chill the fuck out.

Drugs can ruin a career. That's an easy one to stay away from, especially when we're subjected to random drug testing.

Alcohol and sex, though, it's easy to fall into those habits. I've seen it with some of the guys, especially when the puck bunnies show up, flirting and throwing themselves at us. I've got a good enough head on my shoulders to pry them away. Not that I haven't ever indulged in a little fun, but that isn't what I want lately. It doesn't meet a need that I have. It hasn't for a while.

Sitting in the front seat of my brother's car that I borrowed to pick up Amber after she called me sounding frantic and worried, I thought the only thing I'd be stressing over was what happened to her at the party.

Thankfully, she seemed okay, albeit a little shaken up when I picked her up.

It was difficult keeping my eyes glued to the road with that mini-skirt riding so high up her thighs that I swear I could catch a glimpse of satin, or was it silk? Before I know it, I've pulled the car over, she's on my lap, and I'm thrusting and grinding, ripping her panties, and giving her an orgasm without even touching her pussy.

Well, not with my hands, tongue, or cock.

It's like we're two teenagers, dry humping in a car, and it's not what Amber deserves for her first time.

And when she strokes me through the fabric of my blue jeans, I'm about ready to burst. I don't want that, and saying no to her is nearly impossible.

My willpower is crumbling because of her.

I steal another taste of her lips, and that's when it reminds me of sour cherry. Another taste and its more recognizable—fruit punch and rum. Delicious, and I realize she isn't entirely sober.

How much did she have to drink tonight? "You've been drinking," I say, and I hate that it almost sounds accusatory. "You taste like rum punch."

"I had a drink."

I can hear it in her tone that she's holding back. She had more than one drink. Every time I've seen Amber with a drink, it's never been just one.

She's young, curious, living her best life, and if that involves underage drinking, I'm not her babysitter. But I'm also not about to take advantage of her.

"Your first time isn't going to be in a car, drunk, with your roommate." I gently pry her back to her side of the car, keeping a safe space between us.

"Are you sure about that?" The look in her eyes is primal and electric.

I suck in a breath, reminding myself that as much as I want her and I want this, it isn't going to happen tonight in my brother's car.

"I'm taking you home." I clear my throat and refocus on getting us back to the apartment, pulling out onto the road.

Amber is quiet, and I'm glad that she's keeping space between us because if she had unzipped my jeans, I don't think I'd have been able to say no to her. It had been difficult enough to put an end to what we started in the car.

"I thought we were going back to your friend's party?" she asks, glancing at me curiously.

I can't show up with a raging hard-on, and I'm going to have a nasty case of blue balls if I don't get home and fix my massive problem that aches like a motherfucker right now. My cock twitches just hearing her voice, unassuming and innocent to the throbbing sensation that is unrelenting.

"We need to take a detour. If you're planning on coming," I wince at my own choice of words, glancing at her, "you're going to need panties under that thing you call a skirt." I point at the tiny piece of fabric that barely covers her ass.

"You don't want me to flash my kitty at all your hockey player friends?" she jokes, and I don't smile.

There's nothing funny about her suggestion.

"Jasper." Her hand reaches out to touch my shoulder, and I wince. The thought of her with another man, especially one of my teammates, burns brighter than the heat of the sun.

I swallow the anger, rage, and jealousy bursting inside of me just thinking about them bending her over, fucking her.

She's not mine.

It shouldn't matter.

But I can still feel her heat and warmth, my cock bursting at the seams inside my jeans, and her hot pussy grinding against me. I can smell her scent, the sweet aroma that I crave a taste of on my tongue. I want to watch her shudder and hear her moan my name as I make her come again and again.

"What?" I bark as I pull up and park the Porsche out front of our apartment complex. It's short-term parking, three hours, but I don't intend on leaving the car overnight here. I'll take care of business, freshen up, and head back to the party, hopefully without Amber.

I need space from her, if only because I don't know how much longer I can hold off what I want. *Her.*

She's silent, and she follows me up to the front entrance. She keeps fiddling with the hem of her skirt, tugging it down a little lower to reveal her midriff. I suppose it's better that her hips and stomach show than that her ass is on full display.

I watch her as we head into the elevator. She's tugging the hem farther as if that will keep me from getting a good look at her cheeks.

When the doors shut and it's just the two of us

alone, I reach over, my hand cupping her bare bottom and giving a squeeze.

Amber sucks in a breath. "Reconsidering your offer?" Her voice is raspy and filled with trepidation. She's nervous. It's cute, but I wish that by now, she could relax around me. I'm not going to force anything or push her into something that she's uncomfortable doing. Another reason that fucking her or letting her give me a BJ in the car is not a wise idea.

I force a smile, my cock straining against my pants. "If you're coming with me tonight, you're going to have to change into my jersey."

She tilts her head, staring up at me. "I can do that," she says. "But do I have to wear anything underneath?"

This woman is going to kill me.

We exit the elevator, and I retrieve my key from my pocket, unlocking the door and letting us inside.

The window shades are open, offering a spectacular view of the city skyline at night. I flip on the lights, allowing us to see where we're heading, and Amber begins stripping out of her clothes, leaving a trail as she heads into my bedroom.

"What are you doing?" I ask, watching her

saunter with her hips swaying and her back to me, dressed in absolutely nothing.

"You told me to wear your jersey. I thought I'd give you a free little peek at what's going to be underneath."

She's toying with me. I know she's not trying to play games, but she's been drinking, and as much as I want to fuck her senseless and show her what it's like to be ravished, I'm not doing it under these circumstances.

But she's making it hard for me.

I already had one drink tonight. I don't know how many she had, but clearly, she's not thinking straight.

I yank open my closet, retrieve an Ice Dragons jersey with my number on it, 45, and the back reads Greyson. "Put this on and maybe some pants, too," I grumble, tossing it at her. I drop my keys, wallet, and phone on the bed as I head for the bathroom.

I stalk inside and shut the door since she's invaded my bedroom.

My cock twitches, and dammit for trying to be a gentleman. I unzip my jeans, my cock springs free, and I push my pants all the way off. Might as well be comfortable while I beat one out.

I run my thumb over the head, and already, it's

sensitive and throbbing. I can't help but think about Amber and that short, little skirt and her wet pussy against my cock.

I suck in a breath, trying to slow down and keep from being overly vocal.

"Are you okay in there? Need a hand?" Amber asks, and she knocks on the door.

I want to shout at her to go away, that she's done enough already. I glance at the shut door. I didn't lock it. In haste, I forgot to, or maybe on a subconscious level, it was intentional.

But at any second, she could barrel inside and witness me with my cock in my hand, pumping vigorously as I slam my eyes shut and imagine burying deep inside her warmth.

Do I want to fuck her?

I'd give anything to be inside of her and to feel her body tighten around me like a vise as I make her come. That feeling alone is enough to make my cock twitch, and I reach for a tissue.

There's movement and rustling on the opposite side of the door. The bathroom door squeaks open, and Amber stands there in nothing but my jersey and with a cell phone in her hands as she watches me.

"I swear if you're recording this," I growl at her

and realize she's holding my phone up, and it had better not be on video chat.

Amber's eyes widen, and she shoves the phone to her ear, but she doesn't turn around. There's not even a semblance of privacy as she watches me. "He's indisposed at the moment."

"I can hear him," Kyler says. Apparently, she put us all on speakerphone. "Where the hell are you? I thought you were picking Amber up and would be back by now. Is everything okay? You sound —stressed."

"I'll be there soon," I grit through clenched teeth. I glare at Amber. "Hang up the damn phone."

She ends the call, spins on her heel, and tosses it a couple of feet onto the bed. "Anything I can give you a hand with?" she asks, her gaze on my cock.

She steps forward, closing the gap between us, and drops onto her knees.

"Let me," she says, and I remove my hand as she brings her luscious, ruby lips over the head. She gently takes the crown into her mouth, her tongue dragging on the underside of my cock, teasing me.

My fingers tangle in her hair, trying not to force more down her throat, but I want to feel her entire mouth around me.

She takes me deeper, and the sensation is

overwhelming. I tug at her hair, taking a fistful in my hands. "I'm going to—" I warn her, trying to push her away as I reach for the tissue.

I expect her to back away, but she doesn't. Her fingers tease my balls and holy fuck, I lean on the wall to keep from falling over as her mouth fucks me until I burst on her tongue and down her throat.

She swallows, staring up at me with fervent eyes. "Are you sure I can't convince you to stay in tonight?" she asks.

I'm panting, gasping for breath, and I pull Amber to her feet, kissing her. I walk her backward to the bed, and she scoots back, lying down, while I climb on all fours, towering over her.

My fingers dance over her thighs with a featherlight pressure as she squirms under my touch. She's ticklish, and while I don't intend to torture her with tickles, I do enjoy making her writhe beneath me.

I capture one wrist, pulling it over her head and then the other, pinning her to the mattress.

She wraps her legs around my hips, bringing my weight down on her.

"Are you going to fuck me?" she asks, smiling up at me.

I growl, loving it when she talks dirty. It's primal

and makes me want to fuck her all over again, but this time not just her mouth. "Not today," I say. "But I am going to give you the best orgasm of your life."

Her cheeks redden, and I imagine there's a flush across her breasts, but I can't see it with her wearing my jersey. Which is hot as fuck. I lift the hem of her shirt up around her waist, revealing her gorgeous pussy lips. I scoot down on the mattress, dropping gentle kisses over her thighs.

I hear the sudden intake of breath, and her legs clench. I'm guessing this is new territory for her.

"Spread those perfect little legs of yours. Give me the best view of a lifetime," I say, trying to help her relax. I can't tongue fuck her successfully with her legs clamped shut.

"You don't have to—" she whispers.

"Do you not want me to?" I rest my lips over her pubic bone, nuzzling her with my chin and lips, dropping soft kisses over her mound. I spread her lips just a little, and she inhales a shaky breath and then exhales slowly. "You've never done this before," I say, trying to coax it out of her.

"Is it that obvious?" she asks with a nervous laugh and covers her face with her hands.

I don't tell her that it's kind of obvious because she's buttoned up so tight that even if she begged me to fuck her, it wouldn't be good. It would hurt, and I don't want to do that to her.

"That's why we go slow and take our time," I say. Not that I haven't had a few flings that were nothing more than a quick fuck, but that isn't what Amber is after, certainly not her first time.

"Now this feels like a sex-ed lecture," she laughs and covers her face with both hands.

I climb back up her body, reaching her wrists, pinning them together above her head. "Trust me, it's not like any sex-ed you've ever experienced," I say.

With one hand, I keep her pinned down, and with the other, I glide down between her thighs, teasing her pussy lips, tracing a soft, lazy path over her skin.

She's restless under my touch, her hips rising to my hands, wanting more. That's a good sign. Her legs part a little more for me. "How about we go slow, just fingers?" I suggest, sensing that she's not comfortable with oral yet, even though she just went down and gave me the most amazing blowie of my life.

I chalk it up to nervousness. "You're gorgeous," I say, releasing my grip on her wrist and tugging the jersey up and over her head, wanting to see every inch of her naked, to admire her beauty.

"You're just saying that," Amber says and scrunches her nose. "I'm not an athlete." She pokes me in the chest and helps me remove my shirt, leaving me naked above her.

"I wish you saw yourself the way that I see you. You're perfect."

She blushes and bites down on her bottom lip. I lean in, capturing her lips with mine. If she's going to bite that lip, I'm going to free it from between her teeth.

Her lips open as I lean in for a kiss, and already, our tongues are dueling. I guide a knee between her thighs, and she instantly parts her legs for me. This time, her mind distracted as my fingers move down across her breast.

She's quiet with heavy breaths as I listen to the soft moans of what she likes versus what she loves. Amber is reserved, and she is holding back.

My touch is gentle and light, and she whimpers for more as I tease apart her folds. She shifts back, restless and growing antsy from my fingers stroking the outside of her pussy.

"You're such a tease," she mumbles, and I kiss a path down her neck.

"You have no idea," I say with a laugh. "But I promise that it'll be worth it."

Her eyes are heavy and dark, fueled by desire. With one finger, I tease apart her pussy lips, and she's already wet. The heat seeps from her core, and I gently guide one thick finger inside her warmth.

She stretches her legs wider, and if I was going down on her, it would be a perfect sight. My mouth captures her nipple, bringing it gently between my teeth as I work a second finger into her tight pussy.

She inhales sharply. "Too much?" I ask, not wanting to hurt her. She's going to need at least three fingers to stretch her before she'll be ready for my cock.

"No," she pauses and moans softly, moving her hips in tandem with my fingers. "It's good."

I can't help but smile as I feel her rock against my palm while I stroke the inside of her pussy, curling my fingers and teasing her insides as they swell.

I use my thumb to circle her clit, and her lips part, hips rocking as she's gasping for air. Already, I'm driving her wild, but I haven't felt her clench down yet. I haven't felt or seen the telltale signs of her impending orgasm. But it's coming.

She bites her bottom lip, and I kiss a path from

her breast back up to her neck, sucking and nipping the sensitive skin as she purrs under me.

"You don't have to hold anything back from me," I say, wanting her to be as vocal as she needs to be. "Listening to you is a turn-on." I don't point out that watching her hips rock and having two fingers deep inside of her pussy is also making me hard. Again.

Wetness coats my fingers as I keep stroking and teasing the same spot, and she opens her eyes and meets my stare. Her cheeks are red, more warmth seeps out, and I'm sure that she feels it, too, because her eyes widen. It's nothing to be embarrassed about, but I see the trepidation across her face.

"Babe, you getting your body ready for me is sexy. I want to rail that tight pussy of yours. Claim it for myself."

Her lips part, and she gasps as I add another finger, stretching her. "That's good," she purrs, and her hips are gyrating against my hand, rocking back and forth as her insides clench down around my fingers.

Her eyes shut, and her back arches off the mattress, beginning to chase the orgasm. I can feel every shudder of her walls, like a vise against my fingers, clenching and keeping them nestled tight inside as I continue the motion.

"Oh, fuck," she mutters, her back arching off the bed as she gasps and moans, leaning up toward me. Her fingers claw at my arms, my body. She wants me.

As much as I want to drive my cock into her, it's not going to happen tonight. Listening to every moan that she makes is like a symphony. Perfection.

"Jasper." The sweet sound of my name on her lips is highly satisfying. So is watching her come undone. It's freeing.

She finally collapses on the mattress, panting hard as I untangle from her body and lay beside her on my side, watching her. "Fuck, that was incredible," she whispers.

I quirk a smile. That's a definite ego boost. "Good," I say and lean in, kissing her lips softly. My fingers dance across her hips, not wanting to stop touching her, ever.

I knew one taste of the forbidden would be addicting. I just didn't realize how much so.

Amber rolls around to face me and scrunches her nose. "The bed is soaked."

"Whose fault is that?" I tease, pulling her to lie above me so that she's not in the wet spot.

She straddles my waist, staring down at me. "Definitely yours, since you did that." Amber gestures at the mattress, grinning at me. "That's officially your side of the bed. The wet side."

———

We hurry outside, Amber dressed in my Ice Dragons jersey, and I'm in the same collared shirt and jeans as when I picked her up. It took every ounce of energy to climb out of bed when all I wanted to do was sleep and curl up against her naked body.

But how would I explain to my brother why his Porsche got towed? He'd never let me borrow the car again.

Amber glances at her watch as I open the car door for her, and she climbs in. "Are you sure the party isn't over?"

I've gotten a dozen texts from Kyler demanding to know where the hell I am and what's taking us so damn long. I hurry around to let myself into the driver's side.

"It's still happening, but my brother has quite a lot to say." I toss her my phone and let her read the full list of messages.

She glances through the texts while I focus on the road, pulling out into traffic as I head for the party at Noah's house. It started at the bar nearby, but Kyler texted me that they walked back to Noah's to hang out since the puck bunnies had shown up and had gotten handsy with Asher, who is married.

Amber reads through the dozen or so messages that Kyler left, and a few pop up while she's on the phone. "Asher just texted, asking if we're coming."

I try not to snicker like a high schooler. "Yeah, just text him back. Our ETA is fifteen."

"Okay," she says, tapping away at the screen and hitting send. "Listen, um, is Emerson at the party?"

"She is," I say and can sense hesitation from Amber. She's not the only one wondering what we're doing. We're roommates, and I swore that I wouldn't cross this boundary, but hell, it was worth every second of it.

"Can we, maybe, not tell her about tonight?"

"Which part?" I ask, glancing briefly at her before returning my attention to the road. I make a hard right as we veer away from the main rush of New York City traffic as I try and maneuver through a few side roads.

It's still crowded, even at this late hour. The city never sleeps.

"The part where you had your fingers shoved up inside me," Amber says.

I can't help but chuckle. "I don't think that will

come up in conversation, but if it does, I'll make sure not to mention it."

"You know what I mean," she says, exasperated.

"It'll stay between us." I reach for her hand and intertwine our fingers together. "We can keep our little romance a secret if you want."

She doesn't need to know that the guys on the team warned me to stay away from her.

"You don't mind?" she asks, and her eyes widen. "Charlotte might find out, but I'd rather not mention it to my sister."

I don't mention that I'd rather Kyler not know, either. "We may need to come up with an excuse for why it took us so long to get back to the party," I say.

"I'll think of something."

Amber follows me inside the condominium when we arrive at Noah's house. He's got a swanky penthouse suite and plenty of room for hosting guests in his two-bedroom.

I'm accosted by Kyler the minute that I step inside the penthouse. "Keys?"

I hand over the keys to the Porsche.

"Everything okay?" he asks, glancing me over, like he's trying to figure out why the hell I was late, and I don't think that banging his fiancée's sister is on that list of reasons for our delay.

The guys are all still hanging out in the kitchen and living room. Emerson, Kate, and Ava are sitting at the dining room table with a bottle of red.

"I guess I should mingle?" Amber says and glances at me. "I'll be over there," She points at her sister, and I nod as she heads in the opposite direction.

Kyler smacks me on the back. I'd like to think it's a warm greeting, but he wraps an arm around me and walks me down the hallway of the house, away from the guys.

"Do you want to tell me why you're fashionably late, brother?" Kyler is pressing me for information. From his tone, I'd figure that he was worried, but I'm not sure that he isn't suspicious, either.

"I told you when I left, I had to pick up Amber from a party on campus. I drove back to our place, and she took a few minutes to get dressed and get her head cleared."

"Is she okay?" Kyler asks, glancing past me toward Amber. "Did someone do something to her?"

I can hear the rage stewing.

"Nothing she couldn't handle. She was hit on by some scumbag." I don't elaborate because she never told me the specifics, but she seemed mostly fine.

Kyler nods and glances at me, hard. His stare

unwavering. "Why'd it take you two hours to get back here with my car? Did you take it for a little joyride?"

"In New York City?" I scoff at his suggestion. "Like I said, it took a bit for her to get ready, and she was hungry. Plus, I thought I should sober her up before bringing her out with her sister."

"Wait, she was drinking?" Kyler drops his hand from around my shoulder and folds his arms across his chest.

I grimace. That's something I probably should have kept to myself.

"Just some punch at the party. Like you didn't drink before you were twenty-one."

"I had Bristol before I was twenty-one," Kyler says. "There wasn't a lot of free time to party and hook up with girls."

"Do you mind if I rejoin the guys?" I'm not asking his permission. I point at my buddies from the team and then head back in their direction.

"Glad you could make it back to the party," Noah chimes and gives me a pat on the arm. "Nice of you to look out for your roomie."

"Well, she is family," Kyler cuts into the conversation, joining us.

I don't want to think of Amber as family, not in the way that Kyler intends. I decide it's best to steer the conversation away from Amber as quickly as possible. I glance at Asher standing next to Noah. "I heard the puck bunnies were merciless tonight."

Asher laughs. "That's one way to put it. I swear Kate was going to murder Jemma for putting her hands all over me."

"And we would all defend Kate, too," Parker chimes.

"How did that even happen?" I hate that I missed the party, but I don't regret what happened between Amber and myself.

"Kate went to the bathroom," Asher says, explaining how Jemma swooped in the minute that his wife disappeared. "I kept telling her I wasn't interested."

"And she kept shoving her hand on his dick," Parker adds.

"She was persistent." Asher exhales a heavy sigh. "And I'd never hit a woman. Forcibly remove her hands, of course. But Kate saw the whole ordeal and clocked Jemma in the face."

I can't help but laugh and glance over my shoulder at the table, only now noticing that Kate has a plastic bag of ice on her knuckles.

"How's she doing?" I ask.

"Oh, she's fine. Jemma isn't much of a fighter. She

pulled Kate's hair, and Ava stepped on her feet. I don't think we'll be invited back to the bar for a while."

Shaking my head, I can't hide the smile on my face. "Usually, we're the ones getting kicked out, not the other way around."

"Crazy night," Asher admits, "but worth every minute to see the look on Jemma's face when Kate slugged her. That was hot."

"Two chicks fighting is always hot," Owen says. "How is Emerson's little sister doing? We noticed it took you a while."

"She's doing better," I say, forcing myself not to turn around and glance at her. "It took a minute to get ready, change into something more appropriate."

"Like your jersey," Noah says, raising an eyebrow.

"Trust me. It was more appropriate than the skirt she wore to the campus party." Just thinking about her in that miniskirt makes my cock stir. Fuck. I can't start having these thoughts about Amber, not here, not now.

Kyler grins. "You made her change before you brought her here." He pats me on the back. "She's like a little sister already to you; that's cute."

Inwardly, I cringe at the use of his words, *little*

sister. She is definitely *not* my sister. "Just looking out for my roommate."

"I haven't seen her and Emerson at a game together," Noah says. "They should come, wear Greyson jerseys and fight over who the best brother on the team is."

"Are you trying to start drama?" Kyler glares at Noah. "Because everyone knows I'm the better player. This guy is my sidekick." He points at me and grins.

"Sidekick, my ass," I snort. "You think way too highly of yourself."

"Who has scored more goals this season?" Kyler asks.

"You're center. I'm right-wing—"

Parker wraps an arm around Kyler's shoulder, pulling him away before this debate gets any more heated between us. "How about we discuss your wedding plans."

Noah gestures for me to follow him, and he pulls open the sliding glass door, leading me to the balcony where it's brisk but beautiful with the city lit up. "Nice view," I say. The view from my place is pretty spectacular too, but it's nice to see a different vantage point.

"Yeah, it's pretty great." Noah pauses and turns

around, his back to the view as he leans against the railing. "What's going on between you and the sister?"

"What do you mean?"

"You two are living together!" Noah's eyes widen, and he rubs his temples, clearly frustrated. He can't know that Amber, and I fooled around tonight. It's not possible. We both cleaned up. I'm not like wearing a giant sign above my head that reads *almost got laid*.

"Yes," I say, not sure where he's going with his question. "We're just friends."

"But you're living with her! I thought I told you to stay away from Amber. That you're going to make a mess of shit with the team, your brother, all of it when he finds out you're screwing her."

"I'm not banging her," I say, staring him dead in the eyes, refusing to blink.

It's not a lie. I haven't had sex with her yet. Technically, she's still a virgin.

"So, you just jumped at the chance to invite her to move in with you? Live together, what is that?"

"It wasn't my idea," I admit, although I'm glad she did agree to move in with me. "Kyler asked me to have her move in. You know about the apartment fire. She didn't have anywhere else to go, and he flat-out asked me to take her on as a roommate."

Noah is shocked by the revelation that this wasn't my idea.

"Why would he do that?" He runs a hand through his hair.

Because he doesn't know that I'm falling in love with her; if he did, he'd never have suggested it.

"I don't know," I say, biting my tongue.

"Bullshit. We've been friends since the moment we met. Don't lie to me," Noah says.

"Kyler doesn't want her living with them while they're engaged and about to get married. He's worried it'll interfere with their lives as newlyweds."

Noah exhales a sigh. "Okay, that actually makes sense. I've never been married, but I could see where that might make things complicated." He rubs the back of his neck. "So, he doesn't know about your little crush on Amber?"

"It's not a crush," I lie. It's so much more than that now. It's out of control.

An obsession.

"Right. Well, your *not-a-crush. You* have that under control?" Noah asks, unconvinced that I can handle it.

"There's nothing to have under control; like I

said, not a crush." It's the truth. It doesn't have to be a crush anymore. Now that it's real and I've had a taste of Amber, I want more.

A crush implies feelings that haven't been acted on.

We definitely acted on those desires tonight.

I clear my throat and nod toward the door. "Anything else?" I ask. I could use another beer, and listening to Noah is killing my mood.

Why does everyone think that I can't handle being with Amber? Just because I haven't gotten serious with a girl doesn't mean that I can't or won't, eventually.

Do they think I will break her heart and mess everything up? That's not what I plan on doing. Though, who plans on hurting a girl on purpose? And if they do, they're a sick fuck.

"That's all," Noah says, and he watches me as I head back inside out of the cold. I close the door, leaving him on the balcony. I chance a glance at the girls, and Amber's eyes are on me. She smiles faintly. It's forced, like she's trying to have a good time, but she doesn't fit in. She sips at her glass of water while the other girls all have wine in front of them.

I shouldn't get involved. I'd pour her a glass, hand it to her, and tell her sister to fuck off.

But she's twenty.

Even if I drank when I was twenty, and she obviously does as well, this is one battle that's not my place to involve myself in.

I grab a beer from the fridge, and Amber stands, coming to meet me in the kitchen. It's just the two of us alone, although we're only a few feet from the guys. Their backs are to us, busy and not paying us any attention.

"Do you want something to drink?" I ask, holding the fridge open.

"Not much but beer and hard liquor," she muses. "Emerson already said she'd kill me if I had any wine. I didn't mention the punch earlier."

"Probably for the best," I say. I open a cabinet and search for a cup.

"What are you looking for?"

I find a metal travel mug and hand it to her. "Make some coffee," I suggest.

"I don't want coffee—" her eyes light up when it dawns on her what she could do. "Oh!"

I shouldn't be helping her find ways to drink and hide it from her sister, but we're not driving home. We're at a party and taking the subway home tonight. Plus, I'll be with her.

"You're too good to me," Amber says, leaning on her tiptoes, kissing my cheek.

I turn my head, my lips brushing hers for only an instant before we both step apart and glance away awkwardly. I run a hand through my hair as I head toward the guys, relieved none of them took stock in what happened, their backs to us the entire time.

But once glance at the girls as Amber heads over to tell them she's making a fresh pot of coffee, Emerson glares at me and stands. She pushes herself up from the table and heads right for me.

The air is knocked out of my lungs as she grabs my arm and drags me back outside onto the balcony, slamming the glass shut behind us.

TWENTY-ONE
AMBER

I SHOULD RESCUE JASPER. I watch as my sister drags him outside into the cold and onto the balcony. She is livid, and I'm not sure what just happened. I feel like I missed something.

Is it about me?

The coffee pot is taking forever. I can't waltz outside and use that as an excuse for why I'm interrupting whatever tongue-lashing she's giving him.

"Everything okay?" Ava asks, glancing at me and then at where I'm looking. She must sense my discomfort, or maybe she knows something that I don't.

"My sister seems pissed at Jasper," I say, waiting

to see if either Ava or Kate chimes in as to why her sudden change in demeanor.

Did she say something to them?

"Is everything okay?" Kate asks, reaching for my hand on the table as I sit across from her. "She's just worried about you."

"That doesn't sound like Emerson," I say, pinching my lips together. The number of times my sister has called me or reached out before the fire is few and far between. We're worlds apart, like revolving around two different suns apart. Sometimes I wonder how we're even related.

My phone buzzes on the table, and I glance at the text from Charlotte.

Where did you go?

She only now realizes that I ditched the party. I love the girl, but she's a bit self-centered when it comes to boys. It's not anything new with Charlotte. She's always been a bit boy-crazy.

I glance at my phone, debating on whether I should respond.

"We heard you were at a campus party," Ava says, and she's staring at me like I'm a child, worried that I did something I shouldn't have. Is there disappointment on her face? I don't know her that well, but she reminds me so much of my sister in her look of judgment that it's scary.

Or maybe I just feel guilty.

But why?

I grab my phone and send Charlotte a quick text to let her know that I'm fine.

Had my roommate pick me up. Got hit on by a loser. Long story. Tell you later.

My text is longer than I intend, and I hit send and stand. "I'm going to check on my sister," I say, heading for the glass doors.

Jasper and Emerson are on the farther side of the balcony, neither noticing as I quietly open the sliding door and step outside.

"I'm just worried that something might have happened to her," Emerson says, her hands shoved into her sweatshirt pockets.

"And when she wants to talk about the party, she will. But until then, give her space," Jasper says.

I clear my throat, making it known that I'm outside and I can hear them.

My sister spins around to face me. "Amber," she says and lets out a sigh. Is it disappointment? She's made it clear that she doesn't approve of me drinking until I'm twenty-one. She's probably unhappy with my choice of attending a campus party too.

"If you have something to say, say it to me. Don't go behind my back and interrogate my roommate," I say.

Emerson nods and glances at Jasper. "Could you give us a minute?" she asks.

"It's cold. Don't stay outside too long," he says. "You may be wearing a sweatshirt, but your little sister has short sleeves on."

I press my lips together, and my stomach fills with butterflies. I'm torn, hating how he refers to me as her *little sister* but also swimming in warmth at him, acknowledging that I'm chilly.

He sees me.

Notices me.

Cares about me.

Unlike Emerson, who always seems wrapped up in her world. There is so much that I don't know about my older sister, like why she left the FBI after working so hard at Quantico. We hardly ever talk. Four years age difference is like a lifetime between us. I'm not sure how or when it happened, but the wall is made of stone.

"I'll make it quick," Emerson says, and I watch as

he strolls back into the building, sliding the door shut.

The air is even colder without him nearby, and I shiver, wrapping my arms around myself to keep warm.

"You're wearing his jersey," my sister says, nodding toward the oversized Ice Dragons hockey jersey that I have on.

"He told me to wear it tonight. I thought it was like a hockey party or something," I say with a shrug.

Her eyes tighten, but she doesn't point out the obvious fact that I'm the only one wearing one of their jerseys tonight, and I'm not the girlfriend or wife of a hockey player.

She doesn't have to say it aloud. It's unspoken, and it's loud and clear.

Emerson's jaw is tight. "I don't know what game you're playing with him, but stop."

"There's no game," I whisper, and my mouth is dry. "Is that why you dragged him outside? To ask him if we're sleeping together?"

She shifts uncomfortably on her feet, tapping her heels. She's dressed to the nines, looking dynamite. That dress probably cost more than her salary, wherever it is that she works now. "You're not screwing him, are you?" Emerson asks.

"Not that it's any of your business, but no." I huff, annoyed by her lack of concern about my actual well-being. "I'm going inside." I push past her, knocking into her shoulder as I head for the sliding door on the opposite side of the balcony.

Emerson grabs my arm, spinning me around to face her. "I don't know what happened tonight at that party you went to. Jasper won't say, but I think you need to take a few minutes and cool off before you go back inside."

"You don't know me," I snap and yank my arm back from her reach.

"You don't think I've been there? Forced into doing things that you have no desire to do?" she asks. Her tone is dark, and my stomach twists. "You're lucky Jasper showed up, before shit got really bad."

There's a heaviness to her words, a rawness that cuts me and burns all the way through. I no longer fight to move away from her for the door and slowly turn to face her. My tone is softer, gentler with her. "This isn't about me," I say.

She clears her throat. "This is about you," Emerson says, but she doesn't sound convinced. Her eyes are glistening with tears.

"I'm fine. I got hit on by a college jock with a brother who plays for the Island Bruisers. He was an ass, and I left the party. That's all there is to it." I leave out the tiny part where I had some rum punch, and the *loser* called me an *Ice Queen*. The story isn't really as tragic or horrible as she has somehow made it out to be.

My sister sniffles and nods, pressing her lips together. "That's it?"

"I promise I'm fine. Jasper took care of me. He picked me up. I'm good." He did take care of me in ways that still make me tingle, and I can't help but wonder what happens tonight, after the party, when we get home.

"Well, I'm glad Jasper was there for you, but you don't only have to rely on him because he's your roommate. You have me too, sis."

That's not the only reason that I was relying on Jasper. I trust him and have confided in him more times than my own sister over the past couple of months. Again, not something that I want to share with her.

"We're friends, Jasper and me. If it were a problem, him picking me up, I could call a cab or something next time." I don't think he said anything to Emerson, but maybe I'm relying on him a little too much.

She nods and pulls me in for a hug. "I just don't

want you getting yourself into trouble that you can't get out of," she whispers and kisses my forehead. "Jasper travels a lot for the team. You can always call me if he's not around."

"Thanks." I nod and pull back slightly, glancing at her. "Are you okay?" I feel like she's holding something back, but I haven't the faintest clue what it might be.

She forces a smile, same as always. Emerson never tells me what's going on in her life.

"I'm good. Actually happy," she says and smiles; it's the first time she's looked genuinely happy in a long time.

"Okay, good. Can we move this party back inside? I'm freezing." I don't wait for her answer as I head back into the apartment. My arms are chilly, and I head for the coffee that I made. While I don't need caffeine at this hour, I want something to help warm me up, and I don't think I can waltz over to Jasper for that in front of his teammates or my sister.

When the party finally dies down, and Noah kicks everyone out, Jasper accompanies me outside and onto the sidewalk while we make our way to the subway.

"We could just hail a cab," he suggests.

If we do that, we're stuck waiting with the other

couples. While I don't mind Ava and Kate, I'd prefer to have some time alone with Jasper.

Owen left a few minutes before we did and is nowhere in sight. I'm guessing if he took the subway, we might catch up to him when we reach the subway platform. At this hour, trains are few and far between.

"What fun is that?" I hurry a few feet ahead of Jasper, and he grabs me by the jersey, pulling me against him and wrapping an arm around my hips.

"Hold up," he says, and his body heat warms me, as does his hold around me. "I hope tonight wasn't too boring with the girls."

I glance at him, unable to hide the smile. "It was nice." I'd have rather been wrapped in Jasper's arms as he hung out with his teammates, but that would have meant not hiding our new relationship.

Is it even a relationship?

My stomach somersaults just thinking about all of it. I lean into Jasper, wrapping an arm around his waist, pulling him closer and tighter. I need his strength to help subdue the butterflies from surfacing.

"Nice is code for boring, or it sucked." Jasper chuckles.

"No," I counter. "I had a nice time, but I'd have rather spent it with you—in bed."

He stops walking and pulls me into his arms, his lips landing on mine, hungrily devouring me. The night air is cold, and my cheeks sting from the chill, but none of that matters with his hands wrapped around my waist and lips against mine.

"Me too," Jasper whispers, pulling back. "You're freezing, and you're not dressed for the cold." He holds an arm out, hailing a cab.

"It's fine," I whine. The truth is that the subway takes longer to get home. It gives me more time to think, explore, and cherish the moments together with Jasper until we return to our apartment.

I crave the cold air and the silence of the night, the stillness that blankets the city. It allows my head to clear and my thoughts to consume me without being overwhelming.

And the main thought, the one invading my head, my body, and all my senses, is of Jasper.

Where the hell am I sleeping tonight?

His bed or mine? Or is he joining me in my bed? Are we sleeping alone?

I'm overanalyzing the simple question with every possible scenario and what the outcome might look like tomorrow.

The few cabs that pass us already have passengers. "Let's keep walking. If we can grab a cab on the way before we get to the subway, we'll take it home." Jasper is all business in his tone, even in the way he walks and carries himself. He's focused and dedicated to whatever task is set in front of him.

He keeps an arm around my waist as we walk alongside one another toward the subway. It's another block, but I can see the entrance.

I'm practically stomping my feet to keep my legs from buckling from the cold. Jasper stands behind me at the traffic light as we wait for it to turn. His arms are wrapped around me, his body heat warming me as his hands rub up and down my bare arms.

I should have worn a long-sleeved shirt under the jersey, but I wasn't thinking that far ahead. The Porsche had heat. I wasn't considering how we'd get home after the party. Apparently, Jasper hadn't thought about it, either. I guess we had been a tad bit distracted.

The traffic light changes, and we hurry across the street and down the steps through the turnstile to the subway platform.

There are more people waiting than I would have thought for this late hour. It's not nearly as cold, either, without the wind whipping around. Jasper is nestled against my back, his arms tucking me in like a blanket, cocooning me. He rests his chin on the top of my head.

"What's your schedule like for next week?" I ask, trying to distract myself from the worry itching at me, edging closer as I keep thinking about what happens when we get home.

"Practice. Games. More practice." Jasper laughs. His breath is warm, and he pulls me tighter against him. "We have a bunch of away games for the next week."

That's probably for the best. It will give us some time apart to figure out what it is we're doing.

I don't say anything. I just watch for the next train as I stand on the platform, pressed against his warm body.

"I'm going to miss you when I'm gone," he admits, his breath tickling my ear as he pulls me even tighter. I didn't know that was possible until I feel his erection pressing into my back.

"Me too," I admit, letting my eyes fall shut. It's easier to confess how I feel when I'm not staring into his gaze. "Any chance Charlotte and I can take a road trip and cheer the team on?"

I glance over my shoulder at him, and his smile

eases every fear inside me. "I'd like that, but don't you have school?"

"Oh, right." I exhale a heavy breath. "I could miss a day."

"No," Jasper is firm in his answer. "You're not missing your classes. Your education is important."

"Okay, Dad," I grumble and playfully glare at him.

"If you're trying to be sexy, it's *Daddy*," Jasper teases and then wrinkles his nose. "Um, no." He doesn't want to be called Daddy, and I don't want to call him that, either. He doesn't give me older man, Daddy vibes. We are practically the same age, only a year apart, not even.

The double doors open, and the train pulls up and slows to a halt. We step on amongst the crowd, boarding together. There's no place to sit, and he's pressed tight against me, one hand around my waist, the other holding the metal bar above his head.

"I do want you to come to one of my games again," Jasper says, and I shuffle around to face him. He keeps his hand on my hip, his fingers caressing me through his jersey that I'm wearing, and he tugs me closer, pressing his lips on mine.

I melt into his kiss. His body and his lips make me tingle. My heart pounds loudly, drowning out the sounds of the train as we roar through the tunnel.

"I'd like that," I say as we're bumped apart from the jolting of the subway changing rails. He pulls me closer, his hand on my lower back, keeping me pressed against him.

"But you can't wear the rival's jersey, *babe*. If you do, I'll be forced to punish you."

I chuckle at his words, staring up at him with a devious grin on my face. "Is that a threat, *babe*?" I ask, using his little nickname right back at him.

He growls and covers my lips again. This time, his tongue pushes past my mouth, and I open my lips, granting him entrance. We jolt and shift with the train, but neither of us breaks apart. He holds me tighter, keeping me to him, protecting and embracing me. My body is warm and tingly, set aflame from just his kisses that are warm and teasing me of what is to come.

The voice over the loudspeaker notifies us that our stop is next. "That's us," I say, patting his chest, trying to give us both a minute to catch our breaths.

I pull back only slightly, and he escorts me toward the doors when I realize two people with phones are holding them up inconspicuously.

Are they recording us? Maybe they're just watching videos on one of the social media apps.

My breath is shaky as the train slows at the next station, and I hurry off and onto the platform, heading for the escalator. Jasper is right on my heel and grabs my hand, quick to catch up to me.

"What's on your mind? You've been tense since we left the train."

"You didn't notice anyone filming us?" I feel paranoid. It's not like we're doing anything illegal or illicit.

Jasper shrugs, and we approach a traffic light, forced to wait for it to change. "It goes with the territory. I get all sorts of people snapping pics of me when they realize who I am. Usually, it's when I'm in my jersey, but you're wearing my jersey. They probably put it together. And we make a great couple. Who wouldn't want to watch us make out?"

I turn to face him, and his breath mingles with mine. I shiver, but this time, it isn't from the cold.

"Does it bother you?" he asks, pushing a strand of hair behind my ear. The light changes, and he ushers me forward.

I follow his lead, letting him walk me back to our apartment complex. We head inside; the lobby is warm, and it's a blast of heat that is overwhelming as my fingers and nose are numb.

Jasper reaches forward and presses the button on the elevator. I miss his body, his touch, his proximity. I gently rock back into him, and he notices. How could he not?

"We'll be home in a minute," he whispers into my ear, a hand on my hip, steadying me.

I take a deep breath in, and I can smell his scent. It's everywhere, surrounding me, from the jersey to his body standing behind me, barely touching me.

The double doors to the elevator open. I step inside the small space, and he follows, pressing the button for the floor, and his arms are snuggly wrapped around my waist, pulling me against his chest.

His arms are warm, his touch soothes me, and we've reached the twenty-fourth floor before I know it. "We're here," he says, indicating that I should probably untangle from him and step out onto the floor.

He retrieves his key from his pants pocket and unlocks the door, gesturing for me to step inside first. The house is quiet, and I reach for the light switch as I'm flooded with memories from earlier of the two of us fooling around in his bed.

My breath is raspy, and my nerves tingle throughout my stomach, making me anxious all over again.

He shuts the front door and secures the lock.

"I should get ready for bed," I whisper and turn and head for the bedroom. Am I expecting him to follow me or invite himself to join me? We haven't defined this thing between us, and I don't think three in the morning is the time to do so.

"It's late," Jasper says and rubs his eyes.

I turn and head for the hallway, glancing at his bedroom door that was left ajar, the light still on, and the sheets crumpled from our festivities earlier. I bite down on my bottom lip and step inside my own room, flipping on the light.

He turns off the lights in the living room and heads down the hallway. "Can I text you while I'm away?" Jasper asks, standing in the doorframe of his bedroom.

"I would like that," I whisper.

"Goodnight." I hear his soft voice as he heads into his room, and the door clicks behind him as he shuts it.

I close my bedroom door and flop onto the bed in a heap. I don't bother undressing for bed. I like wearing his jersey, it smells like Jasper, and I want to be wrapped up in his scent while I sleep.

————

I awaken the next morning, and Jasper is gone long before I have to be up for class. There's a note on the kitchen counter along with several twenty-dollar bills that he stacked and left behind.

Eat while I'm away.

I'll eat, but I don't need to spend his money. I push the cash aside on the counter, shoving it into the corner where he can collect it when he gets home.

I put on a pot of coffee and force myself not to text Jasper first thing in the morning, which is hard, considering I want to comment on his note and the money.

But I don't want to seem too desperate to text him. He's busy with practice, or at least on the way to practice.

What time did he leave this morning?

I head back to my room, grab a fresh change of clothes to shower, and glance at his bedroom. The bed is made, the lights are off, and the place looks immaculate. Even the hamper that he usually keeps beside the bed is out of sight. It's probably tucked into his closet.

My phone buzzes on my nightstand, and I grab it before hopping into the shower. There's a message from Jasper, and I can't help but smile.

My bedsheets smelled like you last night. Is it wrong that I don't want to wash them?

I SPENT the last hour staring at my phone, trying to decide what I should or shouldn't text to Amber. Noah is sitting beside me on the bus, and my brother is one row in front, so at least he's oblivious to the dilemma.

Noah, however, doesn't miss a beat, ever.

"You shouldn't be that hung up on her," Noah says.

"I'm not," I say and clear my throat. I erase the message again before finally landing on one that's a bit flirty and hit send.

My bedsheets smelled like you last night. Is it wrong that I don't want to wash them?

Noah tries to peer over my shoulder at the text,

but I've positioned my phone so that he can't read what I just sent Amber.

I shove my phone into my pants pocket. I have no idea what time she wakes up for school. I'm always out of the house in the morning before she even gets up for classes.

"You spent the last hour or so texting and erasing messages," Noah states the obvious.

"Whatever. We're on the bus, and I'm bored." I'm using it as an excuse because he's right, she's getting in my head, and she doesn't even know it yet.

One night. That's all we had, and we didn't even have sex yet. Not that I can't stop thinking about what it would be like to lick her pussy and drive my cock into her tight warmth.

It's all I dreamt about last night. Repeatedly.

I kept waking up in a hot sweat, and that was after it took forty-five minutes for me to fall asleep. I need to get Amber out of my head.

Usually, I'd work out and spend a couple of hours at the gym, but it's a travel day, and we're riding the bus to the airport for our next game, which doesn't mean that we get away with lounging around all day.

Coach Malone is on us the entire flight, going over plays and discussing our last couple of games.

Mostly, he's recanting every score that we missed. I was hoping to listen to some music and get a couple of hours of shut-eye, but he doesn't seem to agree.

After we land in North Carolina, we're shuttled to the hotel to check in, leave our luggage in our rooms, and then meet up within the hour to bus over for practice.

I'd have rather spent a couple of hours at the hotel gym to burn off the energy coursing through me, thinking about Amber.

I need a good run, to lift some weights, anything to tire my ass out. Maybe some time on the ice will help. She's all I can think about at this rate, and I don't need the distraction.

We gear up in the locker room and head out to the arena, doing drills and practicing while we have access to the rink.

It's a good practice game with the guys, and we're cautious that no one gets hurt before tomorrow's game against the Barbarians.

"You missed an easy shot, Greyson," Coach Malone says as I head off the ice.

"Aiden's a good goalie." We both can't win when we're practicing against our own teammates.

"Even so, you had the perfect shot, and you missed. What's on your mind, kid?" Malone asks.

The guys head into the locker room, but Coach keeps me from joining them, blocking my way. I could push the guy aside, he's small and stocky, but I'm not about to bully the coach, not if I want to play tomorrow. I don't want to get benched.

"Nothing," I say, staring him in the face. I made three goals during practice, and he has to jab on the one shot that I missed.

"Something going on between you and your brother?"

I shake my head. "Kyler and I are good."

"Is this about a girl, the one you lost your shirt over?" Malone guesses. I suppose everyone saw me toss my jersey to her.

"It's about nothing," I say, my jaw tense. "The guys and I were up late last night. I hoped to get a few hours of sleep on the flight here. I missed one shot, Coach. Owen missed two. You're not harping on him." I shouldn't be bringing my other teammates into this, but I don't see why Coach Malone is giving me crap.

"You've got talent, Greyson. It's not about you missing the shot. It's about how you weren't laser-focused. You've got raw talent, and sometimes you could use a little direction. Get out of your head. My job is to help prepare you for the game tomorrow.

That's all this is, a pep talk. Don't go getting your panties in a bunch."

"I'm good. I'd come to you if I weren't, okay?"

"Fair enough," Malone says. He smacks me on the back. "Now, get in there with your teammates before they leave your ass behind."

———————

We grab dinner as a team at a steakhouse down the street. It's a fancy little joint, and we're all dressed in dark jeans and collared shirts, which appear way underdressed when I take stock of the romantic couples in suits and fancy dresses.

It's the kind of place that I'd like to take Amber to on a date. I slide my phone out of my pocket and tuck it under the table, keeping it out of sight while I text Amber.

Did you eat dinner?

I already know the answer. She certainly didn't make it. But I don't like to think about her not taking care of herself while I'm away. What did she do when she lived on her own in her studio apartment? Did she eat on campus every day?

Miss me already? I'll find something to eat.

It's nearly seven o'clock. If she hasn't ordered

dinner, she's not going to do anything about it. The fridge is pretty bare, not that she cooks. I send her another text.

Are you at home?

I rejoin the conversation until my phone buzzes, and I briefly glance at it before excusing myself for the restroom.

Yes. Stalking me?

Why won't she order dinner with the money that I left her? I exhale a sigh and slip off to the back hallway near the restrooms. I glance at a few local menus and put in several takeout orders, having them all delivered to the apartment.

Yes. You'd better not be planning on going out tonight. I ordered you dinner. Plenty of it, and it'll all be delivered within the hour.

I shove my phone into my pocket and head back to the table with the guys. Amber texts me again, but I don't answer her, not right now. I can feel it buzzing, and it's more than one text.

If she's pissed, so be it. The girl needs to eat, not starve herself, because she can't afford food. I know that's the reason she's not eating. It's the same reason that after the apartment fire, she only bought a handful of outfits and wore the same clothes every day.

She's too proud to accept gifts, let alone handouts.

After dinner, we walk back to the hotel, which is a nice stroll and helps work off the food. My phone is buried in my pants pocket, and as much as I want to read the texts from Amber, now isn't the place or the time.

My phone buzzes with another text.

I'd like to think it's along the lines of *thank you,* but it also could be *fuck you* because I wouldn't leave her alone.

I also may have overdone it a bit with the food. I don't know what she likes, so I ordered from four restaurants and three meals from each. That'll give her plenty of leftovers; knowing Amber, she probably has Charlotte over.

I hit the gym for a few hours with Noah, Chase, and Aiden when we return. Parker insists that he'll join us, but he's got to give his wife a call before it gets too late.

"How much do you want to bet that Parker doesn't show," Aiden says. "I'll bet he's back in his room having phone sex with Ava right now."

I grab my towel and toss it at him. "You're such a jerk."

"Oh, come on, you don't think your brother is

doing that with his fiancée up in your room right now?"

I cringe. Just thinking about Kyler and Emerson grosses me out. I'm happy for them, but I don't want to think about my bro having sex with any girl, phone sex included.

"He's tucking his kid into bed," I say. "They do this video chat thing where he says goodnight to her." I lay down on my back to bench press weights, and Noah spots me.

"Video chat, huh?" Noah chimes in and wiggles his eyebrows. "Yeah, I'll bet the minute the kid is in bed, that video is showing off his family jewels."

"You guys need to get laid," I mutter. "Maybe even find yourselves a girlfriend or something. You have too much time on your hands."

Noah grins proudly. "I've got plenty of girls on my roster. When was the last time you had a hook-up, Greyson?" Noah asks.

"None of your business."

Noah is smirking. "You haven't hit that with the roommate yet?"

"Leave Amber out of it!" I snap and slam the weights down, the noise echoing through the gym.

Noah and Aiden exchange a quick glance at each other. Chase is the only one who stays out of it. He's running on the treadmill and apparently put in his earbuds. Lucky bastard.

"Well, what I said about bro code still stands," Noah says, gesturing for Aiden to spot me while he does leg presses on the machine across from us. He's also cautiously keeping away from me, which is probably smart because he's pissing me off.

"Duly noted," I seethe.

"But in all fairness, I wouldn't have suggested she move in with you, either."

"It wasn't my idea." Lifting the weights above my head, it takes all my concentration not to drop the damn thing while listening to Noah and Aiden ramble on about Amber.

"She *is* cute," Aiden says.

Noah agrees. "Hard not to think about tapping that—"

"Have you thought about shutting the fuck up?" I snap at Noah. I put the weights back and climb out from under the bar. My arms and body are feeling the burn, but my head and heart are still highly energized.

He holds his hands up in mock surrender. "I get it. You're just roommates. Which is probably good because she's likely hooking up with some college guy while you're away this week. I mean fuck, if I were her, that's what I'd be doing while my roommate is away. Don't have to tame the screams."

I stomp over toward the machine that Noah is on, and just as I'm about to yank him off it, Aiden grabs my shirt and tugs me backward several steps. "Chill out. He's trying to fuck with your head."

"Having fun?" I shout at Noah.

He grins and nods. "Yeah, I kind of am enjoying it. Greyson has a crush on Amber. It's cute."

I flip him the bird and exit the gym. There's only so much of Noah that I can take tonight. I love the guy on most days, but right now, he's getting to me, and I can't let what he says fuck me up before a game tomorrow.

I head up to the hotel room. While it's standard practice for rookies to share a hotel room, I never grasped how Kyler and I ended up sharing a room together. He should have his own room unless he said something to Coach when I joined.

I slide the electronic key, and the door opens.

Kyler is on his cell phone when I enter, holding it up and doing a video chat with Bristol.

"She's still awake?" I glance at my watch.

"Someone isn't listening to Em or Nanny Lia."

"I am, too, listening. I'm not tired," Bristol says with a loud sigh. I swear, from across the room, I can hear the pout on her face, and I'm not even looking at the camera. She's probably got her arms folded across her chest and demanding to stay up late.

"Uncle Jasper says it's bedtime," I chime in, trying to help Emerson get the kid to bed.

"Thanks," Kyler says, glancing at me.

I grab a bottle of water from the mini fridge and cool down for a minute after the workout I had downstairs. "I'm going to shower," I say, glancing at my phone to see if Amber texted me back. Sure enough, there are a couple of messages waiting to be read.

I click on her message as I head to the bathroom, and Kyler pays me no attention, which is a relief, or else he might ask why the hell I need my phone in the bathroom. That's one explanation that I'm not interested in giving him. Neither is the part where I'm texting Amber back.

I open her message, and a huge smile reaches my lips.

Dinner was delicious, all twelve meals.

I try not to laugh at her remark. I know she didn't eat everything, but that's her way of thanking me for it. There's a second text after the first one.

You really outdid yourself. At least now I can eat for the rest of the week. I promise I won't let it go to waste.

I shut the bathroom door and lean against it. I type away, texting her back.

Glad you came to your senses.

A smirk reaches my lips when I see three dots indicating that she's writing back. My heart jackhammers in my chest, waiting on her response. I thought working out at the gym and practicing on the ice would have tired my ass out. But when it comes to Amber, she makes me feel more alive than ever.

You didn't give me much of a choice.

I chuckle under my breath and flip on the bathroom fan. I strip down and slide open the glass shower door, turning on the spray.

You don't take orders very well.

I click send and then grimace, hoping that didn't come across as too harsh. I did leave her cash and a note. I wanted her to spend the money on food, but I know she's too damn proud.

I don't take orders at all. I'm not a waitress. What are you up to?

I chuckle at her response. I'm not sure she really wants to know, but I text it to her anyway.

Getting naked.

She immediately texts back.

This is the one time you can send a dick pic. Prove it.

I snort and contemplate going in the other room and snapping a picture of my brother Kyler, who happens to be a dick at times, just to joke around with Amber. But if she actually wants to see my dick, who am I to say no.

Are you sure? This isn't like a trap, is it? Where you send it all over the internet to unsuspecting ladies who don't want to see my dick?

My phone rings, and it's Amber calling me. I answer it right away. The shower rains in the background, as does the bathroom fan, but I don't turn either off. At least I've got a teensy bit of privacy from my brother while locked up inside.

"Dick pics are okay if they're solicited," Amber says. "Just never send a girl an unsolicited one. If she doesn't ask for it, she doesn't want to see it."

"Noted," I say and smile. I hope that she's not speaking from experience because I'd kill whoever sent her an unsolicited dick pic. "Are you asking to see my dick?"

She chuckles, and I wish we were having this conversation on video chat because I'm sure as hell that her cheeks are bright red, and she's probably got her head in her hands. She wears nervous well. It's flattering and adorable on her, even though she would disagree with me.

"Only if you're not expecting a pic in return," she says and giggles. "I do not look sexy."

"You're always sexy," I say. I can't imagine her looking anything but desirable.

"I'm curled up on the sofa in sweatpants and a T-shirt, *babe*," Amber says.

"Are you alone?" I ask. There's background noise, but I assume it's the television that she has on.

"Why? Would you be jealous if I had someone over?" she asks.

My throat tightens, and my stomach knots. Who the hell is she entertaining at *this* hour? "Do you have someone over?"

I swear I can hear rustling and movement. Is she forcing someone to be quiet, covering their mouth to keep them from laughing or speaking? The silence drags on, and I know without a doubt that I'm not imagining it.

"What the hell is going on, Amber?" I growl.

TWENTY-THREE
AMBER

"I TOLD you he'd get jealous easily," Charlotte chirps, and I elbow her to shut up and grab a throw pillow, covering her face with it.

I'm not trying to murder my best friend, just shut her the hell up before she ruins the flirtatious vibes between Jasper and me.

"Is that Charlotte?" Jasper asks, and I swear I can hear the relief flow right through him.

"It is," I say, "and she was just leaving."

"Am not!" Charlotte pipes up. I'm not on speakerphone, but Jasper is loud on the phone, and with the sound of the fan and shower in the background, I have the volume turned all the way up to hear him clearly. "Girls' night. We're having a sleepover. Imagine it, Jasper. Naked pillow fights!"

He growls, and this time, it's unmistakable. It's not out of anger or jealousy. He's turned on. I smile, hearing his sound, and imagine his hands stroking his shaft.

"Go in your bedroom. Lock your door," Jasper orders.

I wave to Charlotte as I hop off the sofa and hurry to my bedroom.

"You're ditching me for a boy?" Charlotte calls after me. Like she hasn't done that to me countless times at parties or the bar.

"Payback is a bitch." I grin and give her a salute before slamming the bedroom door closed. Except, I didn't go into my bedroom.

I went straight for Jasper's and shut the door.

"Undress," Jasper commands with authority, and I lock the bedroom door and shimmy out of my sweatpants and panties.

"Yes, boss," I tease and put the phone down for only a second while I take off my T-shirt. "I'm naked."

His voice is thick and heavy, fueled with desire. "I want to see," Jasper whispers.

"I'm not taking a photo." I don't trust that it won't end up on the internet.

"Video chat with me."

"Seriously?" I ask, and he sends a video request.

I sigh and point the camera so that he can't see any of me naked from the video. I'm neck up and fumbling backward toward his bed.

"Is that my bedroom?" Jasper asks as I lie down on the mattress, scooting back toward the head of the bed.

"I didn't notice," I answer cheekily. "Is it?"

"You're going to kill me," he says, shaking his head with a wry smile. One hand is holding the phone, and I'm pretty sure his other hand is stroking his shaft, or at least teasing his cock.

He looks damn fine with no shirt on and gives me an ample view of his face and chest. "Point the camera lower," I say, and he chuckles.

"You want to see my cock?" He tilts his head, staring into the phone as if he were looking straight into my soul.

It's not like I haven't seen his cock before. My tongue and mouth were wrapped around him yesterday after the campus party. But it feels like a lifetime ago, and it'll be days before we're physically near each other.

"I do," I say, and my mouth is dry. I run my tongue over my lips, and he smiles, raising an eyebrow.

"Damn, that's hot when you do that tongue thing."

I'm pretty sure I'm blushing, and I scrunch my nose, trying desperately not to freak out or have a panic attack over the fact I'm having phone sex with Jasper. When I get stuck in my head, I tend to freak out.

"Are you going to let me see you, *babe*, or are you just enjoying the show that I'm giving you?" he asks.

I am enjoying every minute of his naked body, and when he gives me a half-second view of his cock, I swear my ovaries are going to explode. The man could put a baby in me, and I'd be down for it, and I'm the girl who never wanted kids.

"You're being a tease," I say and shuffle back on the bed, propping myself up on the pillows.

"Oh, a nip slip!" Jasper teases as I get comfortable. "You've got great breasts. You should show them to me more."

I laugh under my breath. "Right, I'll flash you and the team to show my support at your next game."

"You'd better not show your tits to anyone but me," Jasper growls. "But a celebratory boob flash after a game sounds wonderful. As long as I'm the only one who gets to enjoy those tits."

"These tits?" I ask and flash the phone at my breasts before bringing the camera back to my face.

"Damn, girl. Do that again."

A muffled knock comes from the other side of the phone. Jasper shouts, "Go away!" I can't hear the response, but he groans, unpleased with the situation. "I swear my brother is trying to cock block me."

I can hear a few muffled words from the other line, like *shower* and *girlfriend,* but I'm not entirely sure what the hell was just said.

"I can't help it if you're not getting laid!" Jasper retorts, and his brother mutters something else unintelligible through the phone.

"Do you need to go?" I ask, sensing his frustration.

Charlotte knocks on the bedroom door. "I hate to interrupt, but are you two almost done? I'm waiting for you to put on the movie."

Clearly, our getting interrupted is killing the mood.

"Now, your bestie is trying to cock block me?"

"She's your biggest supporter, second to me," I say. "But I don't think this is happening tonight."

He growls and repositions the phone back up at his face. "Yeah, you're right. Rain check?"

"Yes, but can I cash in when you're back home, and it's not phone sex?" I ask.

Jasper chuckles. "I'm holding you to that. You, me, one hot date and a night that you'll never forget," he says.

He knows the right words to tug at my heartstrings. "Break a leg tomorrow!" I say and grimace, realizing that maybe that's not the best phrase to say to an athlete.

Jasper snorts and shakes his head. "If I do, I'm blaming it on you."

"Kick their butts. And I'll see you in a couple of days?" I don't want to sound overly eager and like I'm expecting to hear from him daily. We're not officially dating. And while I've never done casual, I don't want to chase him off or scare him.

"We're roommates," Jasper says with a laugh. "Better believe it."

We both hang up and as disappointed as I am that our little phone sex tryst didn't pan out, the thought of him taking me out on a real date makes my insides tingle. I climb off the mattress and head for Jasper's dresser, stealing a T-shirt that falls down to my knees and a pair of his boxers, walking out into the living room.

Charlotte is texting someone while situated on the sofa, stretched out. She moves her legs when I join her in the living room.

"Ready?" I ask, grabbing the remote and queuing up the movie. It's a rom-com flick that's fairly new that neither of us saw in the theaters. I'm not expecting much since it flopped at the box office, but it's something new to watch that neither of us has seen.

She points at the bowl of popcorn on the living room table that she made, and I grab it, bringing it to the sofa to share. "I should grab us something to drink before the film starts." I shove the bowl in her lap to hold while I grab two girly beers from the fridge.

On the fridge is a magnet in the shape of a hockey stick, with a bottle opener as part of the design. I use it to pop the tops off the beers, bringing the drinks back to the sofa.

"Thanks," Charlotte beams and taps my girly beer with hers. "Have fun with the new boyfriend?"

I chuckle. It was fun, but it didn't end like how I'd have hoped. "Sure, until his brother interrupted."

"Ouch. Does he still not know about the two of you?"

I shrug. "What's there to know?"

Charlotte turns to face me, the bowl of popcorn in her lap. "You tell me."

I haven't told Charlotte yet about what happened between Jasper and me last night after he picked me up. I'd been vague, only stating that he'd given me a ride home.

The girl can read me like an open book. "Did you two bump uglies?" She wiggles her eyebrows suggestively.

I laugh nervously and sip my drink, hoping it'll alleviate my nerves. "We didn't bang or bump anything together."

"But you're not denying something happened!" she says, pointing at me. "Details, girl. I always tell you all mine."

Another sip of beer, and I laugh. "Yes, but I don't ask for them."

She ignores my remark. "So, what did you both do if you didn't bump nasties? Butt stuff?"

I wrinkle my nose and grab a piece of popcorn from the bowl, tossing it at her face. "No!"

"Oral?" she asks, and my eyes widen. I can't hide anything from Charlotte, even when I try and keep what we did a secret between Jasper and me.

"You did!" Charlotte is far too giddy with

excitement. "Oh my gosh. Did he go down on you? Or did you blow him? Tell me it was good. I'll bet he has a huge dick."

I grab another piece of popcorn to throw at her face, but she catches it midair. Damn her!

"Well?" Charlotte asks, waiting for me to elaborate.

I reach for the remote, wanting to end before it turns into a full-on firing squad, and I feel pretty close to that at the moment.

"I don't kiss and tell," I say, hoping that'll put an end to her interrogation.

Charlotte snaps the remote from my hands and keeps it out of my reach. She's a couple of inches taller than I am, so there's not much use in me trying to fight her for the remote. But that doesn't mean I'm going spill all the details about what happened last night.

"Right. Well, he picked you up from the party. What happened after?" Charlotte looks genuinely interested, but she just wants the dirty deets.

"I got hit on by this jerk I have class with, and I wanted to leave. I couldn't find you, so on my way to the subway, I called Jasper to have someone to talk to since it's a long walk."

"And?"

"He offered to come and get me." There's nothing scandalous in him picking me up. We are roommates and friends. I definitely would consider Jasper, a friend. "End of story."

"Bullshit!" Charlotte laughs. "That's not all that happened. So, come on, spill it."

I'm smiling but glance away. "Not happening. We're just friends."

"Right," Charlotte says with a knowing look. "Friends who have phone sex and sneak into his bedroom and are wearing his clothes while he's away?"

I glance down at the clothes that I'm wearing. "My laundry is dirty."

"What about the outfit that you had on when I came over?" Charlotte is full of questions, and nothing seems to get past her.

"Are we watching the movie or staying up all night gossiping about my lack of a sex life?"

Charlotte quirks a grin. "Yeah, I don't believe this innocent charade anymore, but if you don't want to tell me, fine. I'll get it out of your boyfriend when he's home."

"He's not my boyfriend," I say, but even I don't sound convinced.

———

I'm busy with classes and work for the remainder of the week. With Jasper out of town with the team, I request a couple of extra shifts at Mad Tea House. I need the money, and the apartment feels empty when I come home at night alone.

I haven't seen Charlotte except for lunch on campus between classes. She texts me daily, asking if there's any steamy news from my hockey boyfriend, and sends me snippets that she finds of him playing hockey online, clips from the game that he played the previous day.

I swear she stalks him more than I do—more than I did, anyway.

But I like seeing the videos of him playing, and when he's back in the city, I want to surprise him and show up at one of his games. And maybe this time, I'll actually wear *his* jersey. Although, it is fun to rile him up.

The evening shift at the tea shop is busy, and I'm surprised when Emerson shows up, bringing Bristol with her.

"Is this the Mad Tea place?" Bristol asks with wide eyes. She untangles from my sister's hand and runs around the tea shop glancing at the walls and the Alice in Wonderland-themed décor. Most of it is out of reach except for the children's table that we have situated in the corner, with a mural of a tea party on the wall.

"Yes," Emerson says. "What flavor do you want?" She reads off the descriptions to Bristol as I wait for the two of them to put in an order. It's been busy all day, but the past hour has finally settled down.

I prepare Emerson and Bristol's drinks and can't help but wonder if there's another reason my sister decided to show up where I work. She's never been here before, at least not while I've been working behind the counter.

Emerson doesn't live near campus. It seems like she came out of her way to see me.

"Is that your sister?" Maggie asks. She's working the counter with me today since Samantha bailed on her shift again.

"It is, and her soon-to-be stepdaughter."

"That's sweet. You can take a break and visit with them for a few minutes. The place is quiet. I've got it."

"Thanks," I say, taking off my apron and stepping around to join Emerson and Bristol at a nearby table.

"What are you guys doing here?" I ask.

Bristol gobbles up her tea and chomps on the fruit bits in the drink that she ordered. She has a huge grin on her face. I swear she ordered the sweetest drink on the menu.

"There's a game Friday in town. I can get us seats together if you want to come and support the team."

"That sounds fun. I have work in the afternoon, but it's a night game, right?"

"Yeah, an evening game. You'll have to wear Greyson's jersey if you come."

I can't help but wonder if she heard about the two other incidents where I was wearing an Island Bruisers jersey. I don't bring it up or ask which Greyson I'm supposed to be representing.

"I think I can find one in his dresser."

"You go through your roommate's dresser?" Emerson asks, raising an eyebrow.

Bristol giggles, and I glance at the kid, unsure that she understands what Emerson is talking about.

"I may, at times, borrow a jersey or whatever," I say dismissively.

"Like the one you wore to the party last weekend?" Emerson asks.

Bristol sips her drinks and stares at Emerson with a smug smile. "You borrowed one of Daddy's jerseys."

"I did, and I regret every second," Emerson says.

Bristol is beaming proudly, like she concocted some wicked plan to get Emerson into trouble. I wouldn't put it past a six-year-old to scheme and my sister to fall for it.

"This sounds interesting," I say, waiting for Bristol to elaborate.

Emerson glares at her to keep her mouth shut, and I feel completely left out. "You can tell me later," I whisper to Bristol.

My sister snorts and rolls her eyes. "We're not doing that," Emerson snaps.

Bristol holds out her pinky like she's promising me that she'll tell me later, and we're good. Is that the new meaning of a pinky promise?

Kids these days. I link my pinky with hers before standing. My break is long since done, and Maggie has been kind enough not to point out that I should be on the clock and working.

Did Emerson drop by to invite me to the game, or was there something else that she wanted? She could have just as easily sent me a text. "Thanks for the invite. I'll be there."

———

The week drags on. Jasper and I exchange a few brief texts, nothing scandalous or hot. He lets me know that he'll be home late Thursday but not to wait up because their flight is delayed due to storms in North Carolina.

I don't even hear him come in Thursday night, and he's gone Friday morning before I get up for class. But I can tell that he came home last night. There's a suitcase in his bedroom, the door open, and his fresh scent fills the living room, as does coffee.

He put a pot on before leaving, and I swear the man knows the way right to my heart.

My day starts out great, perfect until I head into class for statistics, take a seat, and Atlas Storm decides to grab the chair next to me. I swear, his name is as pompous as he is.

If it's not bad enough that I hate the class, dealing with Atlas puts a damper on my mood. But I don't want it to bother me. He's a nobody—a college athlete who is hoping to bank on his brother's name and fortune.

He could be a decent player. I've never seen him play.

"Are you coming to the Bruisers game tonight, *Ice Queen*?" Atlas asks.

"You're an asshole," I say, refusing to answer his question.

I should be relieved he's not asking me to *his* game on campus because there is zero chance that I'd want to attend and cheer him on in the stands.

The Ice Dragons are playing the Island Bruisers tonight but not at their home stadium. Since both teams are based out of New York, the Ice Dragons don't have far to travel. It's practically like being at home without the fans' support.

Which is why Emerson suggested that I come and cheer on the Ice Dragons. They need all the support that they can get. At least, I'm assuming that's the reason for the invite.

Atlas turns to face me. "I can get you seats on the ice, right behind the glass. My brother has connections, which means I have connections."

"I already have tickets for tonight," I say and grimace, wishing I hadn't spoken to him. I don't want to confess that I have plans and will be at the game.

"Are you going with friends or a date?" Atlas asks.

Is he seriously trying to find out if I'm single? What the hell is wrong with him?

I need to put an end to whatever he thinks this is between us because there is zero interest from me.

Who the hell gives the nickname *Ice Queen* to a girl he flirts with?

No one. Certainly, not Atlas Storm.

How is it that girls chase after him?

Well, not this girl.

"My boyfriend plays for the Ice Dragons," I say.

"Your boyfriend?" Atlas repeats, and he sits up straighter, his jaw tight. "I didn't know you were seeing anyone. He wasn't at the party with you last weekend."

"He doesn't attend silly campus parties," I say, trying to excuse the whole thing, and I shift, turning my attention to the professor who stalks into the classroom looking disheveled. That's about how I feel, but I try to remain composed. I don't need Atlas Storm making me flustered.

Atlas laughs under his breath and leans back, folding his arms across his chest. "Whoever your little crush is, he isn't your boyfriend. There's no way you're dating an NHL player," he says.

Am I crazy for telling him about Jasper?

We're not technically dating, but we are roommates, and I think he'd do me a solid if I came clean and told him that Atlas Storm is harassing me in class and I need a favor.

Atlas isn't buying my story, but I'm not sure I've convinced myself, either, which is half the battle.

While it's obvious, Jasper has feelings for me. I'm a little worried about how long those feelings will last. He's focused on his career, and, well, what if the sex is mediocre or downright awful? What happens then?

"I don't care what you believe," I say with a shrug and open my textbook. I'm actually relieved when the professor begins his lecture. As much as I hate statistics, I despise Atlas Storm even more.

He's unconvinced, and I give him the cold shoulder for the rest of the class. The minute that statistics is over I grab my bag and hightail it out the door, my books still in my hands. Usually, I'd put my stuff away before leaving, but I need to get out of there before I say something regrettable.

"Hey! Wait up," Atlas calls after me.

I hurry my pace, but Atlas is taller and has long strides when he walks, easily catching up with me.

I curse under my breath, but the sound is barely audible over the commotion of students pouring out of the lecture halls.

"I'll be at the game tonight with some friends. Since your boyfriend is playing tonight, you should introduce us." Is this his version of a peace offering? A truce?

I spin around to face him. "And why would I do that?" I ask. Atlas and I aren't friends. I don't know why I even let a word of what he says bother me. But I can't just let it go.

"Because I think you're full of shit."

TWENTY-FOUR
JASPER

I'VE BARELY SEEN AMBER. Not because I haven't wanted to but because our schedules haven't meshed together. I want to take her out and impress her with a fancy dinner date, but I've spent all week traveling, and now that I'm home, I'm up early to hit the gym, and she's still in bed asleep.

I've discreetly been trying to find a nice place to take her without asking anyone I know for a recommendation because that would also come with way too many questions.

I shove my phone into my locker. I can't keep checking my messages for texts from Amber. The last one she sent was an hour ago.

Good luck! Don't break a leg. Break someone else's.

I try not to laugh, but I'm sure I'm wearing the

stupidest grin. I have to shut it off. I don't need the guys harassing me or Kyler giving me shit when he finds out what's going on between me and Amber.

With my back to Kyler, he clears his throat. "You've been awfully quiet. Is your head in the game for tonight?" he asks. We're in the locker room, gearing up for a game tonight with my most despised team, the Island Bruisers.

"Why wouldn't I be?"

They're a team known for playing dirty. They even went as far as one of their players threatening one of ours, among others in the league. He was arrested, kicked out of hockey, and consequently put behind bars.

The league tried to cover up the scandal, and I only know all the details because my niece was the target of one of the threats.

My disgust goes back even further with Atlas Storm. We played together on the ice when we were in our early teens, in a hockey league.

The wanker stole my girlfriend, Bridget Malister, and used his brother's name to get into her pants. The fact that Knox Storm was a first-round entry draft pick lit up her eyes. Plus, Atlas promised her tickets to the Island Bruisers games and that she could sit in the Ice Box.

I couldn't compete with that, and I didn't even try.

I ghosted her as much as a kid could, given we went to the same school. We even had a couple of classes together. I wish I could say that I don't know whatever happened to her.

Oh, I know. I even see her from time to time.

She's a puck bunny.

Rumor has it she slept with Knox Storm the moment the opportunity presented itself. Not a big surprise. I don't even give her the time of day or so much as a nod when we cross paths. She's dead to me. As cold as the ice I skate on.

"I'm looking forward to a good game tonight. I heard Em and Amber are going to be in the stands cheering for us," Kyler says.

He laces up his skates, and we head out of the locker room and into the hallway, waiting for the announcement with our introduction.

I inhale a sharp breath. I like the thought of Amber in the stands, cheering for me. I hope that she's come to her senses and is wearing an Ice Dragons jersey with my number on it.

"I'll bet it's the nosebleed section," I say. We're not at our home stadium, where we've got a section of decent seats that we share among our team.

"Nah, I gave her my black AMEX," Kyler says.

"You didn't just buy the tickets outright?"

"I'm not a controlling douche." He shoots me a look. "I let her pick out the seats that she wanted."

"She's not going to spend the money to get close-up seats," I say. While I don't know Emerson as well as he does, if she's anything like her sister, she'll be in the nosebleeds because she won't want to spend his money.

"We'll see," Kyler says and lets the word trail off as we're introduced and make our entrance, skating onto the ice.

Immediately, we're booed and shouted at for being the rival team at the stadium. It doesn't bother me. I'm used to it and tend to drown out the sounds as I get my head into the game.

There's a sea of blue amongst the crowd. Their jerseys and shirts are like the ocean, with speckles of gold like the crest of a wave that are the handful of fans supporting us. There are more fans at the stadium in New York than when we were in North Carolina, but the seats closest to the ice are all drenched in blue.

No sign of Amber or Emerson. At least not from what I can see. But if Kyler says she's at the game tonight, I'll keep my eyes open for her.

The lights flash, and music blares while we skate on the ice before returning to the player's bench, getting ready for the first period.

"Your fiancée is a no-show," I say. "Or I'm right, and she's stuck in the nosebleeds."

Kyler mutters under his breath, but the roar of the crowd makes it difficult to hear him.

The first period is tough. The team doesn't seem to have their head in the game. Me included. Knox has been talking shit on the ice. Not that it's anything new with him, but I'm not in the mood to listen to his bullshit.

We aren't playing as well as we should be playing, and we have no excuse for it.

Distracted, maybe.

But that's not a valid reason for sucking. And that's what we're doing—tossing the puck, handing it to the enemy, and letting them score.

And the bastards are gloating and bragging about how they're the fucking kings of the ice.

At least our goalie, Aiden, has his shit together tonight, or the score would be triple what it is, and we're losing by four. It's not pretty, and we haven't made a single goal.

Kyler, Owen, and I are pulled off the forward line.

"What the fuck?" Coach Malone throws his arms up in the air, waiting for an explanation from us.

We don't have an answer, but Coach has his eyes on Kyler.

"Do you have something you want to say to me?" Kyler grits between clenched teeth.

"You tell me?" Malone's eyes tighten, and I swear I can see the steam coming off him. There's pissed, and then there's getting on Coach's bad side, which is not a place that you ever want to be.

Kyler rolls his lips together and wordlessly shakes his head.

It doesn't take a genius to read the body language between them. Tense is an understatement.

I nudge Kyler. "We'll get our shit together."

Kyler glances in the stands, ignoring me.

"What is it?" I ask and follow his gaze. The girls aren't in the worst possible section, but my stomach flops when I see Atlas Storm sitting beside Amber, and all I want to do is jump the glass and beat the crap out of him.

Do they know each other?

How?

Maybe it's just a coincidence, her sitting beside him in the stands, but I doubt it.

My mouth is dry and filled with bile at the words that leave my lips. "Are they friends?"

"Isn't he the guy who stole your first girlfriend?" Kyler asks, recognizing the douche.

I cough and clear my throat. "He's a dick. But he saved me from losing it to Bridget Malister."

A smile grazes Kyler's features. "Yeah, I can't believe the tween you dated turned out to be a puck bunny."

"We were thirteen when we first went out," I correct him. "And I can believe it after she left my ass over a pair of hockey tickets." She'd been flirting blatantly in front of me with Atlas. And the days when Knox picked up his little brother from practice, she went all out.

Kyler snorts. "Well, the next time you decide to date a girl, Em and I want to meet her and decide if she's good enough for you."

"Are you worried she's been using me for my good looks and athletic talent?"

Kyler's eyes widen. "You're using the past tense, as in, you met someone?"

Nothing seems to get by my older brother. I was hoping I could wait a couple of years before delving into the story of how Amber and I first hooked up. Although, we haven't actually hooked up. Just fooled around, and that was nearly a week ago.

Even phone sex is difficult while sharing a hotel room with my older brother. But now that I'm back home, I'm hoping to set the mood with Amber, take her out, show her a good time. I don't want to rush her into anything, but damn, just the thought of her lips on my cock makes me want to burst.

"Jasper?"

I don't answer him quickly enough, and he's in big brother interrogation mode.

"Is it someone I know?" he asks.

"It's not someone you don't know," I answer in a double negative, avoiding outright telling him yes.

"Who?" Kyler asks. "Is it some girl in another city you met while we were traveling for a game? That red-haired chick in Atlanta, or was it in Chicago? She kept chasing you around the bar when you went to grab us drinks."

I forgot about *that* girl. She was flirty and horribly drunk. I can only imagine the massive headache from being hungover that she sported. I had to sit her down on a stool and tell the bartender to call her a cab.

"Yeah, she lives in another city," I say. The words slide off my tongue with ease.

Amber and I haven't discussed what we'd say to our siblings about whatever it is that's transpiring between us. And since we don't even know what this new thing is, telling them first seems a bad idea.

"I knew you were having phone sex the other night in the hotel!" Kyler says a little too loudly.

Owen glances at the two of us with wide, incredulous eyes. "Do tell," Owen says. "This sounds like a juicy story."

"It's not," I say and glare at Kyler. "You interrupted. Besides, I don't kiss and tell." That's all they're getting out of me. Hopefully, it's enough to settle the beasts and keep them contained while Amber and I explore whatever is flourishing between us.

"Does your girlfriend care that you have a female roommate?" Kyler asks. "I mean, you didn't mention it when I suggested that Amber move in with you. Which, by the way, I fully intend on covering her rent."

"Why would you do that?" I ask.

"I asked you to take her on so that Em and I could have some space."

"I'm not taking your money. Amber is paying her share of the rent."

Kyler looks taken aback by my suggestion that I

would make her pay anything. "You're expecting her to afford half? You know she's in college and works as a barista at some shop on campus."

"She works at a Mad Tea shop," I say, fully aware of her situation. "And I'm only making her pay a small portion of what she was already covering in rent at the last place that burned down."

My brother smacks me on the back. "You're a good guy. She's lucky to have you as a friend and roommate. But I'm still covering the other half of her portion. I pawned her ass off on you."

"I don't need your charity."

"No, but you suck out there, and if you keep floundering around like some fish, you're not going to get another contract when you're a free agent."

"It's one lousy game," I say. I still have time to perfect my career, to get it all figured out before I'm waiting on offers and hoping that I'm picked up for a new contract. I grumble under my breath, "And I hate the Bruisers."

"Me too," Kyler grumbles. "Knox is the biggest jerk of all of them."

"I'm not a fan, either," Owen says. "But I mean, I don't like any team we play. They're all rivals. Now, what was that you were saying, Jasper, about a girlfriend?"

I groan and refocus my attention on the game. "Nothing. I said nothing." I refuse to give them any ammunition to be used against me because they're not about to let it go.

In the second period, Coach Malone gives Owen, Kyler, and me another chance to redeem ourselves on the ice. We do a better job of working together, focusing, and scoring three goals.

We're still down by one, but at least we've managed to catch up, and when we were benched, our teammates kept anyone from scoring against us.

There are worse positions to be in, I suppose.

By the third period, Kyler makes the goal to tie up the score, and I make the goal that gets us ahead by one.

I blow Amber a kiss in the stands, pointing at her, wanting her to know that goal-winning shot was for her.

"Jasper, why the fuck are you hitting on my fiancée?" Kyler growls, misinterpreting the kiss. He shouts at me across the ice, and for a moment, I think he's about to beat the shit out of me, but Knox Storm comes up with a disgusting smirk on his face.

"Two brothers, sticking it to the same girl," Knox says with a sly grin. He's trying to get to me and being obnoxious enough that I swear Kyler can hear him too.

Emerson and Amber are sitting beside one another. The kiss was one hundred percent meant and sent to Amber. But if I tell my asinine brother who it was meant for, I'm not sure he'll be as forgiving.

"Shove your stick up your puckhole, Storm." I slam my shoulder into his body, pinning him to the glass while fighting for the puck as it glides across the ice at our feet.

"Can't get your own girlfriend. Have to steal your older brother's?" Knox says, shoving me backward.

I throw my stick down on the ice. "Says the loser who slept with my thirteen-year-old girlfriend."

"Whoa!" Knox grunts as I land an uppercut on his jaw, and his helmet flies off. "She was legal when I fucked her."

That doesn't make me feel a lot better. "Really? I was thirteen. She ran off to go suck your dick."

That wasn't exactly how it went down. She hooked up with his younger brother, Atlas, before eventually shagging Knox when she was eighteen, or so I've heard. She followed him around like a groupie, probably begging to let him screw her. Disgust fills me like a lead balloon, my stomach heavy and nauseous as I pound my fist into Knox. He throws back as hard as I give.

"And it was amazing lips, asshole," Knox grunts, his fists slamming against my chest.

Sweat drips down my forehead, and finally, a couple of players intervene, yanking the two of us apart, keeping us from tearing each other to pieces.

We're both tossed into the penalty box, and I refuse to glance in the direction where Amber and *that asshole* are seated.

Why the hell is she with him? Is it to torture me?

She doesn't know about Atlas and about our pasts as kids. How could she? It's not something I talk about. Who wants to relive their first heartache and betrayal?

It was years ago and shouldn't matter, but seeing him beside *my girl* makes my insides boil. I trust Amber. Even though I don't know what we are, I still trust her without a doubt. It also helps that we're roommates, and I've never seen her bring Atlas around.

Let it all be a coincidence. That they happen to be two people that bought tickets and are seated beside one another.

I hate myself for fighting with Knox, for letting him get to me. As punishment, I glance at Atlas in the stands. Perhaps it's a little bit of desire, too, that brings me to look in that direction at Amber.

But she's gone. She's not in her seat. Emerson is alone, and Atlas is gone as well.

Every fiber of my being aches. I could easily blame it on the punches to my chest, my neck, even a few landed to my face.

That isn't what hurts. It's the sting of Amber and Atlas alone together.

I trust her, but I don't trust *him*.

I don't trust that he won't touch her. Hurt her. Use her. To get to me.

There's always been jealousy from his side. The fact that I'm now in the NHL, and he's never been selected in the entry draft, has to sting.

I want out of the penalty box. Hell, throw me out of the game if that's what it takes for me to check on Amber and make sure that she's okay.

Every second is agonizing hell while I wait to be released. Time has never ticked by so slowly. The penalty box attendant pays me no attention other than focusing on his task and watching the clock.

"Psst," I whisper, trying to get his attention. "Do you have your cell phone handy?"

He glances at me over his shoulder. "Seriously? You type never learn about discipline." He turns with his back to me. It is a long shot, texting Amber to make sure that she is all right.

There's still no sign of her, and the longer I wait, the more dread fills my stomach. Emerson won't let anything happen to Amber, which tells me she went willingly with that dickhead, Atlas.

DARE I SAY IT?

I actually like hockey.

Well, I enjoy watching the game when Jasper is on the ice. It's not nearly as exciting when he's benched or in the penalty box, which he finds his way into quite often.

The game is interesting, but all I feel is Atlas Storm's presence as he's seated beside me. Sometime early during the first period, the guy sitting beside me gets up, probably to grab another beer, and Atlas steals his seat.

"You know that seat's taken," I say. I shouldn't even give him the time of day, but apparently, I'm ready to commit social suicide, or maybe he's ready to commit social murder, if that's a thing.

I get the distinct impression that he plans on destroying any reputation that I have at NYU because he's a puckhole.

"Your friend?" Emerson asks, glancing briefly at Atlas.

"No," I say, quick to answer.

But Atlas answers with a resounding "Yes," at the same time.

Emerson doesn't take much stock in it. She returns her attention wholeheartedly to the game, which I appreciate. The crowd is also rowdy and cheering on the Island Bruisers. We stand out, the two of us in our gold jerseys cheering from our seats.

"These are shitty seats. You should have taken me up on my offer," Atlas says. His attention is on the ice rink, at least, but I still don't want him seated beside me.

"I don't want anything from you," I say.

I can feel his brooding stare as he shifts in his seat and turns to face me. "Why?" I do everything that I can to ignore him, but he doesn't back down. When I don't answer, he reaches out to put a hand on my arm, and I yank it back.

"Don't touch me," I snap.

"It's not like you have anyone else touching you,"

Atlas says. "I don't buy your line of bullshit that you're dating a hockey player, *Ice Queen*."

I suck in a sharp breath and pray that my sister didn't overhear him. The crowd is loud, but Atlas is even louder.

"Who I date is none of your damned business."

"You're a liar," Atlas says and shifts to face the game. "You have zero chance in hell of hitting it with one of those guys out there. You couldn't even pass for a puck bunny."

"Fuck you," I say and jab him with my elbow.

"Oww."

"Go back to your own seat." I keep my focus on the game. Jasper seems distracted when he practically hands the puck over to the Island Bruisers.

"You suck, Greyson!" Atlas jumps to his feet and shouts at Jasper. Not that any of the players can hear him, but it makes me hate Atlas a thousand times more.

"Fuck off," I say, staring at Atlas.

"Oh, hit a nerve," he snickers. "Wasn't hard to figure out which one." He nods toward my jersey and the number 45 on the front. Jasper Greyson's number.

Emerson keeps her cool. She doesn't say a word, but I can tell she's watching the entire exchange.

"Go back to your seat," I repeat and glance over my shoulder, looking for the six-foot-tall guy who had been sitting in that seat earlier.

"This is my seat. I traded tickets with that dude. There's zero chance that he's coming back here to these shitty seats," Atlas says.

"And why would you do that?" I don't understand him. What possible reason does he have for wanting to sit next to me? Is it that important to him to make my life eternally miserable?

"As I said before, I don't believe that you're dating any of the players."

"We haven't met," Emerson interjects, and I'm not sure if she's trying to destroy any last shred of dignity that I have left or come to my defense. I doubt the latter. "My fiancé is Kyler Greyson."

He tilts his head, staring at my sister. "I knew you looked familiar. He brought you onto the ice and proposed. Publicity stunt much?" Atlas goes right for the jugular with the accusations.

"And you're dating Kyler's brother?" Atlas glances from Emerson to me, still unconvinced.

"We're living together," I say. That's not a lie. We do share an apartment, just not a bedroom.

He snorts under his breath. "Right." Atlas folds his arms across his chest, and he glances from Emerson back to me. "If you really do have connections to the Ice Dragons, prove it."

"Prove it," I repeat, unsure what the hell game he's playing.

"Family, significant others, they have VIP access. Where's your badge?" he asks. His VIP badge dangles from around his neck.

Emerson pipes up, and I momentarily hold my breath. "This isn't our home arena. We don't have a wives' room when we're on the road or a VIP badge for every game, especially when we're surprising the guys by showing up to one of their away games."

"I'll bet it's a surprise," he mutters. "And you have an invitation to the wives' room?" Atlas asks, glancing from my sister to me.

"Yes," Emerson answers. I'm not sure if she's answering for herself or for me. Is that a lie, or does she have access to the wives' room? Is that even a thing?

"Fuck, where did Jasper go?" I ask, realizing that he's no longer on the ice. He's on the players' bench, and the Ice Dragons are getting their asses kicked by a landslide.

"He and Kyler got benched," Emerson says.

I'm surprised that the puckhole sitting beside me isn't gloating. But he's focused on his brother, Knox, attempting to score.

The Ice Dragons do a decent job of keeping the Island Bruisers at bay, which makes the game exciting.

By the third period, Jasper seems to be refocused, and he even blows me a kiss in the stands, which I swear melts my heart and my panties.

"See, I told you he's my boyfriend." I glare at Atlas.

I can feel Emerson's gaze burning as she's waiting for an explanation. I'm surprised she's not grilling me, but she is good at reading people, and my discomfort with Atlas is obvious by now.

"He could have been blowing anyone a kiss in the stands," Atlas says with a shrug. "I don't buy it."

"How many Ice Dragon fans do you see around here?" I ask.

Atlas presses his lips together, but he doesn't answer my question. He has to know that I'm right.

"Doesn't mean shit, Amber," Atlas says. "I still think you're a liar."

"I'll prove it to you." I stand and shuffle through the row, heading down the aisle away from the ice rink.

"Where are you going?" He chases after me.

I'm not really sure what I intend to do. It's not like I can waltz right into the locker room and throw my arms around Jasper Greyson, even though I want to do that and prove to Atlas that he's wrong.

"To see my boyfriend."

"This should be good," he says with a wry grin as he follows me around the stadium.

Except, I don't know my way to the locker room or even how to get on the floor. We don't have seats by the glass, and we can't just head down the aisle without someone checking our tickets.

There are two guards standing at the entrance to one of the long hallways. The guard nods at Atlas. Do they know one another?

"The Island Bruisers locker room is behind you," the guard says, taking note of Atlas's VIP badge.

"I was actually looking for the Ice Dragons," I say as I stalk up closer and try to peer down the hallway.

"Amber!" Jasper's voice carries and echoes against the walls. "Let her through."

The security guard steps aside, gesturing for us to enter.

"Just the girl!" Jasper shouts.

"Sorry," I say with a sly smile and a shrug as I saunter back toward Jasper.

"Stop checking out her ass!" Jasper glares at Atlas while I head toward him. There's commotion from behind; the game isn't over.

"What are you doing out here?" I ask, shaking my head, staring up at him.

"I should be asking you that question, and with him!" He yanks open the locker room door and gestures for me to follow. I'm expecting to see open lockers and a bench, but there's a long hallway entrance. Is that where the press waits to accost the players after a game?

On the right, there are dozens of numbers taped above on the wall with hockey sticks neatly lined up for the players. I glance over every detail, from the numbers matching the players' jerseys right down to the colors of the Island Bruisers everywhere and their logo on the floor.

"He's in one of my classes, statistics," I say and grimace.

"And you brought him on a date to *my game*?"

"I didn't invite him anywhere. His brother plays for the other team."

"I know that," Jasper says. "But he was sitting with *you*."

"Again, I didn't invite him. I think he paid the guy to switch seats or swap tickets with him." I shuffle my feet, slightly uncomfortable under his scrutiny. "Are you jealous?"

"Atlas is a dick."

I can't stand Atlas, but I never told Jasper about the party, and there is no way that he could hear a word that was said from the stands.

"What makes you say that?" I ask.

Do the two of them know each other?

While I agree Atlas is a jerk, I'm not about to air my grievances to Jasper. I get the impression that he might go after him, and the fight wouldn't be on the ice.

"Just past history with him," Jasper mutters and then glares at me. "What were you doing with him downstairs if the two of you weren't at the game together?"

I exhale a heavy sigh. "Long story."

"I've got time."

"Aren't you supposed to be on the ice or with your team?"

"I got ejected from the game, which you would have seen if you were in the stands." He's staring at me, and I shift awkwardly on my feet. I don't have to ask why he got ejected. He was probably fighting with Knox. The two of them were at it earlier on the ice.

"I may have told him a little white lie," I whisper, glancing away. I don't want to feel Jasper's intense gaze burning me from the inside.

"And what lie was that?"

"That I was dating a hockey player with the Ice Dragons."

The rage seeps right out of him, and he laughs, his shoulders sagging as he pulls me against him for a hug. "You were talking about *us*, right?" Jasper pulls back, staring down into my gaze.

My heart races and my mouth goes dry. I nod. It's all that I can give him. The locker room is hot and stuffy, or maybe it's his warm arms wrapped around me that makes it feel a hundred degrees inside.

"Good," Jasper says, and he brushes his lips against mine.

I crave him like I need air, and my fingers tug at his jersey, bringing him closer and tighter. Every fiber of my being tingles with excitement.

"We should do that more, in public," he whispers against my lips.

I nod, willing to do anything this man asks of me. "I think Emerson knows," I whisper. If she doesn't, then she would have made a terrible FBI agent.

Jasper shrugs. "Kyler will find out, but I don't care. I'm falling for you, Amber."

I bite down on my bottom lip, tugging it between my teeth. I don't want to tell him that I've already fallen hard for the man staring back at me. I'm not great with vulnerability and confessing how I feel. I worry it might scare him away.

"Your brother should be happy for us," I say, leaning on my tiptoes to kiss Jasper.

"He should be, but you're his fiancée's little sister." His brow creases and commotion begins to pour down the hallway. The game must have just ended. "Bro code," he says.

"Seriously? It's not like I dated your brother. If he's not happy for us, then tell him to go screw himself." I can't hide the grin, the fact that Jasper wants to be with me, and the only thing standing between us is his silly concern with *bro code*. I don't see the problem.

He pulls me tighter, his lips crashing on mine as the doors open and the team begins pouring into the locker room. Jasper doesn't break apart the kiss. His lips are on mine, letting everyone see that we're together.

Jasper holds nothing back, his tongue pushing its way in past my lips, and I willingly oblige, stepping backward out of the way against the wall as he pins me to the white-painted brick.

"Get a room!" Noah laughs as he breezes by into the locker room.

A gruff voice clears his throat. "Greyson!"

Jasper pulls back from the lip lock, but he still has his hands around my waist. His fingers tease my hips, grazing against my skin, igniting a fire deep inside of me.

His coach doesn't look the least bit thrilled to see me.

"You got ejected from the game, and you're making out with a puck bunny?"

My shoulders tense, and Jasper spins around, growling at the older man. "She's not a puck bunny, Malone. Amber is my girlfriend."

"Girlfriend?" Kyler's voice echoes through the hallway, and he glances from his younger brother to me.

I momentarily hold my breath, hoping that another fight isn't about to break loose in the locker room.

"WAIT HERE," I say to Amber, hoping that she'll listen to me as I head down the hallway and into the locker room with the guys.

She doesn't say a word, just stares down at her hands clasped together in front of her as she leans against the wall.

I walk into the locker room and take a seat at my locker on the bench, undoing my laces. My helmet is already off, and I hang it on the hook nearby.

"How long have you been banging my fiancée's little sister?" Kyler's voice echoes through the locker room. There's no way that Amber doesn't hear the accusation.

"We're not—not that it's any of your business."

"Was it before or after I offered to pay you?"

I scoff at his suggestion. "You begged me to take her off your hands, that she was a burden living with you—" I unlace my skates and remove them, leaving them on the floor.

"I wanted to give her a place to stay, not get her boned by you!"

"I'm not boning her! And fuck you for trying to tell me who I can and can't hook up with." I stand, coming at Kyler. He's got his skates off now too, but both of us still have our pads and gear on aside from our helmets.

"Listen to yourself!" Kyler shouts. "You can't be shacking up with her. She's your roommate! What's going to happen when you fuck this up?"

"I don't plan on fucking it up," I say, getting in his face.

He shoves me backward. "I'm trying to help you. Can't you see that?" Kyler doesn't back down, and neither do I.

"Help me by controlling my life? I'm falling in love with her! And we're taking things slow, not that it's *any* of your business."

"Good, because she's still a virgin. She doesn't need to lose it to you."

I bring my fist back, and Noah is on me before I can beat the shit out of Kyler.

"That's enough!" Malone steps between us. Noah and Owen yank me back several feet. "Shower, now!" Coach points at me to hit the showers while he has a word with Kyler.

After a quick shower, I avoid Kyler for the rest of the evening. He heads to the shower while I make my way back to the locker room to get dressed.

Coach Malone is waiting for me, arms folded across his chest. "This isn't going to be a problem, your new girlfriend, is it?"

"Why would it be a problem? Why does who I date matter to anyone but me?"

Malone nods. "It shouldn't, but if you're going to acknowledge this thing between you and the girl publicly, she can't be wearing the jersey for the opposing team."

"I thought there's no such thing as bad press," I say with a smirk.

"I'm serious," Malone says, stepping closer, and he rests a hand on my shoulder. Sometimes I think he considers himself like a father to the younger players, offering advice. "You have one more year on your contract. You don't need to make waves—"

I cut him off before he can offer any more unwarranted advice. "Amber was wearing my jersey tonight, in case you didn't notice."

"I didn't," he says. "Just be careful. You don't want to let a girl come between brothers."

"A girl he's never even dated! Why does everyone assume that I did something wrong?"

Malone sighs. "No one is saying that. Just don't let her come between you and the team. Okay?"

"She would never do that, Coach."

I finish getting dressed, and I hurry back to the hallway where Amber had been waiting.

She's gone.

I run a hand through my hair and glance at my phone. There are no missed calls or texts from Amber. I hurry back into the locker room and find Noah.

"I need to find Amber. She might have overheard and misinterpreted some of it. If you see her after the game, text me? I'm going to head back to our place."

"Yeah, I'll keep an eye out for her. Good luck." Noah pats me on the back.

I hurry out of the locker room. The crowd has thinned from the stadium, and there are a few stragglers on their way out who stop me for a photo or autograph. I'm surprised that we have any fans at the Bruisers arena, but both teams are in New York.

As soon as I head outside, I grimace that I hadn't

tried to reconcile with Kyler. I'm still pissed, but if Amber is with Emerson, then at least I'd know she's safe.

I don't like the thought of her riding the subway alone or walking in the dark back to the apartment.

I try Amber on her phone, but after the first ring, it goes to voicemail. Her phone is on. She's declining my call. I hurry to the subway. It's unlikely that she's going to take a cab home; there's a chance that I might run into her.

I shoot her a text message. *I need to talk to you.*

No response.

Maybe that's good. She's at least not telling me to fuck off.

Or she could have outright blocked my number.

How much did she hear? Kyler and I weren't exactly quiet, and I don't know when she bailed. Either way, my stomach is in knots while I hurry home.

The train is crowded, quite a few fans recognize me, and some snap photos and video record me for their social media accounts. It's probably good that Amber isn't down here in the subway station, or I'd be getting my ass chewed on camera, and it would become the next viral video.

I don't need that kind of attention.

I glance at my phone, still no answer. At least I can see that she read the text. She didn't block my number yet. I type another message and hit send.

Please tell me you're not with Atlas.

This time, she's typing. I can see the three blinking dots, and I momentarily hold my breath while the train pulls up at the station. I hurry on but don't bother to grab a seat. It's crowded, and there are far more people in need of someplace to sit. I grab the rail overhead, holding it while I wait for her to answer.

She takes a while, but finally, the message comes through, and I feel like I've just been stabbed.

Maybe I should be with him. No one is paying him to be with me.

I wince at her words on the screen. She has every reason to hate me.

It's not what you think.

I text her back and wait for her to answer. Maybe I should get my ass off the train and grab a cab. At least then I could get to her sooner, wherever she is.

The subway doors have already closed, though, and the train jolts forward.

She doesn't answer me. She types. She erases. The three dots appear. Disappear. Appear again. And then they're gone.

I'm not sure what's worse, fighting with her or the silence waiting for her to answer. The fact that she's not willing to fight for us.

Ten minutes later, she finally answers me. I almost wish that she hadn't.

It doesn't matter, Jasper. We're done. It's over. I'm moving out. I'll leave the key in the apartment.

Texting isn't going to fix this. Seeing her is the only way to not make a further mess from this disaster. But she's probably at the house, and I'm still stuck on the subway train. I ring her again, this time surprised when she answers.

"I'll mail you my last rent check as soon as I get paid."

"Dammit, Amber!" I wince when I realize several people are watching me. Is it because they know who I am or my tone that drew their attention? "I love you. Can you let me explain, please?"

"There's nothing to explain," she says. She sniffles, and I can tell by her voice that she's been crying, which just makes my stomach sink even lower.

"I never took the money."

"What?"

"The money my brother offered for you to stay with me to help cover your rent. I never took it."

She scoffs at my words. Maybe she didn't hear as much as I thought in the locker room. There's no sense in burying myself deeper when she's already pissed at me.

"That would be really classy of you to take money from your brother to cover the rent that I'm already paying you. I realize it's not a lot compared to the share you pay, but I-I-I hate you," she spits out.

"You don't mean that," I say. If she hated me, she'd have hung up already. She's still on the line, her breathing growing louder.

There's movement and commotion on the other side of the phone. I can only imagine that she's packing up her belongings, which will take seconds, considering that she doesn't have much.

The train pulls up at the station, and I hurry off, jogging up the subway station stairs and down the street, racing for the apartment. I need to see her, to stop her, to keep her from making the biggest mistake of her life.

"I love you," I say, the words slipping out before I can even take them back, not that I'd want to do that, either.

"You don't. You only love yourself, Jasper." She hangs up the phone, and I want to scream. She doesn't understand. She doesn't know the whole story.

I'm running down the street, one of the benefits of being an athlete in top shape. I hurry to the apartment and inside, repeatedly hitting the elevator button. I hope that it's not too late. I didn't see her leave, but she could have taken a cab before I made it inside the building. She had a head start on me.

Charlotte comes stalking in through the front entrance and for the elevator as I'm waiting to head upstairs. "You," she says, glancing at me, jaw tense. She folds her arms across her chest and glances me up and down. "Real charming, pretending that you wanted her to live with you when it was your brother's idea all along."

I exhale a sigh. "She heard that."

"Wow. You don't even deny it," Charlotte says. She's loud, making a scene, and a few gazes are making it over to us.

The elevator dings, and I hurry inside. Charlotte is right on my heel.

"Don't think you're going upstairs without me."

Even if I wanted to close the elevator door on her, it wouldn't help my case. Charlotte is Amber's best friend. If I can't get through to Amber, maybe Charlotte can be my advocate.

"I wouldn't dream of it," I say. I press the button for the twenty-fourth floor.

"I need you to convince Amber to give me ten minutes to talk to her."

Charlotte shakes her head, unconvinced. "Why? You've already broken her heart. She doesn't need you trying to convince her that you're the victim in all of this—" She waves her hand between us. "As far as I'm concerned, you're a jackass for taking money from your brother while she's paying the rent. Who the hell does that?"

"I didn't take a cent from Kyler," I say. "And yes, he begged me to have her move in with me, but I didn't agree to it because of him. I did it for my own selfish reasons because I wanted to have her around."

Charlotte presses her lips together.

"I love her, Charlotte. And if she walks away, I don't want her going to that jackass, Atlas, just to get even with me."

She tilts her head, staring up at me. "Atlas Storm, you mean the guy from the party?"

My breath catches in my throat. "Did he do something to her?" My hands ball into fists at my side as we reach the floor, and the double doors open. I wouldn't put it past him for being the reason that she left in such a rush and called me on her way to the subway that night.

Charlotte hurries out first, not that she has a key, but Amber apparently is waiting and opens the door for her the minute we're on the floor.

But her eyes widen when she sees me. "You let him up?" she asks, staring at Charlotte.

"It *is* his place," Charlotte says. "Do you have everything packed?"

Charlotte invites herself inside, and I'm right behind them, shutting the door and locking it. Not that I can stop Amber from leaving, nor would I force her to stay. But I would like her to hear the entire story, not just bits and pieces that she overheard from the locker room.

"Can we talk?" I ask.

She's still in my jersey. That's a good sign.

Or she's been too busy packing to realize that she's wearing my clothes. Which is a more likely scenario, knowing Amber. Distracted.

"I've said everything that I need to," Amber says and grabs the black trash bag with her belongings.

"Let me at least give you a suitcase or a duffel bag," I say, and I'd walk in the other room and grab it from my closet if I didn't think she'd bail.

She glances at her friend, Charlotte.

"Let him give you a bag. As long as he's not expecting it to be returned," Charlotte says.

"I don't want anything from him. And I *never* want to see him again."

"I'll return the bag, okay?" Charlotte says to her friend.

Amber sighs. "Fine." She glances at me. "You can let me borrow a duffel bag so it doesn't look like a homeless girl is leaving your place. Wouldn't want to hurt your image."

I inhale a sharp breath and bite down my tongue. She's trying to pick a fight, to make this easier on her. Well, I'm not going to give in and accept her hostility as anything other than her deflecting her feelings.

"I'll help you pack. Bring the trash bag in with me," I say and gesture for her to follow me into my bedroom.

She glances over her shoulder at Charlotte.

"I'll be right here. If you need anything, just holler," Charlotte says.

Amber mutters under her breath, "Some friend," and follows me into my bedroom.

The bed is still unmade from last night. I got in late and was out early this morning. I pull the covers up to fix the bed and then head for the closet, deciding which bag to give her. I grab one with wheels, wanting to make it easier for her. Even though I don't want her to leave, I'm not about to be a jerk about it. Besides, she doesn't have that much stuff, either. Her bag won't be that heavy.

I grab a medium-sized hard-shell suitcase and unzip it for her. She dumps the contents of the trash bag directly into the suitcase, the clothes tangled and twisted.

"How about I fold these for you?"

"How about you leave me the hell alone and let me leave?" Amber snaps.

I grimace and hold up my hands in surrender. "If you want to leave, you know where the door is," I say.

She yanks the lid on the suitcase shut and pulls the zipper with haste. It gets stuck, and I reach across the bed, shifting the suitcase lid to adjust the zipper and slide it closed. "For the record, I don't want you to go, but I'm not about to hold you hostage, either."

Amber doesn't so much as crack a grin. She grabs the suitcase off the bed. It lands with a heavy thud against the floor. She spins around to face me, and there's a fire in her eyes. "Kyler said he paid you to fuck me! Care to explain that?"

She'd been holding back—the anger, the hatred —now it's all boiling over.

"What?" I ask, trying to understand how she interpreted any of what was said as my brother paying me to sleep with Amber because that is the farthest thing from what happened.

"He asked how long you've been banging me and then proceeded to ask if it was before or after he paid you."

I exhale a breath, realizing how it sounds, but she misunderstood. "Kyler asked me to let you live here so that he and Em could start a family together and adjust to their new lives as a married couple."

"They're not married yet, and that's beside the point," she says.

"No, that *is* the point," I reiterate. "Your sister invited you to live with them, but he didn't want you there."

Amber winces at my words. I didn't intend for them to hurt, but it's what happened. Was it a dick move on Kyler's part? Yes, and I'm not helping matters, either, with my attempt at blatant honesty.

She huffs and yanks the handle on the suitcase, lifting it up. "Apparently, both of the Greysons don't want me around."

"Don't go twisting my words," I say. "From the

moment that he asked me to take you in, I was excited."

"Take me in? Like I'm some kind of adoptable pet or lost puppy? I don't need your charity."

I take a step closer, and she moves backward a step, but she drops her hand from the luggage. I want to take that as a good sign, but I'm not sure that it is, at least not yet.

"You're neither of those things to me or anyone else," I say. "You can't blame Kyler for wanting only his fiancée and daughter in the house. They're practically newlyweds, figuring out their relationship."

She scrunches her nose. "If you're talking about their sex life, gross."

I chuckle, relieved she's at least taking the time to listen to me. "I've always wanted you, Amber. Long before you moved in with me. I didn't think it was a good idea because I had a crush on you, and my teammates all kept insisting that if I acted on it, I'd be breaking *bro code* and possibly messing up the team dynamics."

"That's an excuse," Amber says. "Your brother offered you money, and you took it."

"I never took it," I say, stepping closer, my hand reaching for hers. "I never wanted to take it. That wasn't why I invited you as a roommate. He may have suggested it to me, but I never would have asked without his suggestion."

"Wonderful," she mutters and yanks away from my touch.

"No, listen," I say, trying to explain. "I didn't want to hurt my brother. And while it doesn't always seem like you're close with Emerson, I know you wouldn't want to hide from her that you live with me."

She sighs. "Yeah, you're right. That's not something I can hide when she wants to send me a holiday card and asks for my address."

I chuckle and pull her tighter. "I love you."

"I'm still mad at you," Amber says, but the anger seems to dissipate from her body. "You should have been honest. You should have told me that moving in was Kyler's idea."

"And risk your sister finding out that he was kicking you out? At the time, I didn't know you that well. Emerson, well, let's say she's kicked my ass once before."

"What? Seriously? When?" Amber asks, her eyes lighting up, wanting to hear the story. Her shoulders sink, and the tension disappears.

"When we first met, and it was rightfully deserved, since I tricked her."

"Tricked her, how?" Amber asks. She unlatches my hand and takes a step backward but moves to sit at the edge of the bed, staring up at me. She's not going anywhere, at least not right now.

I can finally breathe a sigh of relief. "Did you ever hear the story of how Kyler hired your sister as a bodyguard to protect his daughter, Bristol?"

Her eyes light up. "No!" she gasps with a laugh and tugs on my shirt, pulling me closer.

I want to kiss her, taste her, relish her, and show her how much she means to me, but instead, I stare deep into her blue eyes, watching her, memorizing every detail, every speckle of color in her irises because I almost lost her.

My hands press against the mattress, trapping her, towering over her.

She leans back on her elbows, waiting, staring up at me, her breath coming out in soft gasps as the moment drags on.

"Are you going to kiss me already?" Amber asks, but she doesn't budge. She doesn't make the first move.

Is she hesitating because she's nervous and the bedroom door is wide open? Her friend is in the living room, waiting for her.

"That depends," I say, slowly closing the gap between us.

Her breathing hitches, and her cherry lips part. "On?"

"Are you planning on unpacking that bag?"

I SWEAR the man is a tease. His lips hover above mine. His body is not quite touching me as he traps me against the mattress, and it's quite honestly the perfect place to be.

He wants to know what happens next, and I wish I could easily tell him that I forgive him.

Wouldn't that be the easiest thing to do?

"Are you planning on unpacking that bag, or do I have to do it for you?" This time, he cocks a grin, and I swear my panties melt right there on the spot.

I tug my bottom lip between my teeth. This dance we've been playing for months hasn't ceased since the moment that we kissed. The bond between us has only grown more intense.

It scares me.

Mostly because I haven't had a real relationship. I've never felt a connection with anyone like I have with Jasper.

"You cook, clean, and unpack? You really are perfect," I say, staring up at him as I lean back on my elbows, admiring his physique. He smells clean. He clearly showered after the game, and the scent of fresh shampoo and soap clings to his skin, mixed with his own earthly aroma.

I want to rise up and lick his neck, but I don't feel bold enough to make that kind of move. Not after our fight. But don't they say that makeup sex can be amazing?

Of course, that would imply that we have sex, and we haven't, at least not yet.

"Say that again," Jasper whispers, crawling above me, but he doesn't press his body down onto mine yet. And I desperately crave the contact.

I also really wish the bedroom door would shut on its own since my best friend is just down the hall, and at any minute, she could interrupt us.

I scoot back so that my entire body is flush against the mattress and my legs are no longer dangling from the bed.

Jasper grins, noticing my eagerness. "Where do you think you're going?" he teases and grabs me by the hips, rolling me around onto my stomach.

"Jasper!" I gasp, and he pins me against the bed. Grabbing my arms, he lifts my wrists, keeping them held above me.

My eyes shut as I feel the warmth of his body graze mine. He lowers his hips, and I swear the man can bring me to the delicious edge from just restraining me.

Fuck.

I suck in a sharp breath, and already, my breathing is coming out raspy and thick. If he can get me off this easily, how will it be when we actually have sex? I might actually die.

"You didn't answer my question," he whispers into my ear. His breath teases my neck, and I gasp from the sudden contact of his lips on my bare skin.

"Which is?" I can't recall what he asked just seconds earlier. My mind is in a fog, the room warm, and he's clouding my thoughts.

Jasper chuckles. "I honestly don't remember, either." He kisses a path down my neck and nibbles on my skin, licking and tasting me as I squirm under him.

"I want you," I whisper, grinding my bottom into his cock, teasing him in return.

"Fuck," he growls into my ear. He releases his hold on my arms and keeps his hips pinned to mine. "Send your friend home."

He lifts his hips long enough for me to roll around, but he doesn't relinquish his hold on me completely. And I feel his cock straining against his pants, begging to be released. My gaze moves down his body.

"The things I'm going to do to you, she doesn't need to hear you scream my name."

I gasp, staring up at him in awe.

Jasper leans down, covering my mouth in a searing kiss, pushing his tongue past my lips. I grind my hips against him, pulling him tighter and harder. I want him, crave him, desire the feel of his skin on mine.

There are footsteps in the hallway. "Just tell me if I should get lost," Charlotte giggles, and I know without a doubt that she must have overheard Jasper.

"Get lost!" We both shout in unison.

"Call me tomorrow, Amber! I want all the dirty details."

I cover my face with my hand, and Jasper grabs

my arm, pinning it back against the mattress. The front door clicks, and my stomach tenses.

We're alone.

I tug my bottom lip between my teeth.

Jasper hovers from above, his lips teasing me, just waiting for me to lean into his kiss.

My stomach does belly flops, but it's my nerves that make my voice tremble. "I want you to be my first," I whisper, staring up at him.

"And I would love nothing more than that," he says, brushing a strand of hair behind my ear. I lean into his hand, his warmth, his body, desiring as much contact as possible.

"But?"

I dread what he might say, and those butterflies go rampant.

Jasper shakes his head. "I want you more than you know. I want you to be sure, and I really wanted to take you out on a date before we did this," he says, brushing his lips against mine.

I lean into his touch, and his hand against mine releases long enough for me to wrap my arms around him, touch him, and explore his body. I reach for the hem of his black T-shirt and drag my fingers over his skin.

He's warm, and the more I touch his hips, the

more I want to touch every part of him. "Shirt off," I command.

Jasper sits up, his hands joining mine as he helps me remove his shirt, tossing it onto the floor before climbing back down my body.

"I was serious about the date," he whispers against my lips, his mouth grazing my neck, his fingers sliding under the jersey that he gave me, caressing my bare skin. His touch is featherlight, and it makes my stomach flutter and my heart race.

"Our schedules don't coincide," I say. That isn't his fault or mine. He's busy with the team, the league, his games. I don't blame him for not being around to take me out. That wouldn't be fair to him. "I'll take what I can get." I grin up at him.

"But it's not enough. Your first time should be with someone you love," he says, staring down at me. "Not just someone who is in love with you."

My breath catches in my throat. He said the words earlier, in haste, in the middle of us fighting, and I did my best to ignore it.

But with his intense gaze boring into me, it's hard to pretend he didn't just say those words.

"You barely know me," I say, trying to bring reason into the conversation. Because I do love Jasper, but the feeling terrifies me. I've never felt this way about anyone romantically before, and I don't want to fall hard and get hurt.

"I know that when you get nervous, you laugh and glance away," Jasper says. He drops a tiny kiss to my nose. "I know that you love unconditionally and will stop at nothing to get what you want. You're determined."

He plants another kiss, this one on my cheek. "You're sexy, and you don't even realize how gorgeous you are, which is even hotter. And while I don't trust you in the kitchen, you are so loving and kind that you don't take what you feel isn't earned."

I laugh, not sure what he's talking about. He did peg me right on the laughing when I'm nervous, but I meet his stare, refusing to let him be right about me glancing away.

He shifts down to my stomach, inching my shirt up around my waist, his breath warm as he kisses above my navel. "You've earned everything that you have, Amber. You deserve to be happy, to be cherished, and loved."

Inch by inch, he guides my shirt higher, his lips and tongue teasing me, warming me as I sit up, and he removes the jersey, letting it hit the floor with a thud.

"No bra?" he grins, and I snicker.

"No panties, either," I say, and reach for his hand, guiding his fingers into my waistband, letting him discover the truth for himself.

His eyes widen, and the smile grows on his face. "If I had known, I would have gotten thrown out of the game a lot sooner," Jasper whispers and covers my lips, his tongue pushing into my mouth.

We roll around, me on top, as I lift my hips and shimmy out of my pants.

"Slow down there, tiger," he says, rolling me onto my back. "I'm not in any rush, are you?" Jasper lifts his hips and removes his pants and boxers, and I suck in a sharp breath.

He has me pinned against the mattress, his hips above mine, teasing me. The longer that I stare up at him, the more my nerves begin to resurface.

I don't expect him to have waited for me to be his first, but I can't help but worry about how many girls he has been with before me. What if I don't do something right? Or worse, what if he doesn't like sex with me?

His thumb grazes my cheek and draws a soft path along my bottom lip, releasing it from between my teeth. "Talk to me," he whispers, staring at me.

He's warm, and his eyes shine down with mirth,

and all I can think about is, what if I'm bad at this, and what if he hates it?

"I'm nervous," I admit, hoping that if I voice my fears that, somehow, I can conquer them, and he can get me out of my head.

"It's just me," Jasper says and rolls over onto the mattress. He pulls me against him as we lie on our sides, staring into one another's gazes. His hand trails soft circles against my hip. "We can wait as long as you need. If you're not ready—" He moves to sit up in bed, and I grab his arm. His bicep is enormous, and he smiles when he sees me staring at him.

"What if I'm bad in bed?"

He chuckles and sits up, his fingers tangling in my hair, stroking my head. "*Babe*, you couldn't be bad at sex. Trust me, and if you're the absolute worst, then I promise we'll just have to keep trying to make it better. The first time is always awkward, anyhow."

"You mean the first time, first time, or just the first time with a new partner?"

"Afraid to say virgin?" Jasper asks, tilting his head at me. "It's not a dirty word. There's nothing shameful or embarrassing about it."

"I'm twenty!"

He merely shrugs. "And if you're not ready, we can wait until you're twenty-one or twenty-two."

"I'm naked in your bed. I think I'm ready," I counter. Is he trying to make me die of embarrassment?

"You think?" he asks, his fingers trailing a soft path across my arms. "I need to hear your enthusiastic consent."

I close my eyes and lean closer. "I want you to fuck me, Jasper."

"Look me in the eyes and say that again," he whispers, and I can feel the heat radiating off us like a volcano about to explode.

I shift on the mattress, climbing onto Jasper and straddling him. Staring down into his gaze, I whisper, "I want you to fuck me, Jasper."

His hands rest on my hips, and he grins, rolling us around. "Tell me if you change your mind," he says, and he's on me like a lion in heat. His mouth is on mine, his body nestled against me. He reaches into the bedside table for a condom, leaving the foil packet on the mattress beside us for when he's ready.

"I won't."

He pulls back, and a frown crosses his features. "You won't tell me?"

"I won't change my mind," I say.

"Tell me if there's something that you don't like or don't want me to do," he whispers, kissing a path down my naked skin. He settles between my thighs, and this time, I don't stop him. I want this with him, to explore and discover what I like.

How can I know without ever having experienced it?

I'm sure that I'm blushing. The room is warm, and I glance away as he stares at my pussy.

"Eyes on me," he whispers, and I inhale a nervous breath and meet his stare.

It feels like he's staring straight into my soul. He doesn't look away, not for an instant.

His fingers guide my lips apart, and I gasp from just the contact alone. He's gentle but firm as he trails a soft path against my folds. "That's a good girl," he praises.

I gasp, my breath coming out in soft pants as I settle farther onto the mattress and spread my legs wider for him. I want him to touch me.

He smiles and brings his lips closer to my pussy. "I'm going to kiss you and lick you now," he says. "Do you want that?"

"Yes," I whisper, and the room feels like it's spinning the moment his tongue drags along my slit.

He dives into my wetness and trails a path around my clit, teasing me.

My fingers tangle in his hair, and I struggle to keep my eyes on him as they slam shut. His tongue teases my clit, and he glides one finger inside of my warmth, stroking and teasing me.

Already, I'm clenching down, my insides beginning to tremble from the contact and warmth that floods through me.

"How many fingers do you use when you touch yourself?" he asks.

I press my lips together.

"Amber?" He pulls back, and I whimper in protest. "Don't go getting all shy on me now." He chuckles as he strokes me with one finger.

"Your fingers are bigger than mine," I say as if it's not a fair comparison.

"One? Two? Three?"

I shut my eyes but hold up two fingers.

"Good girl," he says and continues stroking me with one finger. He teases my clit with his tongue and then glides a second finger inside of my warmth.

I moan from the initial stretch and feel as he fills me. His fingers are thicker than mine. It's not even a close comparison as my head lulls back and my back arches, craving more.

Jasper keeps stroking me, curling his fingers inside me, teasing me. I bend my legs and give him more access. "I want your cock," I say as I finally am able to accommodate his two fingers.

"How about another finger," he says, climbing up my body, kissing me as he guides a third finger inside my pussy.

My eyes squeeze shut as he stretches me, and my mouth widens from the initial pain, but it feels good.

I arch up from the mattress, my hips working up a rhythm against his hand, wanting him to fuck me. I'm breathless from the sensations coursing through me. His thumb circles my clit while his fingers are buried deep inside me, teasing and driving me toward the brink.

The first slight tremors trickle through me, and my breathing catches in my throat.

"Don't hold back. Come for me," he commands.

His fingers repeat the same motions, and the initial pain is now pleasure as my insides clench onto his fingers, squeezing and tightening around him.

Warmth radiates as my body tingles and trembles beneath his touch. My toes curl, and my back arches up off the mattress. Like an explosion, my eyes are squeezed shut, yet I see fireworks.

Jasper withdraws his fingers as he grabs the condom on the bed. He shows me the foil packet. "Do you want another round?" he asks.

His cock threatens to burst in excitement, but he doesn't make any of this about him.

I reach between us. My fingers graze the head of his erection, and he gasps between clenched teeth. "I need verbal confirmation," he says.

"What are you, my doctor?" I joke, and when he's still waiting, I nod. For a man with very little patience on the ice, the amount that he gives me in the bedroom is impressive. "Yes, I want you to fuck me, Jasper. Now get over here and stop teasing me already."

"As you wish," he says with a smile and tears the foil packet open, sheathing it onto his erection.

I watch with all of my senses heightened, taking it all in as he positions himself at my entrance. He's teasing me, dragging the head of his cock across my slit.

"Fuck," I growl and reach between us for his cock. Before I can grab ahold, he glides into me inch by inch.

"Bend your knees more," he instructs, and I do as I'm told as he fills me.

The moan that spills past my lips surprises even me. Jasper stares down, concentrating. His arms are positioned at either side of the bed, pressed against the mattress as he buries deeper inside of me. He doesn't move, and I can sense the strength and focus that it takes for him not to let loose.

He brushes my lips slowly, tasting me as I adjust to his size. "Are you okay?" he whispers, staring, waiting for me to answer.

It takes a second for me to answer as the blood feels like it's all rushed out of my head. "Yes," I say and nod.

His lips are back on mine with fervent kisses as he grinds his hips into me and then begins thrusting. He's taking his time, his gaze tight and focused on me.

With each shallow thrust, my breathing becomes more pronounced, and I wrap my legs around him, pulling him deeper and tighter, wanting to feel him on me.

"Fuck," he groans.

My hands are restless, clawing at his back, his ass, and touching every inch of him. I cling to him as though he's the surface of the ocean, and I'm drowning in the deep blue sea.

I sense that he's close. His breaths are more pronounced. His moans echo through the air as sweat glistens across his forehead. His brow pinches, and I can feel him swell as I tremble beneath him.

"Come with me," he rasps into my ear, and his hand slides between us with each thrust, teasing my clit.

The air leaves my lungs, my breath stolen as my insides clench onto his cock, draining him, stealing everything that he has, and making him mine.

My toes curl, and my back arches off the mattress, tangling with him, clinging to him like he's my life preserver.

I tremble and shudder, the orgasm ripping through me. His body above mine brings a newly heightened awareness—a warmth that encircles me like never before—as he collapses above.

Jasper pulls out, climbing off and removing the condom as he heads for the bathroom.

I'm still gasping for breath as I roll onto my side, watching him from the distance. "Is sex always that good?" I ask, breathing hard, my heart still racing in my chest.

"Most of the time." He chuckles and leans down, planting a kiss on my lips. His fingers tangle in my hair, pulling my mouth closer. "It'll get even better."

My gaze tightens as I overanalyze his words. "What do you mean, better?" I can't imagine sex being better than what we just experienced unless I did something wrong. "Wait, was it bad for you?" I sit up in bed, dragging the covers up around myself.

"I've only had bad sex once or twice," he confesses and climbs onto the mattress. He stretches out beside me, pulling the covers from around my hips so that he can have some of the sheets.

"Was just now one of those times?" My voice catches in my throat, and I'm trying not to panic, but his answer has sent my heart racing and my mind spiraling.

"Of course not." He pulls me down to lie with him, rolling me onto my back and pinning me beneath him. "I promise you that it will always be amazing."

"You can't make that kind of promise," I say with a nervous laugh.

"Sure, I can. It's you and me. You're the hottest girl in the world, and, well, I'm pretty fucking hot myself."

I lean in, kissing Jasper. "I like how you're confident in your hotness," I say, smiling up at him.

He rolls onto his back, pulling me with him, his arms wrapped around my waist as one of my legs drapes over his. "I'm more confident in yours," he says. "Do you know that when I first saw you at the bar, I knew I wanted you?"

"What?" I laugh. "When I showed up after your game?" I'd already had a crush on him for months, not that I would ever tell him that embarrassing secret, like how I stalked him online.

"No, the first time. Remember that date you had at the bar?"

My eyes widen, and I scrunch them shut tightly as if that will rid myself of the memory of Tripp, who was quite a trip. "I really wish I could forget him."

Jasper chuckles. "Then, I apologize for mentioning him, but it was that night when I was watching you at the bar, I kept wondering if he was your boyfriend or just a date, until you bumped into me in the hallway and begged for my help."

"I didn't beg."

"Oh, you begged," Jasper recants. "It was cute and quite adorable in a 'save me' kind of way." He pulls me tighter against him, holding me in his arms.

I relax and chuckle, smiling at the memory of when I first met Jasper. "I didn't know that you had a hero complex."

Jasper stares at me. "I don't—" he whispers, but I

can tell he's mulling it over. "But I admit that I can get jealous at times."

"Like with Atlas?"

"He's a douche. And my jealousy is one hundred percent warranted with *him*. He stole my first girlfriend when we were thirteen."

I didn't realize their hatred went quite so far back. In fact, I hadn't been entirely sure they'd even known one another. I knew Knox played for their rival, but I wasn't sure how he knew Atlas. "Seriously?"

"I try not to hold a grudge," he says and nuzzles my neck, his breath warm and sending another round of tingles coursing through my body. "Especially because I have you. And trust me when I say that you're a million times hotter than she ever was."

Smiling, I shake my head. "She was also a kid. You haven't seen her in years. She could have grown up."

"She's a puck bunny, and trust me, you are, without a doubt, the hottest woman alive."

Wait. I make a face of disgust. "Does that mean you're attracted to a dead person? Is there something that you're not telling me?"

His body vibrates with laughter as he rolls me onto my back, and his fingers lightly graze my hips. I wiggle from his touch, and he raises an eyebrow, realizing what that means.

"Someone is ticklish," he says, watching me try to get away as he pins me to the mattress. But I honestly don't mind it. I squirm, attempting to break free, and his cell phone rings, saving me from any more agonizing torture, which I'm enjoying a little too much.

He grabs the phone from the bedside table, looking at the caller ID. "It's my brother," he grumbles and declines the call.

"Are you never going to talk to him again? Because that's going to be hard to do when you play hockey with him like every day."

"It's not every day, and we fight. Whatever," he says dismissively, sitting up in bed.

The phone rings again.

"He's persistent," I say.

"Do you want to answer it?" he asks, shoving the phone at me.

I shrug and hit accept. "Jasper is a bit busy right now," I answer before so much as offering a warm greeting or even a hello.

A soft, feminine sigh exhales a breath. "I wasn't calling for Jasper," Emerson says. "I was looking for you. You didn't answer your phone. I thought I might try your roommate."

Jasper is watching me attentively. "Tell my brother he can suck my—" I cover his lips with my hand.

"It's my sister," I say to Jasper, glaring at him to watch his mouth and his tone.

His eyes light up, and his shoulders relax. "Oh, well, then tell her I said hello and that her fiancé is a—"

I grab the nearest pillow and smack him with it to shut him up.

"You did not just hit me with a pillow," Jasper deadpans.

Emerson clears her throat. "Do I need to let you go? You sound busy with your roommate." The way she keeps calling Jasper my roommate is annoying me, like a pesky mosquito bite that won't stop itching.

Jasper sits up in bed, watching me attentively.

"Listen," I say and press my lips together, trying to decide how I'm going to word this without making a fool of myself in front of Jasper.

"We're dating!" Jasper shouts, making it known without so much as a hint of guilt on his face. His tone settles, but he's still obnoxiously loud. "Did she hear me?"

I snort. "Of course, she heard you. I think half the apartment complex heard you."

"Only half? Should I go outside on the balcony and shout it for all of the city to hear?" Jasper asks. He wags his eyebrows, and I reach for the pillow. But he's faster than I am and snatches it before I can retaliate. Besides, he has two free hands, and I'm still holding his cell phone with my right hand. He's at an advantage.

"Well, I'm happy for you, but can I talk to him?"

I inhale a deep breath through my nose. "Why?" I ask. I'm reluctant to hand over the phone. Is she going to give the 'big sister, if you hurt her, I'll kill you' speech?

"Jasper and Kyler need to make up. We can't let it affect their practice or their game."

"What do you propose?" I ask.

"Whose proposing?" Jasper asks. "Are you going to ask me to marry you? Because I think I should be the one doing the asking."

I yank the pillow from between his hands. "Go get ready for bed," I say and point at the bathroom.

He's still naked from our earlier festivities, as am I, which I don't mind, but I'm trying to keep him from overhearing whatever my sister is scheming.

"Fine, but if you're proposing, I expect flowers, a ring, and you to get down on one knee. I want the whole package, *babe*." He climbs off the bed, and I roll my eyes, watching as he saunters into the bathroom, giving me a nice show of his ass. I'm fairly sure it's on purpose.

And I'm not wrong or disappointed because when he turns around, he blows me a kiss before shutting the bathroom door. I can hear the sink run and assume that he's brushing his teeth. He didn't take any clothes into the bathroom with him, which means in a minute or two, he'll be back in the bedroom, and I won't have much time to talk to Emerson in private.

"Be quick," I say. "He's out of earshot."

"The boys have off tomorrow. You're bringing Jasper over, and we're going to make both boys apologize and make up."

"And if he doesn't agree to it?" I ask. I don't know how I'm going to convince him to accompany me to Kyler's house, not if they're still fighting.

"Use your womanly charm. He made it abundantly clear that he has feelings for you."

I grimace. "You heard that?"

"Like he said, the apartments around you all heard him. He's loud, and if he's anything like Kyler, he's not going to let this feud between him and his brother go. Do what you need to, but don't fuck this up."

I huff under my breath. "This isn't my fault."

"They're fighting about you. Jasper wasn't playing his best game on the ice tonight, and according to Kyler, he's been distracted at several games you attended recently."

I climb off the mattress and stalk across the floor, yanking open one of Jasper's dresser drawers. I pull a T-shirt out and slip into it while Emerson is venting at me like this is my fault. Which it isn't.

"Am I not supposed to go to his games?"

The bathroom door swings open, and Jasper is wearing a frown. "Give me the phone." He holds out his hand, waiting for me to deposit it in his palm.

"How much of that did you hear?" I ask, staring at him. He's unwavering, and he steps closer.

I relinquish the phone—after all, it's his—and take a step back. The heat that Jasper is radiating is overwhelming.

"Why are you telling my girlfriend that she can't attend my games?" One hand is curled into a fist, but his tone remains more civilized than I might expect. He's trying to keep his composure. Maybe he doesn't think that he should yell at a lady. Well, my sister deserves a tongue-lashing if she thinks she has any say over my relationship with Jasper.

I HAVE no intention of eavesdropping when Amber sends me into the bathroom to get ready for bed. It's clear she wants a word with her sister alone, and I can give her that space. I trust her, and besides, it's her sister she's talking with, not Atlas Storm.

But when I hear her sounding defeated and the words, "Am I not supposed to go to his games?" My insides boil.

I brushed my teeth. I stared at my reflection in the mirror for far too long. I was trying to mind my own business, I really was, but I don't like how Amber's sister is treating her.

"Give me the phone," I command, and if she doesn't hand it over to me any second, I will grab it from her. I'm trying to remain calm and patient, but I don't like the thought of Emerson butting her head into our relationship, where it doesn't belong.

I never judged her and Kyler with their weird relationship antics. Who the hell pretends to be dating and lies to their kid about their relationship? I kept my thoughts to myself on that matter, which is right where Emerson needs to keep her opinions—out of our lives.

"How much of that did you hear?" Amber is doing that nervous tic where she's chewing on her bottom lip. I invade her personal space, prepared to take the phone when she places it into my palm.

"Why are you telling my girlfriend that she can't attend my games?" I'm stewing. The fact that Emerson thinks she can boss Amber around is crazy.

"She's a distraction. Kyler has been telling me how you're fighting with the opponents more, getting kicked out of games, not just thrown in the penalty box."

I scoff at her words. "It's hockey. Fights break out all the time," I say dismissively. She doesn't know what she's talking about. Amber hadn't even been at the last several games because they were out of state. I played like shit in North Carolina too.

"That's an excuse, and you damn well know it," she says.

Amber's chewing her bottom lip raw, and I reach out, running my thumb over her lip as she untangles it from between her teeth. "You and your fiancé will not dictate my life or Amber's."

"I'm doing this for you," Emerson says. "Can you honestly tell me that your head has been in the game lately?"

She doesn't know what she's talking about, and neither does Kyler, who has probably filled her head with nonsense.

"My head is right where it belongs, and so is my heart, in case you or my brother give a crap about that."

"I'm not trying to fight with you," Emerson says.

"Well, you could have fooled me." I bite down on my tongue. It's like walking on thin ice, and I can feel the ground at my feet crack and shift right before I plunge into the icy water below.

"I'm trying to look out for both of you. She's never had a boyfriend. How do you think she's going to handle the media when they come tearing apart your lives, wanting to know every juicy detail?"

Unlike Kyler, who has always vied for media attention, I prefer not to be front-page news in the sports section.

Amber's eyes are sullen as she stares up at me.

She's tugging at the hem of the shirt she's wearing, *my shirt*. With one hand, I reach for her fingers, threading them together as I speak to Emerson on the phone. "I know. We'll figure it out together. You don't need to protect your little sister."

"I'm not little," Amber protests, standing on her tiptoes to make sure that her sister can hear her on the phone.

She's certainly not little, but I'm six-two, and Amber is just over five foot. Her tenacity is adorable, and I lean down, planting a kiss on her nose. "I'm done talking about it. It's late; we're going to bed." I end the call and silence my phone, not wanting to be interrupted.

"And now you see why I'm not particularly close with my sister," Amber says, slumping down at the edge of the mattress.

"She's looking out for you, but she's being a tad bit overprotective," I say, agreeing with Amber that Em needs to mind her own business on this one.

"That's putting it mildly."

"Do you want to shower?" I ask. She's already in my T-shirt for bed, but after our little romp in the sheets, I could use another shower, and it gives me the opportunity to fulfill one of many fantasies involving her.

Smiling, she tilts her head to the side. "Are you trying to get me naked? Because it's working."

"You still look pretty clothed to me," I say and reach for the hem of the shirt that she's wearing. She lifts her arms, and I let my fingers dance over her hips and up her sides as I gradually tug the cotton material over her head. I toss the discarded shirt onto the floor. "That's better."

My fingers roam over her bottom. "How sore are you?" I ask, suspecting that she might still be aching from what we did earlier.

"Throbbing," she laughs into my neck, "I think you bruised me."

"Shit." I tense and run a hand through my hair. My fingers glide up her back as I pull away slightly to meet her stare. "I need you to tell me if I'm going too fast or too rough with you."

"I'm kidding," Amber says, and her fingers tease down my stomach. My cock twitches to life. "It was perfect, but I am a bit achy down there."

"How about we just take a shower, get cleaned up, and curl up in bed together?" I suggest, brushing my lips against her neck.

"That sounds fine, but if you keep kissing that spot and doing that thing with your tongue, you're going to get me soaked before we even step into the shower."

I groan at her words. She's going to kill me with her sexy talk, but at least I'll die a happy man.

————

"Where are we going?" I ask as she drags me to the subway, not so much as giving me a hint of our destination.

"I can't say." The grin on her face is wide, and I can't help but wonder what she's scheming.

"A date?" I'm hopeful. It's my day off, the first one in quite a while. Although I spent the morning downstairs at the gym in the building, I didn't have to meet up with the team for practice or training.

Her tongue darts out the corner of her lips, and I want to kiss her and taste her, let the world know that she's *mine*.

But the words her older sister said keep replaying in my head, and she is right. Amber has never been in a relationship, and her first real boyfriend is in the spotlight. I want to shield her from unwarranted attention, protect her like the innocent little dove that she is. But hiding our relationship from the media and the news will only make it more dramatic.

I take her hand, giving it a squeeze. "You do know dating me doesn't come with anonymity. One photo posted on social media, and everyone will be gossiping about us," I say, leaning in and bumping her arm with mine.

I need to know that she's okay with that part of my life. It's not always shiny and perfect.

"Let them talk." She leans up on her tiptoes and kisses me. "I have nothing to hide."

"Good, then you can tell me where we're going," I say as she leads me down the stairs to the subway station. We cross through the turnstile, and she glances at the map briefly before leading me to the correct platform.

"As long as you tell me what's in that bag you've been hiding under your bed." She smirks all too knowingly.

Did she peek inside and see the dress that I bought her?

I still haven't given it to her, mainly because I can't stand the thought of another man laying eyes on her while she's wearing it.

"Did you look in the bag?" I ask.

"No, I respect your boundaries."

"But you knew the bag is under my bed."

Her nose wrinkles when she laughs and glances away, guilty as charged. I suppose she's not going to tell me where she's taking me. Knowing Amber, she's probably going to take some long, roundabout method to confuse me.

When we approach the platform, and I recognize the train that we're taking, a stone sits in the pit of my stomach. "We're going to Kyler's house, aren't we?" I ask, pinning Amber with my stare.

She purses her lips, debating on whether to answer.

"Dammit," I grumble. "I'm not going over there to apologize."

"I know. You both are too proud," she says, and I open my mouth to correct her that he might be proud, but I'm right. She puts a finger to my lips. "We're just going over for lunch. Besides, when was the last time you visited with your niece?"

"I can't believe you're bringing Bristol into this."

The first train approaches, but it's not the one that we take. Ours is a few minutes behind it. "Any chance you want to explore the city? We could go to the art museum or get tickets to a show?" I'm willing to do anything else right now.

"Tempting, but I've already made plans, and your

teammates are coming by in a couple of hours for a barbeque."

That's a better surprise. "Kyler's hosting?" I ask, hoping that maybe it's at one of the other guys' houses and my older brother will bail on the event.

"He is, and we're going there early to help with the food prep and let you two work out your differences."

"Differences? If you mean Kyler overstepping and shoving his nose where it doesn't belong, then sure, as long as he apologizes to both of us."

"Apologizes to both of us," Amber repeats slowly. "I'm not mad at him."

She ought to be steaming, and if she knew half of the crap that was said, she'd be angrier, but I don't want any of that hostility pointed at me.

I don't elaborate. There's no sense in causing hurt feelings or creating a bigger rift between all of us. I'm not thrilled that Amber planned this get-together behind my back, but I know she's trying to do the right thing.

And if it doesn't work, then I have to deal with his ass at practice tomorrow. At least I'll have somewhere to release the pent-up frustration and anger on the ice.

"If Kyler is hosting, that means I don't get to take

you out on that long-awaited, hot date this evening." I don't want to admit I'm disappointed. I want to take Amber out and let her experience what it's like to be my girlfriend. None of this hiding-behind-closed-doors crap.

"We can go out after the party with the team. Grab dessert or something when we've had enough socializing."

I'm not sure the guys will let me bail early, but tomorrow is a practice day, so they're not going to be out until the early hours of the morning, either. And the party is at my brother's house, who has a kid. He'll probably kick our butts out by nine o'clock.

I wrap my arms around her waist from behind, my lips teasing her neck as I brush her long locks to the side. "I want more than dessert with you," I say.

She chuckles and spins around in my embrace. "I like the sound of that." She rises up on her tiptoes and presses a kiss to my lips. "The train is almost here."

By the time we get to my brother's house, her infectious laughter has brought up my mood, and I'm not stressing or dreading dealing with Kyler.

I press the buzzer to the electric gate and wait for someone to let us inside. While I know the code, the fact that my brother and I aren't on the best terms means I don't want to just waltz in uninvited.

"Ever climb one of these?" I gesture with my thumb at the metal fence, smiling at Amber.

"No, and I don't plan to," she says and smirks. "But I dare you to do it."

Well, in that case, I can't say no, nor do I want to.

I make sure not to climb the guard gate because of the pointed arrows at the top. No sense in risking a maneuver that might put me out of commission for a while.

Kyler's voice rumbles through the intercom system, and he doesn't seem the least bit pleased to see us. "What the hell is my brother doing?"

"Letting himself in," Amber chimes.

"You know I never back down on a dare," I quip, jumping down inside the gated yard.

"I swear, if you get hurt before our next game—" Kyler mutters and presses the button to release the lock, opening the gate.

Amber skirts inside through the driveway, where the gate is open.

We head up to the front entrance, and the door flings open. "Uncle Jasper!" Bristol squeals, and as we head inside, she throws herself on me like a football player might tackle their opponent. Except, she's not doing it to take me down. This is her playful version of hello.

"Long time no see, kiddo," I say and lift her into my arms, giving her a hug.

"Daddy says you've been getting into trouble. He's mad at you."

I haven't seen Kyler yet, but he's home, based on the fact he answered the gate. Although I suppose that he could have done that remotely from another location as well.

"Where is your dad?" I ask.

She shrugs and wiggles to get down. I plant her feet firmly on the floor before letting her go. Bristol hurries across the hallway for the kitchen. "They're here!" she shrieks with delight.

I slip my shoes off and offer Amber a hand while she removes hers, as well, in the foyer before we head to the kitchen together.

I smile at her. Today is quite a bit different than the first time that we entered the house together. We barely knew one another but had shown up to support Kyler's proposal.

Amber's gaze is on me, a smile tugging at the corner of her lips. "We should mess with them."

"What do you have in mind?" I'm game for screwing with Kyler any opportunity that I get.

"We should tell them we're engaged," she says and smacks me playfully on the chest. I grab her hand, intertwining our fingers together.

"*Babe*, I don't want to pretend."

She presses her lips together, and her eyes widen in shock. "I swear, if you're going to propose, I'll kill you. We just finally admitted that we like each other. This isn't a race to the finish line to see who gets wed first."

I chuckle and lean in, kissing her cheek. Kyler and Emerson have been engaged for a few months and haven't set a date yet. But I'm sure when they're ready, they will. "I do like a little competition," I say, mulling it over playfully as I stroke my jaw. "But first, I need to get the ring."

She pinches my arm. "You are not taking Emerson and Kyler with you to go ring shopping. And you'd better be joking with me right now."

"We *are* living together," I tease, wrapping an arm around her waist as I escort her down the hall toward the commotion from the kitchen.

"Yes, one step at a time." She pats my chest as we join my brother, his fiancée, and my niece in the kitchen.

"I'm baking cookies!" Bristol exclaims. She grabs the child-size step stool and brings it to the counter.

She's already put on a ruffled apron, which is quite adorable.

Emerson helps roll up Bristol's sleeves while Kyler is grabbing the ingredients from the pantry.

"You do know they make rolls of cookie dough," I say with a smirk.

"Homemade cookies taste better," Bristol says, pointing at me. "I'm eating yours if you don't want any."

"Do you want to help?" Kyler asks.

The tension seems to have dissipated between my brother and me. Is it because Bristol is in the room?

"I think three people is enough for one batch of cookies," I say.

"Who said anything about one batch?" Emerson asks as she heads for the oven, turning it on to preheat. "Bristol signed us up for a bake sale at school and forgot to tell us that she needs three hundred cookies by tomorrow."

Bristol giggles and scrunches her nose with a huge grin. "You would have said no."

Amber rolls up her sleeves and heads to the sink, washing her hands. "Do you have another apron?" she asks.

"Not one that I'd suggest wearing." Emerson grins and winks at Kyler.

"Gross," I say. I love my brother, but I don't want to think about him and Em banging. I've walked in on her sucking his cock, and it's an image that I wish I could scrub from my eyes.

"What's gross? Cookies are good," Bristol says and glances between us, confused. Thankfully, that comment went completely over her little head.

My older brother clears his throat and nods at me in the direction of the hallway. "Do you have a minute?" he asks.

I'm not sure if he's heading toward apologyville or planning to tell me what a fuck up I am for dating Amber.

"Should I have brought my hockey gear?" I ask, wanting to know if I should be planning for a fight.

"I deserve that," Kyler says as he walks me out into the hallway, away from the kitchen. "I didn't want the girls to overhear us, mainly, my little cookie monster, who will give us both shit and repeat everything out of context."

I laugh under my breath. "Just like you as a kid. Rebellious and a pain in Mom's ass."

Kyler rubs his brow. Neither of us speaks about our deceased parents. Just bringing it up fills the room with tension and dread. "Now, I'm a pain in your ass," he says with a smirk. He's deflecting, and I'm actually appreciative of it.

"You won't hear me argue with that," I say.

He's all I have, at least he was, until I made it onto the team, and they became my extended family. But now I also have someone else, a girl I would do anything to protect.

"Did you mean what you said in the locker room? That you're falling in love with her?" Kyler asks.

I press my lips together. "What business is it of yours whom I have feelings for?"

"Amber is practically family, and you're my brother," he says. "Besides, I thought you had some chick on the side in another state? You were having phone sex at the hotel—" His voice trails off, and the grin spread across my lips is the most obvious indicator of the girl I had been talking to.

He stares at me in horror as the realization dawns on him that we've been hiding this arrangement between us.

"How long?"

"It's really not any of your business," I say and lean back against the wall. I fold my arms across my chest. He looks flustered, and I'm not sure why he cares. Does he honestly think this thing between Amber and me is a fling?

"Were you two shacking up when she moved in?"

"I've been a perfect gentleman, and no, we weren't hooking up back then. We were friends. We still are. We're just exploring this new development between us, which we both want. It's consensual, and that's all I'm saying about it." I drop my hands to my sides, shove them in my jeans pockets and stroll to the kitchen.

Kyler grabs my arm and pulls me around to face him.

I've seen the maneuver before; usually, he does it on the ice when he's about to beat the shit out of his opponent. I hold up my arm to block him, and he laughs under his breath.

"For a man getting laid, you're high-strung," Kyler says.

"You're an asshole," I mutter as he squeezes my shoulder.

"Are we good?"

"That depends. Are you going to leave Amber and me alone and let us figure out our relationship together without you and your fiancée meddling?"

Kyler releases his hold on me, but I don't pull

away. "You know I have about as much control over Em as you do, Amber," he says.

Exhaling a sigh, I nod. "Yeah, we're good." That's about as good of an apology as I'd expect to get out of my brother. We don't do feelings when it comes to our dynamic. And apologies mean someone is hurt, and neither of us ever likes to appear weak. Blame it on all the years of hockey that we've played, but we've learned to bottle our shit up nice and tight.

"Come on, let's help the girls with the cookies," I say, heading back into the kitchen.

Kyler grumbles. "We should wait until the rest of the team gets here. Make them help us."

Laughing, I doubt that it would work. "And the minute you suggest it, they'll bail. Unless Ava and Kate are coming with Parker and Asher."

"That's sexist!" Amber exclaims, overhearing us as we head back into the kitchen. "Just because they're girls doesn't mean they like baking."

"Or know-how," I say with a sly grin. I don't think Amber was intending to speak about herself, but she isn't the most skilled dinner or pastry chef.

She, however, isn't mixing the ingredients, which is probably for the best. She's rolling up the balls of dough and smushing them onto the tray.

She elbows me as I approach, and I come up and

stand behind her, my arm wrapped around her body, helping her form and shape the cookies to make them a little more uniform.

Amber wiggles back against me, and I glance around, trying to see if anyone is paying us attention. They're not. Kyler grabs a stool to sit on and glances over his phone while Emerson measures the ingredients and Bristol mixes the batter.

"You'd better get over here and help," Em says, glaring playfully at Kyler.

"There are plenty of cooks in the kitchen." Kyler gestures at us.

"Daddy, help us!" Bristol chirps and points at the oven. "Someone needs to watch the cookies bake."

"I'm on it," Kyler quips and moves off the stool for the oven. He glances at the timer above the oven. "We still have plenty of time." He smirks and returns his attention to his phone.

"What's got you so enthralled?" Emerson asks. She doesn't sound upset, just interested in what's stealing away his attention.

"Just reading a few articles about the Ice Dragons," Kyler says.

"Anything good?" I ask. I usually avoid reading anything the media prints when it comes to us because it's never accurate.

"Just this," he says, showing us the headline that reads: *Greyson brothers fight over a girl.*

"I didn't realize the press heard us," I grumble.

Bristol glances at us. "Heard what?" she asks with wide, doe-like eyes.

Kyler clears his throat. "I'll tell you when you're older."

Amber glances away, trying desperately not to laugh out loud. She bites down on her bottom lip. I don't get what is quite so funny, but Emerson is grinning too.

"I'm older!" Bristol quips.

They both saw that one coming.

EPILOGUE

Amber

My sister is a jerk. Emerson made it clear to me that she is not extending me an invitation to the wives' room. Apparently, it's a member-only thing, and being the newest addition, she doesn't feel it's her place to make the invite. Plus, we're family.

It's intermission, and she stands, ushering Bristol from the stands. "See you in a bit," she says with a knowing smirk. With the kid facing away, I flip Emerson the bird.

Charlotte chuckles beside me. "It's fine. If you were invited, I'd be sitting alone," she says and nudges me.

I'm wearing Jasper's jersey, one of four that I have hanging in my closet in the apartment. Tonight's game, he's been focused, and I swear, for most of the first period, I thought he didn't even notice me in the stands.

That was until he made a goal and pointed at me. I swear, if he weren't wearing gloves, he'd have probably held up his hands in a heart shape to embarrass me.

"So, I have something to tell you, and I don't want you to freak out," I say.

"Oh my gosh. Are you pregnant?" she squeals, and I clamp a hand over her mouth. The press could overhear, and I don't need Jasper to be the center of a scandal.

"No," I say and glare before glancing down. "If you tell me this jersey makes me look fat, you're dead."

"Of course not," Charlotte says. "I just kind of figured, announcement, freak out, that's like the most obvious answer."

"It has nothing to do with me," I say and jab my finger into her arm. "One of the guys on the Ice Dragons has been asking Jasper, who always sits with me at the games."

"If you're joking, I might actually die." Her mouth is hung agape, wide eyes as she stares at me in awe.

"Get a grip." I laugh. "It's just a little crush."

"Him or me?" she asks. "Please tell me it's Noah. Pretty please." She holds her hands together as if she were begging.

I'm not sure that I should tell her, but Jasper mentioned it, and even Noah has asked a few times casually about my friend who joins me at the games. I thought he was just making conversation and being friendly. It turns out it was something more.

"It's a guy."

"Obviously, and you told him I'm single. Didn't you? Because I'm so single that I think my lady bits are covered in cobwebs."

I snort at her description. "You are too much."

"Well, spill it, girl. What did you tell Jasper?"

"I didn't tell Jasper anything. The hockey player who was asking, I told him you might be available if he woos the crap out of you and puts in a lot of effort. You have a lot of interest from men, and you're picky."

"Fuck you." Charlotte's eyes widen. "I haven't been laid in weeks."

"Oh my gosh, poor baby," I mock. "Relax. We're meeting up after the game for drinks, and I think he's going to shoot his best shot with you tonight."

"Who are we talking about? Is he tall, dark, and handsome?" Charlotte leans forward on my every word. "I need details, and I swear if you tell me it's, like, the guy who sharpens the blades on the skates—"

"It's—" I open my mouth and shut it, teasing her.

"Girl, the suspense is driving me crazy. At this rate, you're just going to make me wait until after the game."

"I should make you wait," I say with a sly grin. "But I can't keep a secret any longer. It's Noah Reece."

She squeals and balls her hands into fists, shaking them excitedly. The girl has no filter and no level of self-control. I used to envy her and the fact that she doesn't have anxiety, but I suspect her mouth lands her into trouble too often.

———

Thank you for reading *Daring the Hockey Player*. I hope that you enjoyed Amber and Jasper's love story. Continue the series with Charlotte and Noah in, *Arresting the Hockey Player*.

When my best friend told me that one of the Ice Dragons hockey players had eyes for me, I thought she was joking.

Turns out Noah Reece isn't just gorgeous and a

professional athlete. There's a whole lot more to him that even the hockey team doesn't know.

I shouldn't go digging into his past. The skeletons should be left buried, but I have a habit of not letting things go, and that includes Noah's secrets.

And he's got a bunch of them.

Arresting the Hockey Player is the third book in the Ice Dragons series but can be read as a standalone. No cheating. No cliffhanger. HEA.

GIVEAWAYS, FREE BOOKS, AND MORE GOODIES

I hope you enjoyed Faking it with the Billionaire and loved Kyler and Emerson's story.

Sign up for my Willow Fox newsletter for new release information.

Want to read my books first? Gain early access, vote for your favorite characters to get their own book, ARCs, discounts on audiobooks, and more! Find out more on my website under membership.

If you enjoyed Faking it with the Billionaire, please take a moment to leave a review. Reviews help other readers discover my books.

Not sure what to write? That's okay. It doesn't have to be long. You can share how you discovered my book; was it a recommendation by a friend or a book club? Let readers know who your favorite character is or what you'd like to see happen next.

ABOUT THE AUTHOR

Willow Fox has loved writing since she was in high school (many ages ago). Her small town romances are reflective of living in a small town in rural America.

Whether she's writing romance or sitting outside by the bonfire reading a good book, Willow loves the magic of the written word.

Visit her website at:

https://authorwillowfox.com

Dangerous Boss

Bossy Single Dad Series

Billionaire Grump

Mountain Grump

Bachelor Grump

Ice Dragons Hockey Romance

Faking it with the Billionaire

Daring the Hockey Player

Looking for kinkier books? Try these spicy stories written under the name Allison West.

Boxsets

Academy of Littles

Western Daddies Collection

Obey Daddy Collection

The Alpha Collection

Western Daddies

Her Billionaire Daddy

Her Cowboy Daddy

Her Outlaw Daddy

Her Forbidden Daddy

Standalone Romances

The Victorian Shift

Jailed Little Jade

Prefer a sweeter romance with action and adventure?
Check out these titles under the name Ruth Silver.

Aberrant Series

Love Forbidden

Secrets Forbidden

Magic Forbidden

Escape Forbidden

Refuge Forbidden

Boxsets

Gem Apocalypse

Nightblood

Royal Reaper

Royal Deception

Standalones

Stolen Art